TROUBLED WATERS

A NOVEL

MARY ANNAÏSE HEGLAR

HARPER MUSE

Published by Harper Muse, an imprint of HarperCollins Focus LLC.

This book is a work of fiction. The characters, incidents, and dialogue are drawn from the author's imagination and are not to be construed as real. Any resemblance to actual events or persons, living or dead, is entirely coincidental.

Any internet addresses (websites, blogs, etc.) in this book are offered as a resource. They are not intended in any way to be or imply an endorsement by HarperCollins Focus LLC, nor does HarperCollins Focus LLC vouch for the content of these sites for the life of this book.

Library of Congress Cataloging-in-Publication Data

Names: Heglar, Mary Annaïse, author
Title: Troubled waters: a novel / Mary Annaïse Heglar.
Description: [Nashville]: Harper Muse, 2024. | Summary: "In heartfelt, lyrical prose, celebrated author Mary Annaïse Heglar weaves an unforgettable, distinctly Southern story of the enduring power of family, Black resistance, and the rising climate crisis"--Provided by publisher.
Identifiers: LCCN 2023058495 (print) | LCCN 2023058496 (ebook) | ISBN 9781400248117 (paperback) | ISBN 9781400235988 (library binding) | ISBN 9781400248124 (epub) | ISBN 9781400248131
Subjects: LCGFT: Novels.
Classification: LCC PS3608.E348 T76 2024 (print) | LCC PS3608.E348 (ebook) | DDC 813/.6--dc23/eng/20231229
LC record available at https://lccn.loc.gov/2023058495
LC ebook record available at https://lccn.loc.gov/2023058496

Printed in the United States of America

24 25 26 27 28 LBC 5 4 3 2 1

For Uncle Harold

PART ONE

LOVELY DAY

December 19, 2013

E ven as she typed the last paragraphs of her final paper for the semester, Corinne couldn't hear the feverish *click-clack* of the keyboard under her fingertips or the frantic whispers of the other students. She wasn't in North Ohio anymore, burrowed away in the basement of the massive library at Oberlin College. She was back in Mississippi two springs ago, listening to that eerie stillness as the Mississippi River swelled out of her banks and onto the roads that connected Port Gibson and Vicksburg, quieting the dull hum of traffic. Then, the River had seeped into playgrounds and backyards, hushing children at play and neighbors at gossip. Eventually, the water rose so high, the birds were too confused to sing, and the River silenced the sky. Corinne had lain in her room with the windows open, wary even of turning on the television lest she further anger the Mississippi. There was nowhere to go and nothing to say.

By the time her waters had receded, the River had washed past every watermark on record, even the one set by the Great Flood of 1927.

Earlier in the semester, Corinne had gotten into a bitter argument with one of her environmental studies professors about the causes of the 2011 Mississippi River flood. He'd insisted that it was simply a natural phenomenon.

"Rivers flood," he'd said with a wave of his hand. *"There's no reason to think it was global warming."*

Corinne, on the other hand, had insisted that it wasn't that simple. The 2011 flood was an alleged five-hundred-year flood, and so were the 1993 flood and the 1937 flood. The 1927 flood—the one that had haunted Corinne since elementary school when she first learned about those who'd drowned and the horrors of a river unhinged—still held the record for the most destructive river flood in US history. There wasn't even a century between any of them.

"How was that 'natural'?" she'd demanded.

Her professor had stood back, crossed his arms, and told her to prove it. So here she was, two months later, with a browser window littered with tabbed articles about deforestation and wetlands, La Niña, and pre- versus postindustrial rainfall levels. She felt even more strongly that, had the River been left to her own devices, she probably would have flooded in 2011, but not so viciously. If the earth's temperature had held steady, the rain would have fallen, but not nearly as much. The River may have risen, but the wetlands and the forests would have been able to absorb the water. But as strong as her conviction was, she still wasn't sure she was being convincing enough for her polemic professor.

"Corinne, just send the damn thing so we can be done!"

Corinne looked up from her screen to see Ashley yawning and swaying by the door of the study lounge, her laptop in one arm and a long-empty coffee cup in her other hand.

"I just want to read it one more time," Corinne muttered before she went back to her screen. "I feel like I'm forgetting something."

"The whole thing? Girl, you keep on, and you finna 'forget' to pass the class," Ashley snapped, her Georgia accent thickening with frustration. "Ain't nobody 'bout to fail you over a typo, and at this hour, a stroke of brilliance ain't coming. Just turn it in!"

Corinne pushed her hair out of her face and felt how dry and brittle it had become since she started her final exams. She hadn't so much as sprayed water on it in a week. "If you really want to go back to the room, Ashley, you can," she grumbled. "My professors have run out of sympathy for me this semester, so I actually have to do this right." She still felt a strange mix of gratitude and guilt for all the extensions her professors had granted her last spring. Most of them hadn't even asked what, exactly, her family emergency was.

"Girl, first of all, you know I'm not leaving you across campus this late at night," Ashley shot back. "Second, you're already past the deadline by ten entire minutes. Third, do I need to remind you that you fly out in the morning? Turn in the paper, Corinne. Better done than good at this point."

Corinne knew she was right, but she hated even the risk of losing an argument, especially when there was a grade at stake. She took one last look at the final paragraph, couldn't find a typo, and decided to take Ashley's advice.

"Fine, we can go," she said as she clicked the Send button.

Corinne woke up the next morning to the blare of her phone's alarm. She thought about flirting with a few extra minutes of sleep, but she hated being late, especially to the airport. Just the thought of having to call Grandma and ask her to buy a new ticket during the Christmas rush was enough to make her jump out of bed and into the shower. She dressed as fast as she could and decided she'd deal with her hair when she made it to Uncle Harold's house. Before she grabbed the giant suitcase she'd left waiting by the door, she leaned over the bottom bunk.

"Bye, punk," she whispered.

"Whatever, punk," Ashley whispered back, and then rolled over. "Text me when you get to New Orleans."

"I will. Love you."

"Love you, too, girl."

With that, Corinne dragged her suitcase down the hallway and out into the damp December rain—that should have been snow this far north in Ohio and this close to Christmas—to wait for the shuttle to the Cleveland airport.

By the time she made her way through the security check, the sun was beginning to peek through the clouds. Corinne chuckled to herself as she remembered when the Cleveland airport—with its four terminals and multiple baggage claim carousels—had overwhelmed and fascinated her.

Two and a half years ago, she'd arrived here with her entire life packed into three bags to start her college career at Oberlin—the school Grandma hated without ever laying eyes on it. During her freshman year, when she flew home, she would sit up by the huge window panels to marvel at the giant planes as they took off and touched down. Back then, her only frame of reference had been the tiny airports in Jackson or Baton Rouge, or the itty-bitty ones in Vicksburg and Natchez that seemed only to host little jalopy jets. She hadn't yet suffered through layovers in Chicago, Atlanta, Houston, or Detroit during her eight-hour pilgrimages back to Port Gibson. After a while, she'd gotten stuck in enough blizzards to learn that when she had a connecting flight, she needed to get as far south as possible on the first flight. And since it seemed she was the only person in Ohio who flew to Mississippi on purpose, she'd started flying straight to New Orleans. It was a good excuse to visit her uncle anyway.

In the beginning, the flights had been exciting. Now, all she could think about was how her jet fuel was melting the ice caps.

When she looked at the planes taking off the tarmac, she saw blood leaking from their wings, like crop dusters. She imagined the bodies of the unborn, untold generations in the baggage compartment. She heard their screams in the wind. And while everyone around her carried on as normal, she could smell a gas leak so strong it made her stomach curdle. She'd already promised herself that when she graduated in a year and a half, she would never set foot on a plane again. She didn't dare tell Grandma, though, because she'd start pressuring her to transfer to a school in the South immediately.

But Corinne liked Oberlin. Sure, the first two years had been rough—she'd never even seen that many white folks, for one thing. And it was her first time being a "minority" as a Black woman and as a Southerner. She had no idea what to say when her classmates asked, "What's it like down South?" like they were asking about life on a different planet. And then there was the bone-chilling, bloodcurdling winter. But by the end of the first year, she'd bought a warmer coat and made her community with the other Black students, some of whom were from the South, too, like Ashley.

She made her way through the hassle of Christmas travelers to the Cinnabon stand and gotten the sloppiest cinnamon roll they had and a black coffee. It would be the first taste of dairy she'd had in months, but she figured she might as well start building a tolerance now. There was no way her new diet was going to be able to stand up to Grandma's Christmas cooking. She figured she could renew her vegan vows when she got back to Oberlin in February. Besides, she found a strange comfort in the guaranteed stomachache she'd get as her penance for flying in the first place. *I might as well set the ocean on fire myself*, she thought. She sat at one of those sterile-looking white tables with black plastic chairs to eat her guilt. The warm icing had melted her thoughts far away when her phone blasted "Thriller" loud enough to startle the very-important-looking men in coats rushing from gate to gate. One of them walked away a little slower and with a bounce in his step, like he'd just remembered there was music in the world.

"Hey, Uncle!" Corinne sang into her phone.

"You made it to the airport, baby girl?" Uncle Harold's voice boomed into her ear, and even this early in the morning, she could hear the cigarette hanging out of the left side of his mouth. No matter how fast he talked, it never fell, like he had it under a spell.

"Yeah, I made it. Y'all oughta have more faith in me." Corinne tried to put on her grown-up voice, but just hearing Uncle Harold's voice was enough to take the rocks out of the pit of her stomach.

"Why would we do that? You know we *know* you, girl." He chuckled. "Now, what time you get to New Orleans?"

"I'll be there about 1:00 p.m. your time. Can't wait to see y'all!" She wasn't lying, but she still had to force the excitement into her voice. She wanted to *be* there but hated the hassle of *getting* there.

"All right, well, you call me when you land, you hear?"

"All right."

"And you make sure to call your grandmama *before* you get on that plane." His voice grew stern. "You know how she gets."

"I know, I know. I'll call her." Corinne felt a tightness at her temples as she thought about Grandma's uncanny ability to jump to the worst possible conclusions at the slightest silence. So many times Corinne had called her only to learn that she'd been beside herself imagining her granddaughter dead or kidnapped. "I'll see you soon, okay?"

"Uh-huh . . . You need me to meet you at the baggage claim, or can you walk out to the curb?"

"I'll meet you at the curb."

"Oh, so you done finally learned how to pack?" he teased. "All right, look for the new truck. Orange Chevy. Bye, Niecey."

Corinne hung up and looked down at her sad little black coffee and the melted goo that was left of her Cinnabon, and decided she was done with punishment. She tossed it in the trash and walked to Starbucks for coffee with coconut milk. After all, that cinnamon roll wasn't going to offset anything.

After she got her new coffee, Corinne settled in at her gate with her back to the windows, only to freeze in her seat when she realized exactly where she was. Right across from her was the gate where, seven months ago, she'd waited for the last flight she'd taken out of this airport. Her grief snaked out of the ground and covered her like a vine, smothering her in her own memories.

Two nights before that flight, she'd looked at her buzzing phone at 12:03 a.m. and seen the words *Uncle Harold*. He never called that late. Her heart had begun to thump as her mind raced. *Was there a tornado? Did Grandma have a heart attack?* Instead, Uncle Harold told her that the oil boat that her brother, Cameron, worked on had gotten caught in an electrical storm outside of Lake Charles, and there'd been an accident. His boss had called Grandma and told her that Cameron was involved, but hadn't told her what that meant. Uncle Harold promised to tell her as soon as they knew.

Corinne remembered going limp and falling to the floor with the phone still clutched. Ashley, who had been reading on her bed with headphones on, had to pull her to her bed where she curled up like a possum. She slept fitfully, between nightmares and crying spells. She kept seeing Cameron's angular, mahogany face swirling above her and hearing Uncle Harold's words: *"We don't know yet."* When she finally woke from her trance, her mouth was on fire and her eyes were dry like she hadn't blinked in hours. She had to concentrate just to breathe.

Corinne had tried to tell herself that he was only twenty-four, and no god was that cruel. She had wanted to call Grandma, but she could barely lift her head. So she waited with her hands on her heart in a desperate attempt to keep it from breaking.

After the gray, early morning light faded, Corinne had tried to get out of bed, but nothing worked—not her arms, not her neck, not her legs.

It wasn't until around 10:00 a.m. that the calls had come one after the other. First Uncle Harold, then Grandma, then Grandma again. Repeat. *If it was good news*, she thought, *they would have texted me when I didn't answer the phone.* And at that point, she knew, but she didn't want to hear it.

Ashley had climbed out of her bed and stood eye level with Corinne in the top bunk.

"*Cori,*" she whispered as though they weren't the only ones in the room. *"I could answer for you, but they need to hear your voice. Not mine."*

But when Corinne still didn't move, Ashley took the phone from her limp fingers and answered it. One look at her face and the frog that had lodged itself in Corinne's throat leapt out, and she screamed so loud her skin crawled.

Two days later, she was drifting through the Cleveland airport on her way to Jackson, clutching the bottle of Xanax the college nurse had given her during her emergency appointment. The flight had been booked so hastily, she'd had two connecting flights in North Carolina alone.

Now, more than half a year later, she still carried a bottle of Xanax in her purse because her grief came and went, but when it came, it was ferocious. Everywhere she looked—from the stove to the gas station to the plane she was about to board—she saw oil and knew it was the same nasty business that took her brother while setting her world afire. She hated how numb the pills made her, though. If she was going to watch the world fall apart, wasn't it the least she could do to feel it? How could she mourn otherwise? But as her throat tightened as she looked at the gate across from her, and her spine tingled at the thought of the poison planes behind her, she began to imagine how much more terrifying a panic attack in the sky might be. She decided mourning could wait and swallowed a pill.

While she waited for the medicine to kick in, she pulled out her almost-full notebook to sketch the characters flocking to her gate. There were two men in full army gear, heavy boots and flimsy hats, who looked like they were ready to go into combat at any moment. There was a white family with four small children—the father glued to his phone and the mother trying her hardest to keep her children's squabbles quiet. There was an old Black woman in a wheelchair who never looked up from her crossword book.

When her fingers began to tire and she ran out of room on the last page of her notebook, Corinne thought again of the paper she'd handed in last night, which reminded her of one of her favorite things about going back home, next to cooking with Grandma and laughing with Uncle Harold: seeing the Mississippi River again.

Corinne didn't remember the first time she saw her, but she remembered the first time she feared her. It was in the second grade when her teacher—bored with her job and her students—showed them a documentary on the Great Flood of 1927. Corinne had sat horrified as she learned about the thousands of people who'd died and their gruesome, gruesome deaths by snakebite, gunshot, and hypothermia in the cold snap after the deluge. So many more simply drowned. She knew by then that she—like most of the other children in her class and nearly everyone in her life—was Black. The suffering people in the documentary were, too, and the narrator made it clear that that wasn't an accident.

Corinne started having what Grandma called "premonitions." She woke up in the middle of the night to visions of the
River crashing through her windows or rising through the floor.
She started drawing the pictures she saw in the documentary—
huddled Black masses atop the levees in the Delta, in tents at
the makeshift camps at the Civil War battleground in Vicksburg.
Sometimes she caught glimpses of them out of the corner of her
eye, their faces long and their backs slumped. Only Black people
went to the camps; white folks went to homes and hotels. Black
folks were refugees, while white folks were guests. The camps
were more like prisons, with fetid conditions, little food, forced
labor, and copious poisonous snakes. Corinne's picture of hell.

Grandma had been the only one who hadn't mocked her or
shooed her off when she talked about the ghosts she saw. She
listened as Corinne described the fear in their eyes, their tattered clothes, their arms swollen from mosquito bites. Corinne
had even told her their names, when she knew them. When
she finished, Grandma would bend her face down to hers, cup
her plump, seven-year-old cheeks, and say, *"You know not all
ghosts are bad, right? Sometimes people just want to be remembered."* Corinne would always love her for that.

"Group A to New Orleans, you're welcome to board." The
voice on the intercom jolted Corinne out of her daydream.

She looked around and saw that the seating area had
become swollen and chaotic as everyone jumped up and
began to jostle their way into some semblance of a queue.
Soon, the attendant called for Group C, and it was her turn
to line up. She found her place behind a white lady with

stringy hair and thought about calling Grandma. But then she imagined that Grandma would be mad at her if she called from the line because she shouldn't have waited until she was in a rush. She'd call her when she landed, when her own nerves were calmer.

As the plane bowed into New Orleans, Corinne threw her window shade open to see the watery landscape emerge below her. Even as the wild land turned into manicured neighborhoods, the water remained, curated into canals and bayous like silver ribbons. Eventually, the only thing below her was the tarmac, and she heaved a body-emptying sigh as the wheels skipped onto the ground. She reached for her phone before the flight attendants gave official permission.

"My favorite niece!" Uncle Harold picked up on the first ring. "You here?"

"Yep, Uncle, I'm here." She couldn't help but smile.

"All right then, I'm just driving around in the circle. And, Corinne?"

"Yes?"

"You know I know you ain't call Mama. Call her now." His voice was stern again. "Not now but *right now*, you hear me? Otherwise, you ain't getting in my new truck."

"Yes, sir." Corinne knew how much her grandmother worried, especially now. But there was something about the enormity of her grandmother's grief that frightened her. It felt like it was so big it could swallow them both whole, or suck Corinne into the womb her own mother had come from. She wasn't sure she'd ever breathe again if she let that happen. Corinne decided to call Grandma after she was off the plane and away from all the mayhem of people who stood up too fast, luggage falling from overhead, screaming babies, and that awkward dance of figuring whose turn it was to walk down the aisle.

Once she was in the terminal, she wandered toward the kiosk across from her gate and bought a granola bar so that when Grandma asked that inevitable question, she wouldn't have to lie and pretend Cinnabon was food. Finally, when she was on the escalator to baggage claim and there was no more time to buy or waste, she pulled out her phone, breathed, and pressed *Grandma*.

"Corinne?" Grandma picked up on the second ring, her voice half panicked, half relieved.

"Hey, Grandmama." Corinne tried to sound cheerful.

"Hey, baby! You in New Orleans yet?"

"Yeah, I'm here. About to go get my bag and meet Uncle Harold."

"Did you eat something?"

"Yes, ma'am. I ate before I left Cleveland. I'm even eating right now." She bit loudly into her granola bar.

"Okay, good. I'm glad you got there safe." Grandma sighed, and Corinne knew her knee was shaking. "Why didn't you call me before you left?"

"I'm sorry, Grandma. I was just tired, I guess. I forgot."

"I was worried to *death*, Corinne." Grandma's voice hardened for a second.

"I'm sorry . . ." Corinne didn't know what else to say. There was no way to tell Grandma that her "worrying to death" was *scaring* her to death.

"It's fine," Grandma whispered, even though they both knew it wasn't. "Just get here tomorrow. Make sure your uncle picks up the shrimp and crabs before you get on the road. I already started on a pie for you. Brand-new recipe: pecans *and* sweet potatoes. Might be a masterpiece, might be a mess!"

"Yes, ma'am." Corinne loved it when Grandma experimented with recipes. It always put her in a good mood. "I love you!"

"I love you, too, baby. Can't wait to see you."

Corinne cursed herself for putting off the call for so long. It had taken less than five minutes, but she'd dreaded it for hours.

After she picked up her big polka-dot suitcase from baggage claim, Corinne walked out into a balmy sixty-three degrees and had to shield her eyes from the glare of the sun. Once upon a time, this would have felt chilly to her, but now it was a welcome change from the damp cold she'd left behind in Ohio. She waited on the curb for all of two minutes before Uncle Harold pulled up in his giant truck with his giant grin and a giant hug.

"What you think?" he asked, gesturing widely at his new truck. It was a bright, flaming, glow-in-the-dark orange.

"It's . . . orange." Corinne chuckled.

"Yep, it was silver, but I got it painted orange. If I'd gotten it painted red, they woulda cranked up the en-sho-ance payment, so I got as close as I could." He laughed so hard he bent in half. Corinne loved the sound of his laugh, but she loved the sight of it even more—the way his cheeks bunched up into perfect round balls under his eyes, revealing the two dimples that lived underneath his mustache. When Corinne was a little girl, he used to let her dig her pinky finger into them.

Uncle Harold threw her bags in the truck bed and closed the cover over them. Then he helped her climb into the passenger seat, where she immediately recognized the end of one of Grandma's favorite songs: "Lean on Me" by Bill Withers.

"Call me . . ."

Uncle Harold shot a glance at her as he pulled out into the airport's mini-highway system. "Speaking of calling somebody . . . you call my mama?"

"Yes, sir."

"You better had. Otherwise, we wasn't gonna leave this airport until you did. She was calling me the whole time you were on the plane." He looked at her as he paused at the first stop sign. "Why do you do that to her, Corinne?"

Corinne knew no answer would be good enough for her uncle, so she stared at her feet.

"Niecey, even if you just do it as a favor to me, call your grandma. Her nerves are fried these days. She lost Cameron too. It wasn't just you."

"I understand, Uncle Harold."

"Then act like it, Cori."

"I will, I promise."

When Uncle Harold didn't respond, Corinne turned up the volume on Bill Withers's voice as he sang the first verse of "Lovely Day." She wanted to stop thinking about Grandma and grief and global warming. She just wanted music.

"That's what I'm talking 'bout! What you know 'bout some Bill Withers, girl?"

"I *know* some Bill Withers!"

"Oh, but do you know *the words*, though?"

"Of course I know the words, Uncle! Y'all taught me!"

"Prove it!"

With her eyes fixed on her uncle, Corinne sang the words to the bridge perfectly, but in all the wrong keys. When she got to the chorus, she shouted more than she sang, the wind making a mess of her hair through her open window.

"Get 'em, Niecey!" Uncle Harold turned the volume even louder and tapped the steering wheel like a drum.

"*A lovely daaaaaaaaaaaayyyyyyyyyy,*" they sang together. Corinne was starting to believe the words coming out of her mouth, that maybe there was more beauty than horror in the world.

They sang like that all the way back to Uncle Harold's house. Bill Withers turned into Lauryn Hill who turned into the Gap Band who turned into Shai. Corinne's throat was sore until the next morning, but it still felt good.

LOSING STREAK

December 20, 2013

"Thank you, Jesus," Cora whispered as she pulled into an empty parking spot next to the handicap space. Even this early in the morning, it was a small miracle to get a spot this close to the Walmart entrance, especially so close to Christmas.

She remembered when the Walmart in Vicksburg was just a regular old Walmart, back when her grandbabies were still babies. No fruits or vegetables, no deli, and definitely no bakery. Now, it was part supermarket, part hardware store, part pharmacy, and part clothing store. It was like being at the mall, except that you paid for everything at one register. And even though she'd been shopping here for years, something about the sight of a shopping cart with potatoes, underwear, prescription foot cream, and a screwdriver felt obscene to her. But she couldn't argue with the convenience. She wasn't about to be running from store to store, wasting gas and money on her fixed income and thin patience. Plus, she didn't have that kind of time with Harold and Corinne getting to town tomorrow.

But she still hated the crowds. Cora refused to come to Walmart on the weekends or after 5:00 p.m. on a weekday. By that time, the place was crawling with teenagers and teachers, who always seemed to have candy in their baskets and a wariness in their step. Then came all the other working people who'd been cramped in offices all day, with their carts full of rotisserie chickens, canned vegetables, and frozen french fries. On Saturday and Sunday, though, the store was so crowded it felt like homecoming at Alcorn. Everybody from all over Claiborne and Warren counties was there—white folks, Black folks, young, old, mothers with their babies, couples in the middle of a fight, preachers with their flocks, farmers, Katrina-refugees-turned-exiles. It was the worst on Saturday, when she could never get out of there without someone banging into her with their basket on the way to get a tray of eggs or a value pack of toilet paper. Or worse, she'd run into someone she hadn't seen in months and have to stumble through the customary song and dance of asking about each and every family member and making fake plans to "get together."

At 8:00 a.m., it was too early for the Salvation Army bell ringer to be out and about but not too early for Christmas music. As the automatic doors opened, she could hear the Temptations singing "Silent Night." After all these years, the song still took her back to her college days at Fisk. She'd seen the Temptations around campus a few times but had always been too shy to get close to them. She'd had a crush on Eddie Kendricks, who was singing lead now.

"Good morning, ma'am." An old white woman with a raspy voice and ill-fitting uniform interrupted her song. It was the same woman who would ask to see her receipts when she left the store to make sure she hadn't stolen anything.

"Morning." Cora lowered her eyes and rushed past her. There was something obscene about someone at least ten years her senior referring to her as "ma'am," but it balanced out when she remembered the white teenagers who used to call her father "boy."

This trip, Cora had a list of things she was too embarrassed to even ask about at Port Gibson's Piggly Wiggly. Corinne was coming back from Ohio a vegan. At first, Cora thought it was a new type of eating disorder, but then Harold had explained that it meant Corinne "didn't eat *food*, she ate what food *eats*." Now all her granddaughter wanted was hummus, tofu, almond milk. And tempeh bacon. *What is a tempeh?* Cora wondered. *And when did it start making bacon?*

"*So you can't eat meat at all?*" Cora had asked over the phone back in October.

"*Grandma, it's not that I* can't *eat it; it's that I* won't," Corinne said with that exasperation only a nineteen-year-old could conjure. "*It's not a* religion!"

Cora thought about asking her what was wrong with religion but decided not to go there. "*Not even chicken?*" she asked instead.

"That's meat, Grandma!"

This child has forgotten the difference between a bird and a mammal, Cora thought. *What on earth were they teaching her in those environmental studies classes?*

"What about fish?"

"That's an animal too! I don't even eat cheese or milk. You should try it!"

"What, do I look like starving myself for the hell of it?"

The way Corinne described what she ate now reminded Cora of the way Grandma Cindy said they used to eat in the Depression—beans and greens and hot-water corn bread. And that was on a *good* day. More often than not, it was just corn bread and molasses. But even back then, they used salt pork to season the food—and it hadn't exactly been a choice. They ate whatever they could afford or grow. Now, here was Corinne, who'd never picked a boll of cotton, much less a bale, in her entire life, making meals out of side dishes. On *purpose*. She could call it "planet-friendly" or "healthy" all she wanted to—Cora knew struggle food when she saw it.

She made her way to the produce section. The "triple washed" collard and mustard greens that came in little plastic bags were too clean for her taste. If they didn't have any dirt on them, how could they have any flavor? She missed the summer, when she could get most of her vegetables out of her own garden, especially because she and Corinne usually tended the garden together. Ever since she was a little girl, Corinne loved to crouch down close to the dirt and pick the beans, peppers, and berries that Cora couldn't reach without hurting her knees. Corinne would spend hours down there, pulling up weeds and mixing in fertilizer.

"Frosty the Snowman" started playing through the store's speakers, and Cora's stomach dropped. This had been Cameron's favorite Christmas song when he was a little boy. Wherever he'd heard it—at school, in the car, one time in the grocery store—it put him into a frenzy. If she closed her eyes, Cora could still see his chubby little cheeks curling upward as he sang and danced offbeat.

She gripped her shopping cart as she realized, once again, that she would never have another Christmas with him. She'd give anything to hear his laughter again, to hug his neck. To stop her knees from buckling under her, she tried to flood her mind with memories of the good times—watching football games together and shouting until their throats went raw, or all four of them playing spades and reading one another's eyes over the table. It was enough to get her going again.

She looked back at her list and saw that godforsaken thing called tofu. Probably because so few people looked for it, it was all the way at the top of the produce case, just above the little bottles of chopped garlic and ginger. Cora almost fell trying to reach it.

"You need help?" A visibly tickled twentysomething with bushy hair rushed over from tending the tomatoes.

"I guess," Cora answered. "Can you get me one of all the tofus?" There was extra firm, firm, medium, and silken, and Cora didn't know which one Corinne ate.

"Yes, ma'am." He grabbed the packages with almost no

effort. Then, perplexed at the plastic squares in his hand, he looked at Cora. "What's a tofu?"

"Child, hell if I know." Cora pushed her cart away. "Thank you, though."

Corinne said that tofu took the place of meat for her. Cora had given it a try once and cursed it to high heaven. She'd never felt so disrespected by a food in her life. As much as she hated wasting food, she'd thrown it straight in the garbage and had half a mind to call her granddaughter and cuss her out. When she'd told Corinne about it a week later, she'd laughed at her until she was out of breath. When she finally stopped cackling, she said, *"Well, you have to season it first, Grandma! At least put some salt on it!"* Now, Cora decided she'd let Corinne show her how it was done when she got home. But she'd better not try to put it in her gumbo. That's where Cora drew the line.

Corinne was "grown" now and wouldn't let you forget it. Old enough to vote, to drive, to walk away. If she wanted to eat like it was 1933, then let her. At least she wasn't showing up with any babies, which is more than Cora could say for herself around that age, or even for her daughter, Yvonne. Cora knew that she'd never had the power to stop Corinne from going anywhere. Corinne had always been a willful little thing. Even as a baby, she would wail and wail and wail until someone picked her up, and then she'd lift her pudgy little arms in a victory dance, like she was Muhammad Ali in a diaper.

Cora went over to the deli section next to get the hummus and pita bread Corinne asked for—and sliced ham for herself. Then it was over to the meat section, where she picked up sausage and chicken thighs for the gumbo. Harold and Corinne were bringing the seafood with them from New Orleans. Cora tried not to dwell on the fact that, since Cameron wouldn't be there to eat four bowls in one sitting, she didn't need to buy enough for a double batch this year. She'd cry about that later, not here. Instead, she turned her attention back to Corinne, who had always loved her gumbo—both eating it and helping to make it.

Cora was still hoping that the smells of it coming together would bring Corinne back to her better senses. Or maybe Corinne would faint in the backyard one day and Cora would be there, in all her glory, with a plate of fried chicken to tell her to quit listening to them white folks up north.

When she was a senior in high school, Corinne hadn't told anyone where she was applying to college. Not her grandmother, not her brother, and not even her beloved uncle Harold. When they'd asked, she just said it was "a surprise." Cora had always known that Corinne wasn't going to Alcorn—where Cora had graduated from night school after she'd dropped out of Fisk when she'd gotten pregnant with Yvonne, and where Yvonne had gone to college until she'd gotten pregnant with Cameron. Corinne and Cameron had grown up halfway on Alcorn's campus after Yvonne got a job there. Medgar Evers had gone to Alcorn. So had Steve McNair. But Cora wanted even more for Corinne. She'd wanted her to get out of their little corner of Mississippi.

But Cora had hoped that Corinne's surprise was a scholarship to Fisk, back in Nashville. Cora's father had gone to Fisk, and her mother had worked there. Her brothers had graduated from there. Cora had wanted Corinne to erase the disappointment she'd seen on her parents' faces the day she'd told them she'd withdrawn from school and broken the family's three-generations-long college streak.

Or maybe Corinne was planning to go to Xavier or Dillard, down in New Orleans. Cora had liked the idea of Corinne being near Harold, and of them driving up to Port Gibson together. Then, of course, there was the possibility that Corinne was going to Spelman or Tuskegee. All respectable choices. Far enough away to let her see new things but close enough that Cora could get to her if she needed to.

But Corinne never did reveal the surprise herself. She had let her principal do it when she'd introduced her to open the graduation ceremony as salutatorian. It had been the first time Cora had ever heard the word *Oberlin*.

"*Oberlin*? Where is *that*?" she'd whisper-hissed at her son.

"It's in Ohio, Mama," Harold said in that tone he used when he was trying to calm her, but all it ever did was drive her crazy.

"*Ohio*? Who told this little girl she could go to O-hi-o?"

"Mama . . ." Harold had cocked his head to the side, as if to beg her not to make a scene. She didn't. Instead, she bided her time.

As soon as the ceremony was over, Cora had rushed everyone to the car like an angry hen. She'd been so mad she was seeing double, so Harold had to drive. Corinne had sat up front, since it was "her day," and Cameron had sat in back with Cora. Cora stared out the window the entire drive with her lips pursed and her teeth grinding. It had taken everything in her not to kick the back of her granddaughter's seat.

As soon as Harold pulled into her driveway, Cora had broken the silence that had hung over the car like Spanish moss. "What in the hell has gotten into you, girl?"

Corinne craned her head around, careful not to hit her graduation cap. "What?"

"Don't you 'what' me, girl!" Cora yelled. "What is this *Oberlin* business?!"

Corinne's face, which had been stretched wide in a smile all day long, froze in horror. Harold sat in the driver's seat, perfectly still, and it felt like an eternity before anyone spoke. And when they did, it was the wrong person.

"Grandma asked you a question, Cori," Cameron said.

"But ain't nobody asked you nothing, Cameron," Harold reminded him. "Come on in this house, boy. Let the women talk."

Cora had broken her steely glare at Corinne to look at her grandson, "Go on, Cameron. We'll be in in a minute."

Cameron had climbed out of the car reluctantly, and Cora had waited until the door was shut before she spoke again. "Well, girl, you got something to say for yourself?"

"Grandma . . . ," Corinne started. "I didn't—I—I thought you'd be proud?"

"That my granddaughter is *leaving* me? You thought I'd be *proud* of that?!"

"Grandma, Oberlin is a good school! A really good school!"

"And who goes there, Corinne? Tell me that! A bunch of white folks? And let me guess, that school older than the Civil War?"

"Yes, it is, Grandma. And Oberlin actually has a Black history—"

"Oh, does it now? What, pray tell, is *their* Black history, girl?" Cora spat the words out like blood.

"Well, it was part of the Underground Railroad, for one thing." Beads of sweat appeared at Corinne's temples. "And they were the first school in the country to admit Black students!"

"And how did they treat those Black students? Huh?"

Corinne didn't seem to have an answer for that. Instead, she sank so deep into her seat that her cap came off.

"Yeah, I bet they don't write about that in their little *literature*." Cora felt the tears burning at the sides of her eyes. "You may think you're so smart now, Corinne, but listen to me when I tell you, they don't *want* us there. You remember that!"

"Grandma . . ." Corinne's voice cracked as her lips trembled.

Before she knew she was moving, Cora got out of the car and slammed the door behind her, leaving Corinne alone with the giant dictionary her high school had given her as an absurd graduation gift. Cora had stormed straight to her bedroom, blowing right past Harold and Cameron in the kitchen. But Harold had followed her and grabbed her bedroom door before she could slam it.

"Mama!" Harold admonished.

"I don't wanna hear it, Harold!" Her nerves were too high to think straight. All she wanted now was a cigarette and silence.

"Mama!" He put enough bass in his voice to startle her. "You know she got a full ride to that school in Ohio? You oughta be proud."

"So you knew?" Cora turned around to face him.

"She just told me that part on the way to the car, Mama." Harold sucked his teeth. "I found out when you did."

"Shut my door, Harold," she said as she reached for her cigarettes.

Cora hadn't come out of her room for the rest of the night. After her first cigarette, her heartbeat had slowed enough to let the shame seep in. She couldn't get Corinne's horrified face out of her mind—her eyebrows frozen high on her forehead, her eyeliner smudged with sweat. Cora knew Harold was right. And truth be told, she *was* proud of her granddaughter, maybe even a little jealous. She'd always wanted to be as outgoing—as outrageous—as her. But Cora knew how white folks can punish you for having the audacity to walk through a door even when they opened it. She also knew that Corinne had spent barely five minutes around white folks. She'd never been outnumbered by them. And Corinne hadn't even visited this school all the way out in the nether regions of Ohio. What did she really know?

Cora and Corinne didn't speak for the better part of a week after that. Cora had tried, but all the words got jumbled in her throat. The tension finally lifted after she made a surprise batch of her county-famous banana pudding. The message had been unmistakable when she'd brought Corinne a bowl of her specialty without a special occasion. And Corinne had eaten it up.

That was more than two years ago, and Cora felt equal parts foolish and relieved that Corinne had, by any measure, done quite well, even if she was coming back with strange tastes and a smart mouth. Cora didn't know how much of that was Oberlin's influence and how much of it was Cameron's ghost. She, herself, still thought she heard his voice every once in a while. And the house felt so empty now that she knew he was never coming home. Sometimes she thought about him so deeply, he would reappear, rolling around as a toddler or brooding as a teenager. The only thing that could make it stop was a pint of Blue Bell ice cream.

After losing both her daughter and her grandson, Cora was determined that her losing streak would stop there. So, if the price of keeping Corinne close—and keeping the peace— was a trip to the nether regions of Walmart for her vegan food-stuffs, it was a price Cora was happy to pay. At least she could make sure Corinne ate.

Cora was halfway to the register when she realized her cart felt too light. She looked down and saw that she'd for-gotten bottled water. Then she remembered that yesterday the water had come out of the faucet looking more like mud and she'd had to use a bottle of water just to brush her teeth. She swung the cart back around so fast her purse strap fell down to her elbow.

She moved through the growing bustle of shoppers to the next-to-last aisle and walked past the mountains of soda pop and specialty drinks to the "water section." It never ceased to amaze her that there were so many brands and types of water. There was Deer Creek, Nestle, Evian, and more. Alkaline, purified, sparkling. You could get it in itty-bitty bottles or gallons. Cora just wanted it clean and cheap. Preferably free.

"Young man," she called out to the blue-vested teenager at the end of the aisle.

"Yes, ma'am?"

"Can you help me get a couple of these cases into my cart?" She pointed to the Sam's Choice bottles on the bottom shelf. "I'm not in the mood to throw my back out."

Without a word, he walked over and loaded two cases of sixteen-ounce bottles into her cart. As he smiled at her, she noticed he had a faint dimple in the corner of his cheek—just like Cameron's. She knew the tears would come if she looked at him any longer, so she turned around without saying thank you.

As she squeaked her cart back to the front of the store, she whispered promises to herself that she would not stop for anything. But when she felt the cold air from the freezer aisle, she made a sharp left and put two gallons of Blue Bell's Pecan Pralines 'n Cream in her basket. Just looking at it brought her relief. Out of the corner of her eye, she caught the word *vegan* and noticed a pack of ice cream sandwiches that claimed to be made with tofu.

"Tofutti, huh?" she asked no one in particular. She threw it in the basket. For Corinne.

A Watched Pot

December 21, 2013

Corinne loved how Port Gibson announced itself as Highway 61 entered its city limits. With a big brown sign, it pronounced itself "Too Beautiful to Burn," harkening back to the words of General Grant on his way to capture Vicksburg for the Union. Now, 150 years later, the town was indeed still beautiful, with its majestic oak trees and centuries-old homes. Once in the city limits, Highway 61 transformed into Church Street, lined, predictably, with magnificent churches. Corinne's favorite one was the pinkish one with a gold finger on top of the steeple, pointing upward. Once, when she was a little girl, Corinne could have sworn she saw it bend at the knuckle.

After she and Uncle Harold passed by Little Bayou Pierre, they turned right at the gas station toward Grandma's house. And before long, they were pulling into her driveway. Corinne had barely shut the truck door before Grandma burst out the back door.

"Well, look who finally made it home!" Grandma flung her arms open wide like she was about to hug the air. "The prodigal granddaughter!"

"Grandma . . ." Corinne sighed. Grandma's guilt trips—slick as sandpaper—were the worst part of any trip home. Her words cut even deeper as Corinne noticed that the creases along the sides of her eyes and across her forehead had etched deeper into her skin. Her hair had gone from salt and pepper to a more ghostly gray.

"Oh hush, girl! Get over here and give me a hug!"

"Go on, Niecey." Uncle Harold needled his index finger into her side as he pulled her suitcase out of the covered truck bed.

I don't need you to tell me to hug my grandmama, Corinne thought. *What kind of monster do you think I am?* But she didn't want a lecture about "talking back," so she swallowed her words. She walked over to meet her grandmother and hugged her tight as she kissed her cheek. Grandma felt warm and smelled like bacon fat. Corinne had missed that smell.

"Let me look at you!" Grandma held on to Corinne's hands after she released her. "You sure you been eating out there in Ohio? Looking a little thin, even for someone who don't eat nothing but . . . *plants*."

"I'm fine, Grandma, I promise." If only Grandma knew how she had gorged herself on fries and pasta as she studied for her finals this semester.

"Well, you *know* we still making the gumbo, right?" A sly smile crept into the corners of Grandma's lips, and Corinne knew she was really asking if Corinne was going to eat some. She knew she probably would, but she wasn't ready to say it yet.

"I know, Grandma! We got the seafood in the car, and I came ready to cook."

"But you know tasting is part of cooking, girl." Grandma got more direct. "What you gonna do about that? What with you being a *vee-gan* now?"

"We'll see, Grandmama." Corinne didn't want to commit just now. What if the smell of sausage made her sick?

She turned to look at Uncle Harold, who was now leaning extravagantly and expressively against his orange truck. He slapped the hood and let out a roar of laughter. "Nope!" he said. "Look at that face! She might have converted, but she ain't no puritan yet! She'll be eating gumbo with the rest of us before the night's over."

"Oh, is that the new truck, Harold?"

"It shole is, Mama! I was wondering when you was gonna say something!"

"Harold! It's beautiful! I *love* the color!" Grandma walked toward the truck as if drawn by the magnetic pull of Uncle Harold's pride. Corinne took advantage of the moment and dragged her bag in the back door.

She rolled her suitcase past the kitchen and through the living room, careful not to look at the altar Grandma had laid out on the coffee table. Years ago, it had been covered with pictures and mementos from Corinne's great-grandparents. Then it had been overtaken with her mother's memory. Now it was dominated by Cameron and his many phases, from infant to young adult. Out of the corner of her eye, Corinne could see that Grandma had trimmed the table with Christmas garland and ribbons.

The decorations took her back to last Christmas, when Cameron had stood in this room looking tall and sullen. He'd been fussing and fighting with a tangled string of Christmas lights, cursing the cord as though it were bedeviling him on purpose. His red-brown skin had turned redder the angrier he'd gotten. Like a demon.

"Shit, motherfucker, loosen up. SHIT!" Cameron had always had a temper, and his two years on the oil boat had polluted his language. He said it was because he was a sailor now and that was how sailors talked, but it sounded more like he'd just been waiting for an excuse and a dam had broken in his vocabulary.

Corinne knew he was less cursing the lights than baiting her to say something. She tried not to look at him, not to breathe too loud, but he saw her cringe out of the corner of his eye.

"The fuck you looking at, Cori?"

Neither of them had heard the back door open, but they heard Uncle Harold cough to announce his presence in the doorway to the living room.

"Y'all all right?" Uncle Harold demanded.

If her uncle hadn't come into the room, Corinne would have ignored Cameron, but now that there was a witness, she couldn't pretend it didn't happen. She dropped the garland she'd been unfurling and ran to the back porch, hot with anger and embarrassment. She threw herself into one of the plastic lawn chairs and tried to slow her breathing. By the time she heard the door open again, a rock had formed in her throat. Uncle Harold sat down in the chair behind her.

"You know he don't mean it, Niecey."

Corinne couldn't bring herself to look at him. "It's still not an okay way to talk to your sister."

"He just moody." Uncle Harold shrugged. "He'll grow out of it, watch. Me and your mama used to fight just the same way."

Corinne crossed her arms tighter and stared into the backyard. Maybe Uncle Harold saw her jaw tightening, because he'd softened his voice when he said, "I talked to him, too, Cori."

It had felt so bitter then, but Corinne would give anything to have even that moment back. She wished she'd tried talking to Cameron herself. She could have tried to reason with her brother, tried to calm him or even taken over detangling the string of lights. Her fingers were nimbler anyway. Instead, she'd trusted her uncle that the two of them just needed time, and that, one day, they'd be best friends the way siblings were supposed to be. She missed that blessed inevitability.

Corinne pulled herself out of her memory to notice that outside of the pictures of Cameron everywhere, the living room looked the same, but the smell was different. The air, the furniture, the plants—everything was coated in a thick, stale stench of cigarette smoke. The smell made Corinne nauseous, even though it reminded her of when Mama was still alive, when she and Cameron still lived in Natchez. Grandma had smoked like a chimney then. But when Mama died and they had to move in with Grandma for good, she quit smoking—for them. Then, in May, Uncle Harold had let Grandma "borrow" a cigarette at Cameron's funeral, and that was the end of her clean streak. It was one of the things that made it so hard for Corinne to be around Grandma over the summer, though she could never say that.

Once Corinne made it to her room, the evidence of one of Grandma's deep-cleaning sprees was everywhere—the carpet had been freshly shampooed, the curtains washed, and the walls wiped down. She could smell that a candle had been burned recently, even though it was no match for the cigarette stink. But not even Grandma's dusting could scrape off the coat of grief that lived in this room, so animate it might as well have been sentient.

Behind her bed was the window she'd used to watch Cameron and Uncle Harold throw a football back and forth, and where, late at night, she'd watched Grandma gaze at thunderstorms. It was the same window she'd left open in 2005, after Hurricane Katrina had knocked the power out for a week, hoping for the mercy of a breeze.

The last time she was home, she watched as Grandma sat like a scarecrow in her hummingbird garden, surrounded by her jungle of morning glories and honeysuckle. Grandma had turned her garden swing into a mourner's bench. A part of Corinne had wanted to go out to her, but her feet wouldn't carry her.

Instead, Corinne had spent that summer following every rabbit hole on the internet about the black gold on Cameron's boat—where it came from, who controlled it, and how much there was. The spectacularly gruesome fashion in which it was unearthed in the Bakken shale and boreal forest. She'd read about how this same oil was snaked down to the coast under the cover of pipelines. But when too many of those got shut down due to lawsuits, protests, and accidents, the oil companies had turned to a hybrid network of trains and barges on the arteries of the Mississippi River to get the oil to the Gulf and then to the market.

As she'd skipped from website to website, the bigger picture became clearer and Corinne could see that her brother had been suckered into a scheme, not unlike the days when plantation owners would lure Black boys far away from home with promises of big money that they could send back to their families. The boys would soon find themselves trapped, sometimes at gunpoint, into a sharecropping scheme in another state. If they made it back to their families, they came back maimed, broke, and broken.

In Cameron's case, it wasn't a plantation but some big corporation with a name that managed to sound both fancy and boring. They'd convinced him to come live and work on a boat for six weeks at a time, taking two weeks off, and on and on. When he'd answered that clarion call for a "good-paying job"—something you didn't see all that often in Mississippi—Cameron had thought it was too good to turn down.

They hadn't told him that the cargo he was carrying up and down the bloodline of the nation would turn the River into a weapon of mass destruction. So, sure, they paid him well, but it didn't cover the costs when the oil he ferried made one-hundred-year floods into annual events, or brought hurricanes so far inland they were no longer tropical phenomena. They paid him well, of course, because they were paying him off. *But the thing about money*, Corinne thought, *is that it burns.*

That summer after Cameron died, Corinne had taken to sleeping in his button-down shirts. They'd smelled like his cologne, weed, and gasoline. And when his scent wore out, she'd fetched another one from his room. She began to exist in a twilight between Yesterday and Tomorrow, where she grieved her brother and the ground she stood on at the same time. Eventually, when she looked out of that damn window, she just saw one big black cloud, like an oil spill in the sky.

"*Boo!*"

Corinne jumped in a perfect 180-degree turn to find her uncle with a full-faced grin.

"I gotcha!" Uncle Harold wheezed as he clutched his chest. Corinne sucked her teeth as her uncle laughed loud enough to wake the devil. The sound was so infectious, she had to struggle to stay annoyed.

"Oh, girl, you know you funny," Uncle Harold said as he wiped a tear away. "Get on in there and help Mama with the gumbo now."

"It wasn't even that funny!" Corinne tried to hide her smile as she moved toward the door.

"Yes, it was! You damn near jumped outta your skin!" But as she walked by him, he caught her wrist and lowered his face closer to her ear. "Corinne, Mama's real glad to see you."

"I'm glad to see her too," Corinne insisted.

"Okay, girl. Be sweet."

"I will," Corinne murmured. She wanted to add, "I *am* being sweet," but she didn't feel like arguing. She just wanted to get in the kitchen with Grandma.

One of the ways Grandma showed her love was through food. If she loved you, she fed you. If she *really* loved you, she taught you how to cook. Grandma had tried to teach Cameron once when he was in high school. She had started with him the same way she'd started with Corinne: with his favorite thing to eat. In Corinne's case, it had been collard greens. In his, it had been pork chops. Once in the kitchen, though, Cameron had rushed through every step, using too much seasoning salt and not enough flour. When he finally did lay the pork chops in the skillet, he'd gotten too impatient and had pulled them out while they were still bleeding. "Boy, you gon' land somebody in the emergency room!" Grandma screeched. After that, she'd never allowed Cameron to make anything more complicated than a bowl of cereal.

Entering the kitchen, Corinne found Grandma sitting at the head of a table splayed with a colorful bounty of vegetables, a softer version of the grin Uncle Harold had just a moment ago on her face. She could see where they all got their cheekbones from.

"Come on, let's get this gumbo started before the game gets good."

"Okay, Grandma. Just let me go wash my hands right quick."

Grandma loved football, and so did Uncle Harold and Cameron. Corinne loved how much they loved it, how it made them delirious and hysterical, especially after the boring football games at Oberlin, where students did their homework in between sparse applause. Last year the team had torn down the goalpost after they'd won two games in a row, and Corinne had laughed so hard she snorted.

Corinne and her mother had been the only ones who didn't care for it. While everyone else sat enraptured around the TV in the living room, she and Mama would huddle in Grandma's bedroom with their books, only occasionally remarking to one another about some interesting passage. Mama had loved novels while Corinne loved biographies. She wished Mama had lived to see her grow out of the kids' section of the library and into autobiographies. Once the gumbo was simmering, Corinne would keep her and Mama's game day tradition just like she did every year. She would imagine Mama was in the room with her, reading over her shoulder. Sometimes she'd even read aloud to her, especially when she was reading about one of Mama's favorite authors, like James Baldwin or Toni Morrison. Mama had loved their fiction, and now Corinne devoured their essays.

She could still see Mama's golden skin and hear her honey-smooth voice, one that soothed even when it scolded. Sometimes

Corinne wasn't sure how many of her memories of her mother—where Mama was warm, smiling, and perfect—were her own and how much she'd heard from everyone else. No matter who they belonged to, though, she knew she couldn't live without them.

When Corinne came back into the kitchen with clean hands, Grandma motioned to the chopping board on the counter with an onion and a head of garlic. But before Corinne went to work, she wrapped her arms around her grandmother and rested her head on her shoulder as Grandma rinsed the rest of the vegetables in the sink.

"Girl, what's gotten into you?" Grandma reached a wet hand back to touch Corinne's cheek.

"Nothing," Corinne said sheepishly as she let go. "Just missed you."

Grandma chuckled. "Missed you, too, baby girl." Corinne was sure she saw the glimmer of a teardrop in her eye. "Now! Get the good knife!"

Thus, the ritual began. Corinne diced the garlic and onions into tiny little bits, then chopped the bell peppers and celery. Next, she cut the tomatoes into chunks and the okra into little pinwheels. Meanwhile, Grandma browned the chicken thighs, and the smell of frying chicken fought the stench of cigarette smoke. Corinne started to ask why she was using a smaller pot but realized she already knew.

And then it was time for the roux. While Grandma brought the chicken fat to a simmer in the pot, Corinne assumed her position at Grandma's side with the bag of flour. She was ready to add it to the oil one-fourth cup at a time, on command, while Grandma stirred. But this time, Grandma took the flour from her.

"You're ready." Grandma beamed as she handed her the wooden spoon.

Corinne's mouth fell open. Making a roux was for elite cooks. It was the step where Grandma became a control freak. Corinne had just accepted that it was something she would always watch and never do. "You sure, Grandma?"

"Yep, you stir this time. I'll tell you when it's ready."

Just then, Uncle Harold came in for a beer. "You coming to watch the game, Mama?"

Corinne could feel his eyes glued to the back of her neck. She knew he was coming not just for the beer but to monitor the peace.

"Yeah, I'm coming, Harold," Grandma answered. "I'm just about to teach my grandbaby how to make her first roux."

"Her? You sure she not gon' burn the house down, Mama?" Uncle Harold took a seat at the table behind them.

"Hush, Harold! Corinne might live in the books, but the girl can cook. She got 'the touch.'" Corinne blushed. Grandma had said that since Corinne was eight years old and had mixed her first batch of corn bread batter without disaster.

"Y'all remember when Katrina came through here and y'all made gumbo?"

"Yeah, Harold, I was trying to use up everything from the garden before the storm came."

"I remember too," Corinne said. "I helped Grandma pick everything out of the garden, but it was so dry that summer, there was hardly anything there. There was only, like, five okra and a whole bunch of squash. I think we even threw some collard greens in there."

"We did." Grandma laughed. "I had been praying all summer for rain, and I was foolish enough to think Katrina was my answer. I still haven't forgiven myself."

"Aw, Mama! You couldn't have done all that!"

"I know, Harold, I just . . ." Grandma shuddered. "It gives me the creeps to think about it now."

They hadn't had a lot of time to work with either. Katrina had hit Florida as a little pip-squeak of a storm, so tiny they'd mocked it at MTV's award show in Miami. But then she'd gone back into the Gulf of Mexico, turned around, and come barreling down on the Mississippi coast like it owed her money.

The weather projections had shown the storm covering the entire state—all the way up to the Delta. When Corinne saw that, she'd immediately thought about the levee breach that had led to the Great Flood back in 1927. When Grandma saw it, she'd stood straight up and yelled at the TV, *"A hurricane? Here?"* She'd jumped out of her house shoes and into her real shoes and dragged them to Vicksburg to stock up on anything they could possibly need to ride out a storm: batteries, candles, coolers, and so, *so* many cans. Even if Katrina passed them by, Grandma knew all too well that they were liable to get a tornado or two. There would be no such thing as "lucky," even if they did wind up blessed.

"Yeah, Unc, I bet you were glad you left New Orleans, huh?" Uncle Harold had gotten to Port Gibson one day before the storm made landfall and wound up staying with Grandma for the better part of a year. For Corinne and Cameron, it had almost felt like a present to have so much time with their uncle. He'd taught them how to play spades and pinochle and how to wrap coins and take them to the bank so that they'd give them back paper money. But they'd known it wasn't supposed to be this way.

"Actually, I didn't leave New Orleans 'cause I was worried about me." He tossed back a swig of beer. "I just didn't want Mama up here with two itty-bitty children in a bunch of tornadoes."

"We wasn't *that* little!" As the word *we* came out, Corinne felt her heart twinge.

"Go on now, Harold. I don't need you in here distracting her on her first roux. You know what they say, Cori?"

"A watched pot never boils, but an unwatched roux always burns," Corinne and Grandma said in unison. Grandma handed her the wooden spoon she always used for the roux. As soon as Corinne felt it in her hand, she knew she'd be eating this gumbo.

"Oh, so you *can* listen!" Grandma feigned surprise. "Ready?"

"Yes, ma'am." *I always* listen, Corinne thought to herself. *I just don't always* obey.

Grandma threw the first fourth of a cup of flour into the Dutch oven, and Corinne began to stir it furiously into the bubbling oil.

"Slow down, Cori," Grandma said softly. "You don't want your arm to fall off. Gentle. You ready for the next one?"

"Yes, ma'am."

Grandma sprinkled the next fourth cup into the pot. Then another, then another until the roux got thicker and thicker. First it turned blonde, then a lovely caramel. Eventually, it matched her and Grandma's complexion at a juicy pecan. By now, Corinne had been stirring nearly twenty-five minutes and could feel her arm turning to mush.

"We're almost there," Grandma assured her. "You know your aunt Connie thinks you can just open a can of something, heat it up in the microwave, and call yourself a cook."

"Yeah, I know." Aunt Connie wasn't really their aunt. She was one of Grandma's friends from church, but they'd known her so long, they called her "aunt" out of respect. Corinne remembered the regrettable meals at Aunt Connie's house, where Grandma would sneak out early and take them out to Krystal's or Chick-fil-A.

"Every once in a while, she'll pull out some seasoning salt, some ole Lawry's, and then you really can't tell her nothing." Grandma laughed. "Lord, yes! See, a lot of people today don't know the difference between 'cooking' and 'fixing' food." Then, as though she caught herself being mean, she added, "But you can't really blame her. Her own mama used cake mix and boxed frosting. Talking about 'she made a cake,' knowing full well Duncan Hines made the cake."

"Grandma, you ought to see what these people call cooking up at Oberlin." Corinne had worked in the dining halls at Oberlin washing pots since her freshman year because it was the best paying job on campus.

"I don't even think I want to know." Grandma paused.

"But it's hard to cook well for that many people. Give them women a break."

"How you know I'm talking about women?"

"Well, aren't you?"

"I am, but you shouldn't assume. And anyway, I'll give them a break when you give Aunt Connie a break."

"Now, she has no excuse! If laziness strikes your aunt Connie just one more time, it'll kill her!" Grandma looked at the roux. "Good job, Cori! I think you did it! You made your first roux! How you feeling?"

"Tired!" The muscles in her arm were burning.

"Okay, I got it from here. You can go on and read your little book or whatever you were about to do."

"I thought you was gonna watch the game, Grandma."

"I am! This won't take me long. But you just made your first roux! You get to rest after that. Go on and read your little book."

Corinne could tell Grandma was enjoying this milestone almost as much as a baby's first words. If she wanted to celebrate by making the rest of the gumbo by herself, who was Corinne to stop her?

"You can come back and take the shells off the shrimp later."

"Okay, Grandma."

"My grandbaby made a roux!" Grandma sang to herself as she added the onion and garlic to the pot.

Instead of going to her room and closing the door with her book, though, Corinne plopped down on the couch next to Uncle Harold. "You really came up here just to see about us during Katrina?"

"Yeah! Nobody really thought it was gonna be that bad down in New Orleans. Even if the weather reports said so, I didn't think *that* would happen."

"Why not, though? It was all over the news . . ."

"Because . . . I guess . . . New Orleans is a lucky city. Hadn't had a big storm in like a generation. Plus, who sits around imagining the unimaginable?"

"Yeah, I know. I don't even think the people who predicted the storm could have predicted the response."

"Shit, you call that a response? The people who were in charge of the response saw the same predictions we did, if not better. If anybody shoulda taken them seriously, it shoulda been them!"

"Right, Harold," Grandma yelled from the kitchen. "They need to be in jail!"

At Oberlin, Corinne had read about what happened in the jails after Katrina—inmates abandoned by guards, left to drown in cells or to try their damnedest to kick down the bars. Most didn't make it. Even the inmates on higher floors had suffered in the stifling heat with no ventilation, no electricity, no food, little water, and the smells of sewage wafting up from below. She'd read about a preteen girl, only one year older than she had been at the time of the storm, who was moved to an adult male facility during the chaos, where she spent days in water that came up to her neck.

"It was predictable, though."

"Yeah, I know, Niecey. That's why I keep saying 'predictions.'" Uncle Harold had that slight smile that let you know he was getting annoyed.

"No, I mean it was predictable based on history too. Same thing happened in 1927."

"Oh, here she come with this flood again!" Uncle Harold chortled. "This girl like a dog with a bone."

"But you can't tell her that dog won't hunt!" Grandma cackled from the kitchen doorway.

Corinne let out a half sigh, half chuckle. She knew it was a joke. But she hated it. Yes, it was true that Corinne had been obsessed with the Great Flood since she was a little girl, when she was supposed to be obsessed with Barbie dolls. She knew she talked about it a lot, but that's because it was relevant. She didn't see how everyone else didn't see it.

Everything was a joke to Uncle Harold, though. She envied and resented him for that.

Corinne went to her room and pulled her Stokely Carmichael autobiography back out. She wanted to rush to the part where he changed his name to Kwame Ture.

HOMESICK

December 25, 2013

Harold felt the crisp December air seep from the cracks in the window into the cracks in his toes. As he sprang up from the bed, he made a note to himself to go by The Home Depot in Vicksburg to get some caulking supplies. He couldn't have Mama out here with unsealed windows. *Plus*, he thought, *it's about time Cameron learned how to seal a window*. Then he realized that he was in Cameron's room, in Cameron's bed, and not on an air mattress on the floor or the sofa bed in the living room. And, all over again, he had to accept that there would be no new memories with his nephew.

Even with all the decorations, music, and food, this holiday felt so empty. And quiet. Cameron used to be the first one to wake up on Christmas morning. Any other morning, he would happily sleep past ten, no matter how loud Mama clicked her tongue in disapproval. But on Christmas Day, he was up with the sun, stalking around the house like a clumsy cat. By eight, when everyone else woke up, Cameron would be sitting on the couch by the Christmas tree, wearing a Santa hat and that same sneaky little grin he'd had since he was a toddler.

Harold had pulled Cameron's Santa hat out of the box of decorations Mama had waiting for him when he'd gotten in from New Orleans, and set it on the nightstand next to him. Now, as he ran his fingers along the fuzzy brim, he remembered when Cameron was little-little, before Corinne was born.

On Cameron's second Christmas, Harold had dressed up as Santa Claus and hidden in the closet with all the presents in a bag. He waited until he heard his cue from Yvonne—*"Cameron, where did all the presents go?"*—and then he'd jumped out with a loud *"Ho ho ho!"* When Harold had seen Cameron's chubby little face—paused between joy and confusion—he couldn't help himself. He reverted into his regular belly laugh. Cameron had recognized the sound immediately and had squealed as he rushed to hug him around the legs. For the rest of his life, Cameron swore he remembered that morning and that he hadn't been fooled even for a moment, but Harold was sure he only remembered because they told the story every year. The pictures from that holiday had become part of Mama's decorations. This summer, she'd pulled them out early and sat them on her makeshift altar along with pictures of all the others she had loved and lost.

Harold knew Christmas would never feel the same without Cameron, just like it never did without Yvonne. But he also knew that sitting in this room—which had been his own childhood bedroom as well as his nephew's—was only going to make it harder, heavier. He pushed his feet into his slippers, tied his plaid robe around himself, and fumbled into the kitchen, careful not to wake Mama and Corinne. Best to let them come to terms with this chasm on their own time.

Harold felt his stomach bubble with that familiar hunger that comes after a night of too many beers. He reached into the back of the refrigerator and pulled out the pot with the last bits of Mama's gumbo. Normally, there would be none left this many days later. But this year, Cameron wasn't there to hog it all, and Corinne had only been able to eat one bowl before she'd run to the bathroom and never looked at the pot again. Harold took the last of the rice and poured the precious little gumbo on top of it. He didn't want to wake Mama with the microwave, so he ate it cold for the first time since Katrina.

Ever since Harold moved to New Orleans, Mama made the dish to welcome him home for the Christmas holidays. It started as her sarcastic way of mocking him for leaving Port Gibson. "Since you from New Orleans now!" She'd smirk at him when she put the first bowl in front of him. "Mama, you know you just wanted an excuse to make gumbo!" he'd shoot back at her. After all, it wasn't like it was a foreign delicacy in Port Gibson. She was even using Grandma Cindy's recipe.

By the time Cameron and Corinne were born, Harold and Mama had dropped the banter and Christmastime gumbo was just an unquestioned tradition. Harold brought home the crab legs and shrimp because Mama liked the idea of it coming straight from the Gulf. By now, he even associated gumbo more with Port Gibson than with New Orleans.

His favorite part was the day after, when all the flavors had melded together overnight. The day after that, it was just as good. The bowl in front of him now was just about to cross that threshold from flavorful to stale. But it was good enough to sop up the alcohol from last night. After he finished, he went to the living room and turned the television on the lowest volume and tried to follow the animated arguments on ESPN.

Harold woke up to the smell of bacon and coffee and knew the women were making breakfast. He stumbled into the kitchen. And there they were—Mama in her housecoat and Corinne in an oversized T-shirt and leggings.

"Merry Christmas, Mama!" He bent down to kiss his mother's cheek as she flipped the bacon.

"Merry Christmas, Harold." She squeezed the arm he'd draped over her collarbone. He could feel the weariness in her voice.

"Merry Christmas, Uncle." Corinne turned away from her skillet of yellowish crumbles to hug his waist.

"Merry Christmas, Niecey." He kissed her forehead and drew her into his side. Her silk headscarf felt smooth against his stubble. "What's this you making?"

"That's her scrambled *tofu*," Mama said the last word as though it had betrayed her. "She wants me and you to try some. I'll do it if you do it."

"I might try it." Harold looked over Corinne's shoulder. He'd seen tofu at the Vietnamese restaurants in New Orleans. "Isn't tofu supposed to be white, though? How you get it to look yellow?"

"I used turmeric." Corinne held a bottle of the bright orange spice up for him to see. *She must have brought it with her from Oberlin*, he thought. He'd never seen anything like it in Mama's cabinets.

"What does that taste like?" He braced himself.

"Doesn't really taste like anything, at least not to me. But it's really good for you. It'll be done in a minute. Just need to add in some spinach."

Even though he'd heard of tofu, Harold didn't know exactly what it was, and he resisted the urge to ask. Instead, he released her. "I'll be happy to try it, baby girl. Right after I get me some coffee."

He reached over Corinne's head to open the cabinet that held his favorite mug. It was green with polka dots. He loved it because his sister had given it to him for his birthday way back when, but also because it was about one and a half times the size of a regular mug. Yvonne had always marveled at how many cups of coffee he could drink in a morning. This, she'd said, should save him a trip or two to the kitchen. He poured a scant amount of milk into his mug, filled it with coffee, and took a seat at the table behind Mama and Corinne.

"How'd you sleep, Harold?"

He knew Mama was really asking about how he was managing in Cameron's old room without him, but he knew if either of them said that out loud, they'd all fall apart. "I slept fine, Mama. The wind is getting in through the windows, though. Gonna need to do something about that."

"Yeah, I was trying not to say anything about that . . ."

"Mama, why not? I coulda caulked up them windows."

"Oh, I just didn't want to bother you." She sat a plate in front of him with grits, eggs, and bacon.

"You're not bothering me, Mama. I don't mind helping you."

"I know, Harold. That's why I love you."

"I love you, too, Mama. And not *just* 'cause you can cook!"

As Mama sat her plate at the head of the table next to Harold, Corinne pushed a spoonful of her scrambled tofu onto their plates. Harold held his fork along the side of his grits to make sure her yellow mush didn't bleed into them. He figured he might as well try it first and get it out of the way.

"Oh, this isn't bad, Corinne!" Mama's voice went up a few octaves. For all her talk about Corinne being such a good cook, she still sounded surprised Corinne was able to make tofu taste like something.

"See, Grandma? All you got to do is season it!" Corinne took her seat across from her uncle.

"Don't get smart, now. You must have seasoned the bejesus out of this." Mama took another bite. "But good job!"

Corinne batted her long eyelashes at Harold, and he knew it was his turn. He took a breath and then a bite. It was less chewy than the eggs it was trying to imitate, but the flavors of onion and garlic were familiar enough that he couldn't complain.

"Yeah, Corinne, good job," Harold agreed and was surprised to find he meant it. "I'm gonna stick with my eggs, but this ain't half bad."

Once they finished breakfast, they didn't even put their dishes in the sink before they let their instincts guide them into the living room. The distance between the kitchen and the living room had never felt longer or more treacherous. They each moved like the ghosts from *A Christmas Carol*, with bent backs and chained feet. Harold heard Mama sniffling and reached behind him for her hand.

"I just wish he was here, Harold." She clutched her cigarettes in one hand and squeezed his hand back with the other.

"Me, too, Grandma." Corinne rubbed Mama's shoulder as she passed her to take a seat on the floor by the Christmas tree. They'd all agreed that none of them were really in the gift-giving or receiving mood. When they'd talked about it before, Harold thought keeping the gifts short and sweet this year would make it less painful. But now, the empty tree made everything else feel even more hollow.

"Hand her mine, Cori!" Harold shouted as he helped Mama to her seat in the reclining chair in the corner.

Corinne pulled out a big, sparkly green gift bag with tissue paper hanging out and passed it to Mama.

"Now, Harold," Mama admonished. "We said we were keeping it small this year. What is in this big old bag?"

"Just open it, Mama."

"Oh, it's heavy too!" She pulled out a brown canvas bag with handheld garden tools attached to the side. "This is so nice, Harold! Thank you!"

"You haven't even gotten to the best part, Ma!" Harold took the bag from her, and while she lit a cigarette, he showed her how to turn it into a stool. "Now you can sit on this while you work in the garden. You don't have to hunch your back all over."

"Well, isn't that something!" she exclaimed. "Where did you manage to find this?"

Harold made a zipping motion across his lips. She didn't need to know that he'd spent hours scouring the internet looking for gardening tools for people with bad backs and come across this gem on a website he'd already forgotten the name of. The smile on her face, though, let him know that every second had been worth it.

Corinne handled the gifts gingerly as though one wrong move could break them all. Harold got a new set of fishing rods from Mama and a bottle of cologne from Corinne. Mama got Corinne a new sketchbook and colored pencils, and Harold got her an engraved pocketknife. If she was going to be running all around New Orleans and the outer parishes talking to strangers, he felt better knowing she could at least cut somebody.

"Grandmama, this one is for you." Corinne handed her a rectangular package wrapped in red paper with jingle bells printed all over it. Harold smiled because he knew that she only called Mama "Grandmama" when she was trying to be extra sweet.

"Thank you, baby!"

Mama was a special kind of gift-giving challenge. She had a habit of dreaming up things that no one had ever seen before—like the year she insisted on a gold quilted jacket—and complaining bitterly when she didn't get them. Harold's many years of trial and error had taught him exactly which gifts to get her and which to avoid. With the special somberness of this Christmas, he had tried to get Corinne to tell him what she was getting Mama, but she'd insisted that she knew what she was doing. Her eyes sparkled as she watched her grandmother peel back the wrapping paper.

"Oh." Mama sounded less than excited. "Whiskey glasses."

"Not just any whiskey glasses, Grandma!" Corinne was undeterred. "These are from Nashville. See the map on them?"

Harold looked over Mama's shoulder as she took one of the two glasses out of the package. He could see the white lines sketching out Nashville's neighborhoods and major streets. He hadn't been to Nashville since he was a child, but he could clearly see the intersection of I-65 and I-40. When Mama turned the glass over, he could see *Nashville* engraved in gold lettering across the front.

Without looking up, Mama put the glass back down and closed the box. Then she put her cigarette out on the ashtray on the table. "Thank you very much, Corinne. That must have been very expensive."

Harold saw Corinne's face fall out of the corner of his eye.

"It wasn't about the price, Grandma! You don't like them?"

"I didn't say that, Corinne." Mama got to her feet, still not looking at Corinne. "I think I'm going to go lay down. I need a little nap before we start on dinner."

"Grandmama!" The sparkle in Corinne's eyes turned liquid as Mama disappeared into her own stormy world. Harold knew it was pointless to even try to reach her once she'd slipped through that trapdoor. She walked to her room like Corinne and Harold were ghosts and she was the only real person in the house.

As Mama's door clicked shut, Corinne looked at him with trembling lips before she sprang up and went into her room, leaving her gifts in a pile underneath the tree.

Harold sighed hard. This week of grilling on Mama's back porch and watching football in her living room was supposed to be his precious break before he had to spend all of January as his niece's full-time guardian.

Oberlin had a thing called "winter term," where students took the whole month of January to pursue what they called "self-directed education." Research projects, internships, personal growth—all up to the student. Pretty much anything they wanted to do. This year, Corinne was going to spend the month down in New Orleans with the Gulf South Historical Project collecting anthropological data about the 2010 BP oil spill. Harold thought the phrase "collecting anthropological data" was an overblown way of saying she was going to talk to people and write down what they said. Corinne was going to talk to nurses and waiters and fishermen all over South Louisiana about what they remembered from the spill, from beginning to end.

He'd been bracing himself for it for weeks. He was so used to having his house all to himself—free from the waves of Mama's overbearing, overwhelming worry and her unpredictable moods but close enough to get to her in a pinch. But starting in January, not only would he have a new person in the house—eating up the food, breathing up the air—but he'd be responsible for her. He could already hear the panicked phone calls from Corinne lost all the way in Algiers or in the hospital with a broken leg because she decided to cross Claiborne Avenue after dark. As much as he loved his niece, he wasn't sure he was ready for that level of liability. But now he had to deal with this.

Even though Mama wouldn't say it, Harold knew she wasn't just lashing out over some whiskey glasses. This was one of her revenge outbursts, to get back at Corinne for shutting down on her over the summer and leaving her alone in her grief—even for going to Oberlin in the first place. Ever since Cameron fell off that boat and to his death in May, Harold saw his nephew's ghost hover over his mother and his niece, closer than their own shadows, staring bullets into their backs. The two of them knew how to do so many things together—garden, cook, play cards—but they couldn't grieve together for the life of them. There was always another explosion waiting just underneath the surface. Harold had become an expert at defusing the bombs, but it was exhausting. He got up and went to Corinne's room. She'd left the door open, but he knocked anyway.

"Cori." He tried to sound soothing. "You really should have talked to me about this."

Corinne just stared at him with furrowed brows and shiny cheeks. Her pain was so palpable, he felt a twinge of guilt for pointing out what she should have done, so he switched to the important part.

"You know she doesn't like to talk about Nashville, Niecey. What on earth would make you think she'd want to think about it today of all days?"

"Uncle Harold." Corinne motioned for him to sit next to her on the bed. "I've been so homesick at Oberlin. So homesick. I miss everything, from the humidity to the River to just the way people talk down here. The way it smells. I miss it so much it hurts. And that made me think about Grandma and how much she must miss Nashville. Especially after all this time away."

"So you thought she must be homesick too?" He silently blessed her heart.

"Well, yes! I thought that must be why she complains about Port Gibson all the time."

Harold laughed. "All the damn time! But I'm not sure she'd *like* anywhere." A puff of Corinne's hair had fallen out of her scarf. He pushed it out of her eyes and lifted her angular chin. "But Nashville is a really, really painful place for her. And you know why."

"I mean, I know a little bit. She went to the white people schools up there. But anytime I try to get her to talk more about it, she either blows up or shuts down."

"Corinne, she didn't 'go to the white people schools'; she integrated them. That's a very different thing. Something neither of us can understand."

"You know that's what I meant—"

"But it's not what you said, Cori. Words matter, especially when you're talking about something this sensitive." He squeezed her shoulder. "And the words you don't say matter just as much as the ones you do. So when Mama doesn't talk about Nashville, she's still saying something. You should listen."

Corinne leaned into his shoulder. "You remember when I put up that poster of Ruby Bridges on my wall?"

"And Mama damn near lost her mind? Yeah, how can I forget?"

"You know, I thought she'd be proud. I coulda put anybody on my wall, but I chose somebody who went through what Grandmama went through."

"But that's the thing, Cori. Ruby *didn't* go through the same thing Mama went through. For one thing, when Mama went to that white school up in Nashville, it was still the fifties. Ruby did it in the sixties, and that's different, in a different city. For another thing, two people can live through the exact same thing and come out changed in whole different ways. Like with Katrina. You ever hear of two Katrina stories that sound the exact same? People lived on the same street in the same flood and got stories that don't sound nothing like each other. Only thing they got in common is water and wind and pain. When you got that poster, it just brought Mama back to her pain. You can't control how somebody else hurts. Can't predict it either. And there's always only one type of pain, Corinne, and it's always yours. It's the only thing you can feel."

"Seemed like she was madder at me for 'not knowing,' to tell the truth. But it wasn't for lack of trying. I asked all the time, but I'm not a mind reader or a time traveler."

"I know what you mean." Harold sighed. "Look, she won't even talk to me about it, and I've been trying way longer than you. She'd talk me and your mama's ears off about her high school, so much so that your mama named your brother after it. Or about that dog—"

"Dandy!"

"Yes, lord. She's told me so many stories about that dog I feel like I met the little nigga myself." He sighed. "But my point is that maybe it's not for you to understand, or even to know. Maybe it's just for you to accept. Accept that she's been through something you can't understand."

"So what do I do now?"

"Simple: drop it. You and I both know *all that* wasn't just about Nashville. It's just easier to get mad at that than it is to deal with the fact that Cameron ain't here—"

"See, that's not fair!" Corinne tensed up. "You were just scolding me about how I wasn't the only one to lose him, but neither was she!"

"Now did I say anything about fair, Corinne? I'm just telling you what is, and it's obvious. You should have thought twice about those little whiskey glasses, sure, but sometimes the way people mourn doesn't make sense—and this is *her* house and she is your *grandmother*. We just have to give her grace, even when it's not fair." Harold could feel the tension relax in Corinne's shoulders.

"Now watch, she's gonna go over there for a minute and then come back out sweet as pie, ready to start cooking. And when she does, I want you to be just as sweet and go help her in the kitchen."

"I do more than just help now!"

"I know, honey, I know." He laughed. "You gon' make me some scrambled tofu once we're back in New Orleans? It really wasn't half bad."

"Of course, Uncle." Corinne reached over to hug his neck, and the world was whole again.

TOMORROW

December 1, 1958

Cora woke up shivering in a pool of her own sweat, her heart beating out of her chest and her mind full of images of broken glass and singed schoolbooks. She realized that she'd kicked her quilts onto the floor again. She scrambled to pull them back around her tiny body as the cold air began to pierce her skin. She buried herself in her quilt and tried to rock herself back to slumber before the sun rose.

But sleep was not a simple thing to find now that she'd learned to fear her dreams. Ever since last August, when Mama and Daddy had walked her down Lischey Avenue to Glenn Elementary, she had the same nightmares over and over. In one, she was followed home by either one lone white man or a gang of them in a car, and then stolen away and strung up by her toes, her mouth bound so she couldn't scream. In the other one, the one she'd just had, she would be sitting at her table or walking to the lunchroom and then—*boom!* The dynamite exploded, and everyone ran. The windows broke and the walls fell down. Almost every time, someone pushed her down and she was crushed and forgotten underneath the charred debris.

Now, on the other side of the wall, she thought she could hear Mama and Daddy mumbling in the kitchen. They, too, seemed to sleep a lot less since she started at Glenn. She thought of going out to the kitchen but didn't want to wake her two brothers in the bed across from her, or hear Daddy's fussing about how she wouldn't be able to concentrate if she didn't get a good night's sleep. Instead, she tried to replace the bombed-out pictures from her nightmare with her memories from Thanksgiving the week before, when the house had been full and warm and Mama's mother and all her sisters were here trying to out-cook each other, while Cora and her brothers and their cousins tried to outrace each other in the backyard. Then, at dinner, they'd all eaten until their stomachs bulged.

Perhaps the only good thing that had happened since Mama and Daddy enrolled her in the White Folks School was that her imagination had become her superpower. She could make the world inside her head so real she could touch it, taste it. Now, she used it to taste Grandmama's chess pie again. She could feel the gritty texture on her tongue, and the sweetness lulled her back to sleep.

⸺

This time, Cora woke up to a warm, wet lick on her cheek and an overwhelming gust of dog breath. She opened her eyes to see her half German shepherd, half who-knows-what smiling down at her with his ears pointed up straight. He looked so proud of himself, like he'd rescued her from another world.

"Dandy!" When she squealed his name, he broke into a dance exuberant enough to shake the bed. Daddy had brought him home for her last year, back when the phone still rang off the hook and Daddy and the neighbors sat all night in the living room with their guns. He'd even let Cora name the dog, much to the chagrin of her older brothers, Harvey and Gerald. Cora noticed that even though the tiny puppy had ears too big for his head, he still had a strut, like he had places to go and people to impress. So she'd called him Dandy. Now he was almost her size. She wished she'd grown as much so fast.

Once she stood up, the smell of dog breath was replaced by the smell of bacon, confirming that it was, in fact, time to get ready for school. Her stomach swelled with a trepidation that would sit there all day, like Thanksgiving dinner. She swallowed her tears, squared her shoulders, and went to the bathroom to wash her face and brush her teeth.

Mama had starched and ironed Cora's blue dress so hard that it rustled as she put it on, but it was warm, and she was grateful for that. She made her way to the kitchen table and took her seat in front of the plate of bacon, eggs, and a little bit of grits Mama had made for her. She had to eat faster than usual today because Mama had to go talk to a man at Fisk, all the way in North Nashville. Harvey and Gerald were still getting dressed. They could leave for school later since they could walk by themselves. Cora wished she could go with them, just to see what it would be like to walk with other Black children. In the beginning, her parents walked her to and from school every day. Now, Cora walked home from school by herself, but Mama still liked to walk her in the morning.

As Cora shoveled the eggs into her mouth, Mama took her station behind her and tamed her hair into pigtails. They didn't talk about why Mama had to go to Fisk, Daddy's alma mater, but Cora knew she had lost her job at the PET Milk Company because of where Cora went to school. She knew that out of a mix of sympathy and respect for the family's sacrifice, the president of Fisk was trying to create a new job for Mama.

"Slow down, Cora," Mama chided. "You're going to mess around and choke." Cora felt a wave of shame pass over her temples. Since she started school, it was like she'd forgotten how to do anything right. Everything that was right at school was wrong at home. She was either too fast or too slow, too quiet or too loud, too fat or too skinny. And every time she adjusted, she wound up getting yet another penalty.

Cora had never wanted to blaze any trails, but it hadn't been up to her. She hadn't found out Daddy's plans for her until she was clutching his hand through a snarling, spitting crowd of white folks as Mama and Daddy took her to enroll at Glenn Elementary, along with Jackie Faye and her parents. *So this*, she'd thought, *is the way to school*. She'd looked down to avoid their faces, even though she barely came up past their hips. August air in Nashville was always thick with humidity, but their panic had made it so heavy it felt like the sky was falling. The air smelled like gunpowder and tasted like fear.

Nothing had made sense. Fully grown men and women—doctors, salesmen, secretaries, pastors, fathers, mothers—were screaming, shrieking at little children, nearly frothing at the mouth. The newspapers and later the history books would say that the mob was "angry." But when Cora had managed to bring herself to look at their faces, that wasn't what she had seen at all. She'd seen terror, pure and unmistakable, of two little Black girls going to the first grade. Hysteria.

She remembered Daddy squeezing her hand hard as they approached the stairs to enter the school. A group of skinny white teenagers had stood in his way with their arms folded and sinister grins across their faces. Daddy had trained his eye on one of the police officers who stood off to the side, like he neither heard nor saw the crowd. When the officer had finally met his gaze, Daddy had shouted, "Well? Aren't you going to do something about the people blocking the sidewalk?" The officer had fumbled over and shooed the teenagers away. As they retreated, they had walked backward so they didn't have to break eye contact with Daddy.

Others in the crowd had called Mama and Daddy by their first names: Jewel and George. It had chilled Cora to the bone to hear her parents' first names—words that were so sacred even *she* couldn't say them—turned into slurs in the mouths of these fanatics. *And if they knew their names, what else did they know? Did they know her name? Her address?*

Cora had even recognized some of the faces scowling down at her. One of them was the Avon Lady, who had been syrupy sweet when she had sold Mama her lipstick. Another was the milkman who had always called Mama "Mrs. Sterling" when he'd come to the house. Daddy had always made it a point to stand straight and tall whenever the milkman stopped by, and now Cora understood why. Another had been Mama's boss when she worked at PET Milk. Now, they were beet red with a fear and fury that made them look like demons. The pictures that Cora saw later in the papers would never capture that redness, just like they couldn't capture her horror.

When they got to the top of the stairs, the principal, Mrs. Brent, had been there to meet them.

"I don't know whether I can stand all this." Mama had sighed.

"I don't know if I can either, Mrs. Sterling," Mrs. Brent had admitted. *"It's the most ridiculous thing I've ever seen."* Then she'd turned to look at Cora and Jackie Faye and smiled. *"I guess you've never had so many people talking to you before. It won't be like that when you come back for class. You'll just be here with the other children."*

Mama had told Cora that the mobs were so swollen because so many of them had come from outside the city limits, several counties out. She said some "segregationist" had come all the way from New Jersey and convinced them that a bunch of five- and six-year-olds were working for the "Communists" and the "Yankees" to invade elementary schools around the city. When Cora had told Mama about the ones she recognized and asked how they could believe something so crazy unless they already wanted to, Mama had just sighed and hugged her.

Daddy had told her that the same drama was playing out at other white elementary schools all over the city. But Cora never met any of the other children except Jackie Faye. At the beginning of first grade, they'd walked to school and back home together, always with one of their parents. But when the white folks had bombed the brand-new Hattie Cotton School, Jackie Faye's parents took her out of Glenn. Even though it happened in the middle of the night and no one was hurt, the bombing was just a few miles away—and way too close for Jackie Faye's parents. If they had lived on the other side of the railroad tracks, they would have been zoned to Hattie Cotton. Cora was jealous of Jackie Faye every day for the rest of her life.

If the bombing had left Cora alone at Glenn, at least it had also dispersed the mob. It was like they'd just realized that someone might get hurt—including white children. The day she went to school after the bombing, when the smoke was still in the air, there had been just a few straggling protesters across the street, but they only stared at her. Still, the ice between her and her classmates and teachers had hardly melted. When she got to class, one of the trashy white boys had told her, "My daddy told me to ask you if it was worth getting that school bombed." Before she could answer, her teacher had shushed them.

The death threats didn't stop either. One afternoon that first year, even though Daddy had strictly forbidden it, Gerald had answered the phone. On the other end, a white woman drawled, "How'd you like to find Cora Mae dead in an alley *one day after school?"* Her brother had run into their shared bedroom with bugged eyes and told her. Mama had whipped him less for defying Daddy than for running his mouth. Cora had dry-heaved all night.

Cora hadn't needed to hear the death threats to know what the people who had stood in that crowd were capable of. And even if they weren't waiting outside of her school anymore, she knew they still lurked: at the grocery store, on the buses, at every school assembly. She had felt their eyes on her everywhere, even when she slept.

Now, at least, there were two more Black kids in the school, even though they were both in the first grade. The city of Nashville had decided to integrate successively as Cora's cohort advanced from grade to grade. That meant that now the first grade was integrated, while Cora barreled ahead integrating the second, and next year the third, and finally the fourth. Blazing trails was lonely work.

———

As Mama walked her to school, Cora winced at the sharp December bite. The air still felt heavy, but now it was also cold. Cora listened to the echo of her patent leather shoes as she climbed the concrete stairs at Mama's elbow. It was still early and empty when they reached the top of the staircase. There were only a few other families around, but none close enough to hear. Cora remembered again the joy of playing with her cousins and eating with her aunts. A sudden chill ran up her spine, and she gripped

Mama's hand with all her might. Mama didn't ask why; she just squeezed back.

"I don't wanna go," Cora whispered through her scarf.

Mama leaned down to cup her face. She smelled like talcum powder and salt. "I know, baby. I don't want you to go either."

Mama tied Cora's scarf tighter, kissed her forehead, and sent her into the building, where the janitor stood holding the door. The janitor, a Black man like most of the school's service staff, gave Mama the customary nod and followed Cora to her classroom like a friendly ghost. Years later, Mama had told Cora that that janitor had promised her and Daddy that if anything ever happened to their little girl, she wouldn't be the only one hurt. Then he'd flashed them the knife he carried with him every day.

"We have exciting news today, class!" Mrs. Block, who rarely rose from her seat, stood up in her near-uniform of pencil skirt, frumpy blouse, and cat-eye glasses. Her gravity-defying beehive looked even more ridiculous as she towered over the globe on her desk. "We're going to be putting on a Christmas play! And *all* of you will be in it. All your parents will be there, and the whole school. We'll get to show the whole community how talented and special you all are. Isn't that exciting?"

As some of the students oohed and aahed, Mrs. Block added an extra sway to her step as she strutted from table to table announcing high-profile roles.

Jennifer was going to play Mary, naturally. She had the blondest hair and the bluest eyes. David was going to play

Joseph. He was the tallest, had the dustiest brown hair and the pointiest nose. When Mrs. Block got to the back of the room, she paused by Cora's table, glared down, and flattened her voice. "Sit up straight, Cora."

When it was time to leave the classroom for recess that afternoon, Cora filed into the line like all the other students, but she paused when she made it to the door. She looked up at Mrs. Block, who was holding the door open. Her thin, pink lips turned from a smile to a straight line when she met Cora's eyes.

"Excuse me, m-m-ma'am?" She hated the stutter that had crept into her throat over the past year. Daddy hated it, too, and tried everything he could to scare, beat, shame it out of her.

"What is it?" Mrs. Block's tone became sharp, not unlike the chill in the air outside. Her volume spiked loud enough that Cora was worried the other kids would hear and make fun of her.

She tried to whisper, "W-w-w-what's g-g-g-gonna be my part in the p-p-play?" She didn't dare look up. Instead, she stared at her reflection on her shoes.

"W-w-w-what's g-g-g-gonna be y-y-your part in the p-p-play?" Mrs. Block mocked her. "Don't you know you're supposed to look up when you talk to a grown-up?"

Cora tried to stop the tears prickling in her eyes as she raised her head. She found a sinister smile etched across Mrs. Block's face, but then something that looked like shame wiped it away, like she had remembered that she was talking to somebody's child.

"I'll tell you tomorrow. Now, come on, you're holding up recess."

Cora knew that she wouldn't get a starring role in the play. Those had already been announced, but she thought she could get a part in the chorus, or even a dancing part. Whatever it was, she wanted to have time to practice. She wanted to get it right—to finally get *something* right.

She told Mama and Daddy that night at dinner and regretted it immediately. They were so excited they did the same thing they did whenever they found out there was going to be a Black person on *The Dinah Shole Show* or *I Love Lucy*—they called the whole neighborhood. You could hear the phone ring all the way down Arrington Street. Then they called Mama's family around Nashville and even made long-distance calls to Daddy's family over in Mississippi. Cora decided that if this was what it felt like to be a movie star, it was the last thing she ever wanted to be.

The neighbors were all so sure Cora was "going to show those white folks," especially if there was a dance involved. Everyone, it seemed, had some acting or dancing expertise to pass on to her. Grandma Cindy insisted on coming up from Mississippi for the grand event. She had to take the train from Vicksburg to Birmingham, and then from Birmingham to Nashville. "No way I'm going to miss my grandbaby taking the stage with these white folks!"

Cora only told her mother that Mrs. Block hadn't told her what the part was. She told everyone else that it was a "surprise"—which was only a half lie. It was a surprise; she just wasn't in on it.

"Whatever it is, honey, you just do your best and we'll be right proud, you hear?" Mama told her. "We'll be right there with you."

But it went on like that for weeks: *tomorrow, tomorrow, tomorrow.* The never-ending, never-coming horizon.

When the day of the play finally arrived, Grandma Cindy woke Cora up early to run a fresh hot comb through her hair and fit her into the immaculate, bejeweled white dress that Mama had bought for the occasion. Grandma Cindy used her special bottle of castor oil laced with fragrant honeysuckle petals. Cora watched her work in the mirror, admiring her gray hair, the only signifier of her age, as she pinned it back in a chignon. Her skin remained a smooth and vibrant chestnut brown, even in the corners of her eyes.

They had Grandma Cindy's specialty and Cora's favorite for breakfast that morning: biscuits. Cora ate two, and when she'd reached for a third, Mama smacked her hand away and reminded her that she didn't want to be busting out of her dress for the rest of the day. Harvey snuck one to her under the table anyway, and she stashed it in her lunch box for later.

Grandma Cindy took her to school herself that morning. She wore all white to show everyone that they were a unit, even with a white hat to match. At the top of the stairs, she knelt down to Cora's eye level and tilted Cora's head up. "Now you hold your head high, girl! You are the smartest, most beautiful girl this little funky school has ever seen, even if they don't want to know it. You hear me?"

Cora nodded and hugged her grandmother's neck. "You go on now. Don't be late. I'll see you after the play." Cora ran into school with a lightness that felt brand-new.

As soon as she walked into the classroom, Mrs. Block came right up to her, beaming. "I've got *just* the part for you!"

Cora smiled. Maybe something had changed? Maybe she'd finally done Daddy proud and "made the white folks see." Then she noticed her classmates staring at her in shock and realized it was the first time she'd ever shown her teeth in that classroom. She rushed to cover her mouth as they whispered and snickered to each other.

"What's my part?" Cora asked through her fingers for what felt like the one thousandth time, but this time without a stutter.

"Well, I can't tell you *now*! That would ruin the surprise, wouldn't it?" Mrs. Block said in that tone Cora was never sure was nice or cruel. She sashayed back to the front of the room and started writing the date on the chalkboard: December 18, 1958.

That afternoon, Cora watched the performance from the auditorium seats for the last time. The class had been rehearsing for two weeks by then, over which time some parts had been reassigned and others created as Mrs. Block had changed the play to her whims and their talents. By now, though, Cora was the only one who still didn't have a part.

After the final rehearsal, Cora went back up to Mrs. Block. "W-what happened to my part, Mrs. B-Block?"

"Oh yes, how could I forget? You have the most important part of all!" She smiled and beckoned Cora to follow her behind the curtain.

When they got backstage, Mrs. Block grabbed the bunched-up stage curtain and handed it to Cora. "Your job is to hold these curtains—*tight*—so that everyone can see the play!" She demonstrated the grip she wanted to see on the curtains, and Cora noticed her knuckles bulging out of her skin. She didn't know white people's knuckles could get whiter.

"W-w-what?"

"We wouldn't have a play at all if the curtain is in the way, Cora. Don't be silly."

Cora's jaw fell, and her whole face followed.

"Now, Cora," Mrs. Block said in a softer tone. "We're doing this for your own good. Imagine if we let them see you?"

Cora looked at her feet like her life depended on it as she imagined the mob from last year storming the stage. What if that happened and the janitor wasn't able to get to her fast enough? What if they strung Daddy up the way they threatened to last year?

"Now, don't be nervous! Just do your best!" Mrs. Block stomped away in her cloggy heels, leaving an echo of *clack-clack-clack*s and a numb seven-year-old in her wake.

Cora felt that hot, hot steam of shame radiate out from her

heart to her toes, her fingertips, and her temples. Her eyelids burned, but she couldn't cry, and it took all her strength to breathe quietly.

She went through the last hours before the play in a daze. Mrs. Block corralled the students into her classroom for snacks and pep talks before the play was set to start. Cora didn't talk to anyone or take any of the cookies or punch. She didn't even take one of the peanut butter sandwiches, even though she loved peanut butter and Daddy told her it had been invented by a Black man from Alabama. She thought about eating the biscuit she'd sneaked out at breakfast, but her mouth was too dry. She heard Mrs. Block mumble something as she walked by her desk, but she couldn't make it out all the way. Everything sounded like an echo.

When the time came, she held the curtain as tight as her tiny hands could manage. Through every reenactment, every carol, every missed line, every rhythmless, soulless dance routine. The "play" had never made any sense, though she'd never dared to tell anyone as much. It was just a collection of random scenes and Christmas jingles. The nativity scene at the end came out of nowhere, like the end of a fever dream. By the time it was over, Cora couldn't tell if she was holding the curtain or if it was the only thing holding *her* together.

She didn't know how long she'd stood there before she heard the crash of applause from the audience and she realized it was over. Everyone rushed out to take their final bow, and Mrs. Block glared at Cora from the center of the stage as if to warn her against coming out with them. Cora took it as permission to leave.

As soon as she stepped off the stage, Grandma Cindy's rough hands grabbed hers and led her out to the car. As they got closer to the door, Mama appeared behind them, walking just as briskly. Daddy was already waiting in the driver's seat. He turned on the engine as soon as he saw the three of them step out of the building. Cora wanted to ask if her brothers had come tonight, but the words were stuck in her throat. When she got in the car, she was relieved to find that they weren't here.

Once she was safely in the back seat, she curled up in her grandmother's lap and realized she hadn't felt the ground under her on the way to the car. As soon as Daddy pulled out of the parking lot, the tears that couldn't come before came rushing out like a volcano. Over her sobs and heaves, she heard the start of one of Daddy's lectures, "You shoulda—"

"Don't you *dare*!" Grandma Cindy hissed back.

"Not tonight, George," Mama whispered, her gaze fixed firm in front of her. "Not tonight."

KEY OF LIFE

January 11, 2014

All the houses on Uncle Harold's street looked so alive, like they had personalities of their own. The house across the street looked welcoming with its teal and yellow. The one next to it was a sassy maroon and gold. The next two—painted bright, devilish red—looked like they were in the midst of plotting a scheme. Still, the colors didn't clash. They laughed and sang in harmony. Uncle Harold's shotgun house was yellow with blue trim, which he said was too close to Southern University's colors for his taste. Even though he didn't own it, he was toying with the idea of painting it purple and gold for Alcorn. *"Everybody here will just think it's for LSU,"* he'd reckoned.

All of the houses had front porches, even if they were tiny. Back in Port Gibson, those were rare, at least on Grandma's street. Instead, most people had back porches that didn't provide for the caliber of people watching Corinne craved. She loved sitting on Uncle Harold's front porch and watching the neighbors the way Grandma watched the birds from her swing in the backyard. Uncle Harold had introduced her to some of his neighbors on her shorter visits before. Now that she'd been here more than a week, she marveled at the mix of warmth and distance he'd cultivated with the people who lived closest to him. She could sense there was a bond there, but she could also tell that he was still a mystery to them, and he liked it that way.

Corinne often waved at them as they walked by or parked their cars. She made up little stories about who they were—how they got here and what their lives were like before, during, and after the storm. Sometimes they'd fill in the gaps in her stories themselves. From the way they talked about the neighborhood—and they were quick to tell her that it was the oldest Black neighborhood in the country—it seemed that every square inch of it was deserving of a historic marker. She watched the way *they* watched the white people who had moved into the houses they'd been priced out of, who jogged on the jagged sidewalks and didn't look up to say good morning. She saw the bitter nostalgia in their eyes when a new For Sale sign popped up and the world ended afresh.

As much as the neighbors were haunted by the storm that had already come, Corinne was haunted by the storms *yet* to come. She had seen the climate projections for South Louisiana, and they didn't look good. In fact, they barely looked survivable. According to one of her professors at Oberlin, New Orleans had a "long history and a short future." Now that

Corinne had witnessed the spirit of the city, though, she didn't know how much of that to believe.

Every story about the pain and loss of Katrina seemed like a thinly veiled love story about the city of New Orleans, and how deeply planted New Orleanians' roots were in the city's soil. It seemed that these people couldn't live anywhere else—not if they wanted to *live*. Corinne noticed that when Uncle Harold's neighbors talked about "loving New Orleans," they didn't mean the buildings or the food scene or the parks. They meant the air, the water, the soil. You could take every restaurant, every store out of this city, and they would still be so deeply in love. She wasn't sure any climate "impact" was any match for that.

Still, she was determined to commit the whole block to memory in her sketch pad. She wasn't the best sketcher, but that wasn't the point. She wanted to remember what it looked like on sunny days and how the wind blew on those precious few cold days. She wanted to capture the warmth in people's eyes, the melody in their cadence. Because when the next storm came—and it was sure to come—there was no guarantee what or who would remain. What if they had to rebuild it all from memory? Or pick it up and take it somewhere else? If she couldn't do anything else, she could remember. It felt futile, frivolous, but she didn't know what else to do.

The porch also provided her an escape as a houseguest who didn't want to make her presence felt too heavily. Especially in Uncle Harold's space. He'd told the family years ago that he was a committed bachelor and, judging by the way he lived, he'd meant it. His two-bedroom house was furnished but not decorated. Clean but not organized. There were random Crown Royal bags filled with pennies and beer bottles overflowing with Mardi Gras beads in every color imaginable. The living room held a simple black futon, a television on a card table, and a coffee table he used as a dining table. Corinne found the smoke-tinged, once-white walls to be oppressive, so sometimes she sat outside just to see some color.

This Saturday afternoon, though, the colors were all muted. It was one of those blustery, rainy days where the rain came in sideways and stung at the touch. The naked crape myrtle trees on the corners did awkward dances at the will of the wind, like snakes sneaking out of a basket. Between the rain and the mild temperature, most people were bundled up inside. But Corinne had put on a sweater and grabbed a blanket before propping herself up to relish the quiet.

She'd been out here for the better part of the day with a mug of tea, finishing her sketch of the two-story house across the street. It was painted a boring black and white but made up for it with an ornate balcony and a mailbox shaped like a fleur-de-lis. It was a welcome break from what she drew during the week between her interviews for the Gulf South Historical Project: the horrifyingly beautiful oil patches in the ocean. She saw the whole world in them, from beginning to end. Sometimes they were too much to behold.

She was putting the finishing touches on the house's upstairs balcony when the screen door burst open and Uncle Harold waddled out, beer bottle in hand. He took a giant, exaggerated step and planted himself in front of Corinne, thrusting his beer-bloated belly into her line of sight. "RUB MAH BELLAY!"

Corinne knew what this meant: his team had won. She didn't know which team; she didn't even know which sport, but she knew they'd won. "They won?"

"RUB! MAH! BELLAY!" He squatted a little lower and waved his beer belly in her face.

She reached out and placed her hand on his stomach like a genie's lamp. Uncle Harold threw his head back and howled in gratification. "Naw, the Saints wasn't even playing. But the Falcons lost!"

"Oh, I see, so you wasn't so much rooting *for* somebody as you were rooting *against* somebody else?"

"Yes, indeed! Ain't that half the point of life?" He laughed so hard his belly shook over his sweatpants. "What you been doing out here all day? Fooling with that little sketch pad?"

"Yeah, I was just drawing. The neighborhood, mostly."

He pulled the sketchbook from her hands. "Well, look at you! You getting better. Might could sell this one down at the Quarter. Start earning your keep!"

"Well, yeah, at some point, we gotta start preserving stuff—"

"Okay, that's it, you get in here with your uncle." He gestured toward the door. "You be getting too damn serious for it to be the weekend now."

"Do I have to?" She tried to grab her sketchbook back from him, but he raised it over his head.

"Get in the house, girl, before you catch your death due to cold. That ain't no invitation. It's an order! That house ain't going nowhere."

If Corinne had told the little-girl version of herself that she'd now be sitting on Uncle Harold's bumpy futon downing her second beer, she'd have been disgusted. She had her first taste of beer when she was five years old, on the Fourth of July. She and Cameron had spent the whole day with Uncle Harold on the back porch as he grilled an absurd array of meats: whole chickens, pork and beef ribs, and deer sausage. Mama and Grandma were in the kitchen making barbecue sauce, potato salad, deviled eggs, and succotash. Corinne had noticed her uncle emptying bottle after bottle of Coors Light and wondered what kind of juice it was. It looked like apple juice, but it bubbled like soda. He'd drunk so many of them so fast that it must have been the best juice on earth. When he and Cameron had gone to the backyard to play catch, she'd tried her luck and found that it was bitter and frothy and gross. She told herself she'd never drink it again, but she threw that out the window in high school. Eventually, she grew accustomed to the taste. Now, on her second bottle, she had a burning question.

"Uncle!" She curled her legs underneath her and turned to face him. "Why come you didn't never marry nobody?"

"What?" A small bit of beer bubbled out of the side of Uncle Harold's mouth as he tried to drink and talk at the same time.

"As long as I've known you, you ain't never had no girl-friend, no fiancée, no nothing. Why come?"

He looked at her out of the corner of his eye. "Your grand-mama tell you to come down here and ask me that?"

"No, I was just wondering." She'd always thought her uncle would make an amazing father, far better than hers had been. When she was little, it had been one of her biggest fears: that Uncle Harold would meet a woman, have children, and forget all about her and Cameron. Now that she was older, she loved the idea of him starting a family and her getting to see, at least from a distance, what a good father would look like. After a couple of years at Oberlin, it dawned on her that maybe he did have a partner, but maybe it wasn't a woman.

"I'm not gay, Niecey, if that's what you asking."

"I didn't say—"

"You didn't have to. I know what that question means after people ask you enough times." He sighed. "Why is it so hard to believe I just don't want somebody in my face all the time? Look, I love y'all, but the thing I love most about y'all is that you ain't all up under me!"

"But you never even thought about—"

"Of course I thought about it!" He laughed. "And decided I didn't want it. You know that's a thing people can do, right?"

"Okay, okay, you right."

"Worrying about the two of y'all is about all I can handle," he said with a sigh. "Besides, girl, I am grown. If I was gonna be gay, I'd be gay." He let out a chuckle. "I'd be the flyest gay nigga out here. Ain't not a damn thing stopping me!"

"I thought maybe you'd be too scared to tell Grandma." Corinne had never heard Grandma talk much about gay people, or sexuality at all, but she knew she went to church every Sunday, and she knew what most of the churches in Port Gibson said about it. Plus, lately, she couldn't imagine telling Grandma much of anything.

"Scared? Of her? What she gon' do? Not have a son no more? You forget she already knows what it's like to lose a child—*two* now. She don't want no more loss." He looked over at Corinne curiously. "What about you then? I don't remember you never having no boyfriend either. Going to prom with a 'friend' your senior and junior years."

She didn't feel like explaining how utterly stupid and boring she found the boys at her high school, so she stayed quiet. Uncle Harold leaned over to pull at her hair. "I'm just teasing, Niecey. You get you a boyfriend, or a girlfriend, whenever you get ready. You not gon' have no trouble!"

"Uncle!" Corinne groaned.

"What? It's just the truth! You always been a pretty girl." He had a twinkle in his eyes that shone extra bright against his oak-colored skin. "And when you find him, you make sure to bring him over here and let me get a good look at him. I'll scare the daylights outta that nigga. Or negress . . . or who the hell ever!"

Corinne laughed so hard the beer came shooting out of her nose. She knew how terrifying her uncle could be, even if he was usually smiling.

"You might need to slow down, Cori. Don't let me find out you been doing *keg stands* with them white folks off in Ohio." He pronounced "keg stands" in the obnoxious, nasal tone he reserved for "white people shit."

"I know what I'm doing." She waved him off. She wiped her face with her sleeve before she got up to get a napkin from the kitchen.

"So how's work been going, Cori? You like it? Think you might wanna come live down here with your uncle once you walk across that stage at *O-buh-lin*?"

"Yeah, I could definitely see me moving down to New Orleans. But I wouldn't want to be all up in your space." She paused. "Maybe somewhere close?" She leaned over to nudge him with her shoulder.

"That'd be just fine." He squeezed her back before she retreated to her side of the futon. "And what you think of the job?"

"It's hard." She let out a sigh. "I hear these awful stories every day: about people who lost everything, everyone. People's family legacies gone—just like that. Fish with three eyes and shrimp with no eyes. Whales so full of oil, when you cut them open, it just spills out like a chocolate lava cake."

"Chocolate lava cake? That sounds delicious," he said with a sly smile.

"I'm being serious, Uncle."

"So you don't like the job?"

"No, I didn't say that. It's hard." She paused. "But I don't see myself being able to do nothing easy."

"And why's that?"

"I don't know . . . because it needs to be done."

"Cori, there's some people in this world who are always looking for the easy way, and then there's people always looking for the hard way. And both of 'em wrong."

Corinne felt her throat tighten and her shoulders shoot up. Just because he could look away from a world on fire didn't mean she could. "I don't *want* things to be hard, Uncle, but they are. And they won't get any easier if I just run away."

"Who said anything about running away? Good lord, girl, you take everything so damn literally!" He got up to get another beer. "One of these days you gon' look up at fifty and wish you'd spent time actually enjoying your twenties. But by then, they gonna be gone."

"If I *get* to fifty, that is," Corinne sneered under her breath. She wanted to say so much more, but she knew she couldn't talk back to her uncle—not in his own house. So she took a slug of beer and sank into the futon.

She must have looked miserable because Uncle Harold stopped mid-stumble on the short walk back from the kitchen, and the frustration that had scrunched his eyebrows melted away. Corinne even thought she saw a glint of pity in his eyes. But he didn't say anything. He just sat his beer on the counter and pivoted to his stereo to put on his Stevie Wonder CD.

The sounds of a crying infant blasted through the air. Then the drums, then the melody, before Stevie Wonder sang his adoration of his lovely, wonderful, precious daughter Aisha.

Uncle Harold spun back over to pick up his beer like one of the Four Tops and then shuffled over to Corinne, beckoning to her with his free hand. "Come on, dance with your uncle, baby girl. You can't keep an attitude while Stevie's on. You know the rules!"

Corinne tried to fight back her smile. Between Stevie Wonder's voice and Uncle Harold's terrible two-step, it was hard to remember what she'd been upset about. She was on her feet before the end of the first verse.

As he spun her around, Uncle Harold reminded her, "Me and your mama used to sing this to you when you was a baby." Corinne braced for the punch line she knew was coming. *"And you would cryyyyyy."*

He dropped her hand and doubled over with laughter. Corinne could see him and her mother trying to soothe her as an irate infant while Cameron ran wild in the background. She could imagine the blow to their pride when it hadn't worked. They were objectively, if unabashedly, bad singers. She didn't realize she was laughing, too, until her belly muscles began to ache.

Corinne had heard Uncle Harold's laugh before. She'd even heard this joke before. But even though nothing was different, everything was. Something told her that this moment was precious and she needed to hold it tight and crush it into her bones. She needed to commit it not just to memory but to ancestral memory, so that anyone who came after her could have it too. One day, someone—maybe her own child—might grow up having never heard Uncle Harold's laugh, and how it could roll across the room, vibrate into your body, and heal you from the inside out. She shuddered to think of how quiet the world would be then. She wanted to remember the cracks and creases on the side of Uncle Harold's face, the apples of his cheeks, and the way his joy could become so heavy his knees would buckle.

She needed to remember his laugh because it wasn't his alone. This laugh had carried her uncle—and his uncles and aunts and everyone that came before them—through things so horrible they were written out of history. Maybe this laugh was what saved them. Maybe it could save her. Maybe they would need this big, intoxicating, infectious, suffocating laugh, as sure as she would need air to breathe. The thought gave her so much joy, she laughed until her cheeks hurt.

"That's right, Niecey!" Uncle Harold shouted. "It's called *Songs in the Key of Life*! Not death!" He broke into his own especially bad version of The Robot, and Corinne tried to mimic him.

They were both sweating by the time Grandma's favorite song of all time came on. The name of the song was "As," but everyone Corinne knew called it "Always." As soon as the first notes played, Corinne rushed to the stereo, on pure instinct, to turn up the volume.

But once Stevie's voice came in, the words threw Corinne's rhythm off. *The flowers don't always bloom in early May anymore*, she thought. *Sometimes they bloomed in April or even March. Sometimes they got so confused, they bloomed in the dead of winter.* According to the climate projections Corinne knew, one day, they might bloom for the last time.

What had once sounded so sweet became sinister. Stevie was saying that he would love you forever because the order of nature was forever. The oceans would never cover the mountains. Dolphins will never fly and parrots will never swim. But Corinne couldn't hear these words without thinking of parrots disappearing with the rainforest or dolphins dying en masse in oil spills today or tomorrow as the glaciers flooded freshwater into seawater. She'd heard enough about mutated creatures in the ocean that a flying dolphin really didn't seem so far-fetched. *If I was a dolphin*, she thought, *I'd certainly try to fly.* It was better than frying in oily, acidic water.

Corinne's two-step slowed to a simple, slow sway as her chest and throat tightened. Her skin began to feel heavy, as if she had been tarred and feathered. She looked at her uncle, still laughing, still dancing. He heard the same lyrics but saw a different world.

Stevie went on about the never-ending march of time and the inevitability of the seasons. Betrayal swallowed her whole, and her sway came to an abrupt halt. Sweat began to drop from her body and her beer slipped to the floor. The crash of broken glass broke Stevie's spell over Uncle Harold. When he looked up from the bottle to her face, he rushed over.

"Niecey?"

She'd fallen into a squat, clutching her chest as her lungs and heart competed for space in her rib cage. She grabbed on to her uncle's arms and he half walked, half carried her to the futon.

"Breathe, Cori, breathe." He was kneeling in front of her, squeezing her hands. "I'm gonna get you some water. You breathe, okay?"

Corinne nodded. "Can you turn it off?" she whispered through choppy breaths.

He looked confused for a moment but nodded back. Once the music was off, she began to breathe longer and sob louder.

She thought about asking him to bring her backpack so she could get her Xanax, but she didn't want him to know she'd been taking them. And she wanted to feel this, even if it was what he would call "taking it the hard way." The only thing that scared her more than global warming was becoming apathetic and complacent. She decided then and there that she would throw away those pills. There was no running from this anyway.

"Maybe I let you have too many beers," Uncle Harold said as he handed her a glass of water.

"What seasons, Uncle Harold?" Corinne had caught her breath, but now the tears were streaming down her face.

"What are you talking about?"

"He's talking about seasons knowing when to change. But what seasons?"

"The seasons of the year, Cori," Uncle Harold said patiently. "Spring, summer, fall, and winter. We're in winter right now. You know that, right?"

"We don't have seasons like we used to. One day it's seventy degrees and the next day it's fifty degrees. In what season do it drop twenty degrees in twenty-four hours? They had a *hurricane* in *New York City* in *October*. Two years ago! And no one talks about it anymore. It's barely even snowing up at Oberlin—damn near in Canada—in 'winter.' And everything keeps getting worse, never better. The world he's singing about is a whole other planet at this point, and you think I'm hysterical if I say something about it."

"When have I ever called you hysterical, Cori?"

"You don't have to say it. I can see it on your face." Snot had run down to her chin, but she refused the tissue he handed her. "The way you roll your eyes if I so much as mention global warming. Like I'm making a mountain out of a molehill."

"Cori, I just don't understand what's the use of you getting yourself all worked up over something that ain't even happening now. Same thing with you and that damn flood from way back in the 1920s. Ain't there enough to worry about right now?"

"But global warming *is* happening now! The globe *has* warmed! I just gave you a million examples!" She paused to sniffle. "I talk about it so much because I don't know what else to do. Just worry about it and bottle it up?"

"Okay, okay." He put his arm around her. "So this really is that serious to you?"

"Yes," she whispered, still crumpled in her little ball.

"Okay." He squatted back down in front of her and took her hands. "Okay, I understand now. Can you look at me?"

She raised her eyes to meet his. "Thank you," she whispered.

"I'll never dismiss you or joke about it again. I promise." He paused. "You still need to blow your nose, though."

She allowed a half smile and took the tissue.

"I love you, little girl."

"I love you, too, Uncle." She buried her face in the crook of his neck and let the sobs come heavy. He squeezed her back like she was the most precious thing in the world.

DOUBLE VISION

January 24, 2014

S he'll have the beignets," Mercer announced to the stoic waitress in her neat white cap and too-long white apron. "And we'll both have a café au lait. Thank you." He grinned across the table to Corinne. "You're going to love this!"

"Actually," Corinne interrupted. "I'll have a black coffee with two sugars. Thank you."

"Oh." Mercer's porcelain skin started to redden. "Sorry about that."

Corinne pursed her lips and gave him her most tolerant nod as the waitress disappeared back into the kitchen. Mercer was her canvassing partner with the Gulf South Historical Project, where they were both interns. The Project was a long-time Black history preservation society, with records dating back well into slavery. Since 2005, though, they'd become more active in environmental advocacy. What was the point of preserving all this history, they reasoned, if it could all just wash away? The folks at the Project weren't sure yet how they would use all the data from the Deepwater Horizon oil spill—lawsuits, insurance claims, or just shoring up the historical record—but they wanted to make sure they got it before it calcified underneath the weight of time and trauma.

Every day this week, they'd driven around Plaquemines Parish interviewing fishermen who'd abandoned the waters when the Deepwater Horizon had exploded four years ago. Every once in a while, they'd hear about folks who'd quit fishing and moved into the city, so they took today to interview some of them. Instead of driving around in Mercer's car, they decided to take the RTA and suffered through a slew of late buses and skipped stops. Half the time, they'd just wound up hoofing it. Add to that the emotional toll of the interviews themselves—talking to folks drenched in the pain of losing the places that made them—and they could barely stand by the end of the week.

Corinne had hated group projects since elementary school, so she was not thrilled to learn that her winter term project came with a "partner." But Miss Daphne, the Project's volunteer coordinator, had insisted that it wasn't safe for her to go out alone *and* that the interviews were more reliable if two people were present. "*Four ears are better than two,*" she'd said. Miss Daphne had an air of calm and certainty that was hard to argue with. No sooner had Corinne accepted the idea of a partner than she found out her partner would be a rich white boy from outside Shreveport. By the end of her first week with him, she'd been shocked and impressed, despite herself, by how unassuming and unannoying he was.

Today, after their last interview, Mercer had gone on and on about the beignets he'd had that morning. Perhaps it was the wave of her hand or the roll of her eyes, but somehow he'd figured out that Corinne had never had them. Mercer's jaw had dropped and his green eyes had gone wide, his slender, tall frame bending over hers in disbelief.

"Okay, that's it. We're fixing that right now."

The next thing she knew, he'd dragged her halfway across town to the Café du Monde in the French Quarter. Corinne knew that there were so many other places they could have gone, but Mercer had insisted on this one, which happened to be the loudest and the most crowded. She tried to tune out all of the clatter from the kitchen and the chatter from the neighboring tables.

Since they'd started working together, Corinne had almost come to trust Mercer. He was earnest, worked hard, and put up with her silent spells, no matter how long they lasted. How much more could she really ask from someone who had to spend all day right up under her? She was about to slip into one of her daydreams when she felt his expectant stare like a laser on her forehead.

"I haven't been to the French Quarter this whole time." The words fell out of her mouth before she could think about them.

"Ever? I thought you came here to visit your uncle."

"Well, we used to come here when I was a kid but haven't had much reason to come since I got older." She sighed nervously. "What I meant was that I haven't been at all this month."

"Oh yeah, me either. I haven't really had much time to go out at all." He looked at her like he'd taken some huge risk with that admission.

"Yeah, we've been working a lot." Corinne shifted her gaze toward the street. "And you still have classes at Tulane."

The French Quarter was New Orleans's oldest and most famous neighborhood, but that didn't stop it from being the most elusive. It had a unique ability to inhabit multiple worlds at once. There were sparkling, brand-new storefronts mixed with some so old they seemed to have grown out of the swamp itself. And at the same time that it burst with life, it was hopelessly haunted. It felt like the jolliest place on earth until you listened for the short pauses between the laughter that wafted through the air alongside the smell of liquor and seafood and the faint scent of oil. Then you could catch the funeral-like current of somberness. Here, "laughing to keep from crying" wasn't a cliché. The laughter was the only thing keeping the city afloat, even though it was below sea level.

The streets thronged with tourists, who you could always identify by the way they ignored service staff. But the Quarter wasn't like the tourist traps in other cities that were utterly devoid of any and all local flavor. You could find actual New Orleanians among the crowds of wide-eyed college students and tourists fresh off cruise ships and airplanes and buses. It was like they were laying claim to the place, declaring their dominance and permanence.

This time of year, it was especially easy to tell the faraway tourists and the residents apart: look for the coats. To anyone who lived in New Orleans or nearby, fifty degrees was officially and unbearably cold. It was cause enough to break out their warmest coats and their briskest walks. On the radio and local TV channels, there had been frequent and urgent reminders to check on your loved ones if the temperatures fell below forty degrees. But the tourists generally lolled around casually. If they wore coats, they wore them open. Some of them even wore shorts, inviting scandalized stares from the bundled-up Gulf Coasters. Corinne was acutely aware that now she, with her open coat, looked like a tourist.

"We used to come here all the time before my mother died," she said casually.

"Oh, I'm sorry! I didn't know you lost your mother." Mercer started to blush and fidget.

"No, no, it's fine. It was a long time ago." Sometimes she shocked herself with the intimate things she said to Mercer. It was almost like she forgot he was listening.

In truth, she'd avoided the French Quarter because it reminded her too much of those childhood visits. How she and Cameron had marveled at the street musicians and dancers. How they'd tripped over the cobblestone streets while crowds of bachelorette and bachelor partyers had tripped over them. She remembered how her mother had loved the muffulettas at Galatoire's, piled so high with salted meats and olive tapenade that Corinne wondered how she opened her mouth that wide.

Mama would tear through the giant sandwich as Uncle Harold chided her about her blood pressure.

"Ain't that your third beer since we sat down?" she'd shoot back. Then he'd drop his head and the subject. It wasn't easy to remember the good times because the memory always ended and then Corinne was back in reality, all alone.

A waiter dropped their beignets and coffee in front of them without saying a word. Corinne looked at the three perfectly powdered square donuts. The oil, still hot from the fryer, was soaking up the powdered sugar. They reminded Corinne of the French toast sticks they served at the dining hall at Oberlin. She looked up and saw that Mercer's pupils had gotten big and watery. She picked up the first square with caution, making her best impression of a lady. One bite, though, and her whole mouth was covered with gooey melted sugar, and she didn't care because it was one of the most heavenly things she'd ever tasted.

"Oh my God!"

"See? I told you!" Mercer laughed as he took his first bite.

"It's so good!" Corinne's mouth was still full, but she couldn't care less. She licked the sugar off her fingers like it had the secret to life everlasting. On her second bite, she swallowed a bit too fast and had to reach for her coffee. She took a sip before she remembered to put in the sugar, but it didn't matter because she already had sugar all over her lips.

"Aren't you glad I brought you here?" Mercer teased.

"Okay, white boy, don't push it." Probably the most interesting thing about Mercer was that he didn't bristle if she reminded him that he was white. In fact, he'd remind her of it, and all the undeserved perks that came with it. Even the über-Left white guys at Oberlin—self-appointed allies, the anarchists who still imagined the South with active slave markets—didn't do that.

"How have you never had one of these?" Mercer asked.

"Well, my mama didn't care much for coffee, and my uncle doesn't care much for sweets, and my grandma hates eating out," Corinne explained. "So there was never really much reason to come somewhere like this."

The beignets were a sweet end to an especially bitter week. By now, Corinne and Mercer had grown accustomed to the horror stories of heavily mutated fish, cancerous lungs, recurring nightmares, broken promises, and bounced checks. They could never tell if the people they interviewed were angrier at BP, the media, or the government. Sometimes it was hard to tell if they even saw a distinction between the three.

But while people in Plaquemines Parish had been grateful that anyone cared at all about their stories, the people they canvassed in New Orleans came as close to slamming the door in their faces as Southerners ever get. Sure, they invited them in, sat them on the couch, and asked if they were hungry, but they weren't eager to talk, at least not about the oil spill. They dismissed their questions about BP and gushing oil like they were batting away gnats on a hot day. *"Why are you worried about something four years old?"* they asked in so many words. *"And so far away?"* They had left those problems behind them in the swamp. They were in the city now. Corinne and Mercer felt like they were reopening wounds and forcing people to go back to some of their most painful memories. And they hated themselves for it.

Miss Daphne had set up the interviews for today. Every time they told her about someone who had left Plaquemines and moved to New Orleans, she'd made notes and gone to work to track them down. She insisted that every story was important and that the longer they waited, the more people would suppress their pain and forget the details. They'd forget where they were when they heard the news of the blowout in the Gulf. They'd forget the dragging drip-drip of news as the oil blackened the sea. They'd forget the confusion and frustration and how what was left of their trust in the government and the media eroded like the coastline. They'd forget the drop in tourism just when the tourist industries were beginning to recover from Katrina and, then, the 2008 financial meltdown. They'd forget the defeat.

"Think how much would be lost if we didn't have slave narratives," she'd commented with her hands on her hips, sounding some twenty years older than her age but looking ten years younger. Then she'd shake her head so violently, her perfect head wrap would begin to slip off. She was an intoxicating, and very Southern, mix of intimidation and warmth.

Before she could remember her manners, Corinne found herself reaching for the last beignet. "Oh my God! I'm so sorry! You want to cut it in half?"

"No, no, no," Mercer said with a laugh. "I-I'm happy to see you enjoying it."

"Thank you," Corinne said with a mouth full of dough. She laughed at the thought of Grandma seeing her eating like a savage in public.

"What's so funny?" Mercer grinned with sugar all over his mustache.

"Oh nothing." She took another bite and smiled bigger. "I'm gonna eat this whole thing."

"Please do!" Mercer looked thrilled.

By the time they left the café, floating on a cloud of sugar, it had turned dark-dark outside. Mercer turned to Corinne.

"You wanna . . . ?" His head nodded toward the River as his voice trailed off.

"Yeah, sure," she said. "Let's walk off the doughnuts." She thought about all the weight Grandma had gained since Cameron died, and how it seemed to keep her down.

As they turned the corner toward the Mississippi River, the water greeted them more like an ocean than a river. The promenade was illuminated by the dim lights of the bridge and the lampposts. The air had gotten colder, and there were only a few brave tourists huddling close together on the benches or barreling down the sidewalk. Corinne couldn't see the moonlight very well through the fog, but she could feel it as it pulled on the dark waters, commanding them to wave and writhe.

They were walking toward an empty bench, but before they made it there, Corinne walked away from Mercer and toward the River as if beckoned by black magic. For a moment, she forgot she wasn't alone. As she got closer, the water began to look less like water and more like oil, barrels and barrels of it. Its ebb and flow then ceased to be an innocent dance between the terrestrial and the celestial. Instead, it became a sinister sprawl.

Corinne imagined the waves heaving together to form a tsunami—like the one that drowned Indonesia in 2004—made of oil. The closer she got, it became even more real and she could see it oozing toward the city, threatening to flatten it and drag all the horn players, bartenders, tourists, historians, and church ladies out to sea. Sucking the soul right out of the city. She imagined offering herself as a sacrifice for the city and the black wave that threatened to engulf it. She planted her feet and made herself into a levee.

It wasn't until she heard her own scream that she realized that she had floated out of her body. Corinne looked down. She'd climbed up on the railing, pressing it into her ribs. That was when she felt Mercer trying to yank her down from the railing with all his might.

"Corinne!" She heard him scream her name in his northern Louisiana accent.

As the sweat on her skin turned cold, she realized it had happened again. She'd had another premonition. No one else had seen the tsunami that had been so real to her just seconds ago. How was she going to explain what had just happened without sounding like some wild, crazed woman? She broke free of his arms and turned around to face him, expecting to find panic, fear, and, above all else, judgment in his eyes. But when she finally looked, all she saw was concern and curiosity, and even a little warmth.

"Corinne," he said seriously. "What's wrong?"

Something about the way he said it let her know that he really wanted the answer and wasn't afraid of it. She felt a wave of relief and a level of safety with him she hadn't realized she needed. *Finally*, she thought. *Maybe someone sees what I see.*

He took her hand and guided her to the nearest bench, where they sat next to each other, staring out into the water. Corinne folded her arms across her chest as Mercer placed his fists on top of his knees, like he was ready to fight anyone who dared intrude.

"Tell me," he said gently.

"So it might sound crazy . . . ," she started.

"Try me."

She sighed. "I thought I saw this giant wave coming toward the city, but it wasn't made of water. It was oil. And it was going to eat the city alive. Just a giant wall of oil, tall as a skyscraper and wide as a cruise ship."

She could see Mercer's brow furrow out of the corner of her eye. "And so you were going closer to it?"

"In my head, I thought I could protect the city somehow? I don't know, none of it makes any sense."

"No, it makes sense . . . It just sounds really . . . *selfless*."

"I guess that's one way of looking at it," she said with a laugh. Then more somberly, "I used to have these things when

I was a little girl, after I first read about the big flood from the 1920s. You ever heard of it?"

"The Great Flood of 1927? *Yeah*, I've heard of it. I'm an ecology major, Corinne. *And* I'm from Louisiana."

"Oh right. When I bring it up at Oberlin, people look at me like I have three heads." She sighed and continued, "Well, when I was in like the second grade, I got really interested in the flood and I read about it all the time. And I started having this thing where I felt like I could *see* the flood everywhere, all around me."

"Well, I think that makes sense. It reshaped the whole country, and especially Louisiana and Mississippi. So in a lot of ways, it *was* all around you."

Corinne didn't realize how much she needed to hear that she wasn't silly or selfish for remembering things she hadn't lived through. She missed when Grandma had done the same thing. "I was only ever able to really talk to my grandmother about it. She called them my 'premonitions,' but at least she listened to me. Everybody else thought I was just making it up for attention."

"Wow, I'm sorry."

"It's fine. It kind of made me and my grandmother closer, because she took me seriously. I think that's why I was able to get over it, or at least get it under control. I stopped having them altogether by the time I was in middle school. But they came back after my brother died and I started reading more and more about fossil fuels and global warming. Now the premonitions aren't just about the flood. Now it's all kinds of disasters: tornadoes, hurricanes, droughts. New floods. It's like at first I can tell it's not real, but if I don't catch myself right away, it becomes real and there's nothing I can do. Does that ever happen to you?"

She turned to face him and found him staring directly at her. "That *has* happened to me. I've never imagined the water turning into oil or physically putting myself up as a sacrifice. But I've definitely envisioned storms where there weren't any, and it definitely felt real."

"What do you think that's about?" Corinne had never felt closer to another person. All this time, she'd thought she was the only one haunted by these visions.

"Well, since we both had the big bright idea to look climate change in the face, in a way it's kinda what we get: the ability to see the future. I call it the 'climate curse.' 'Cause if you think about it, there's nothing in these visions, or premonitions as you call them, that isn't true. Eventually, water *will* swallow up New Orleans, sooner than later at the rate we're going." He gestured to the oil rigs they both knew were out in the distance, under the cover of night.

Corinne bit her lip and then whispered, "I just wish I didn't feel so powerless, you know? Like, what's the point of having this—what did you call it? This climate curse, this double vision—if I can't do anything with it? Like, I see this tragedy of all tragedies coming from just around the corner, but I can't do anything," she said, her voice breaking on the last word.

Mercer reached for her hand. "You're not doing *nothing*. I mean, at least we're looking at it, not running away. 'Cause, lord, would that be easier."

Corinne laughed wryly. "You right, but I want to do something more than just scare myself to death. It's not even all in the future either. These motherfuckers killed my brother last spring."

Mercer squeezed her hand, and it felt clammy and bony. "Well, if you've learned anything from your brother, you know how important the Mississippi River is to all these companies. Imagine how much money they'd lose if they couldn't use it even for a few hours?"

"Probably a whole lot." Corinne chuckled at the thought. Maybe it wouldn't bring the industry to its knees, maybe it wouldn't reverse global warming, but maybe it would be worth it just to throw a rock at the bully.

"Just one of those oil barges can carry like eighty thousand barrels of oil. That alone is worth millions of dollars. I don't know how many barges go up and down the River every day, but it's a lot, and it's becoming a lot more 'cause they can't use the pipelines anymore, so this is their backup plan." Mercer had a diabolical look on his face. He'd thought about this before. "What if we got in their way one day?"

"What do you mean? Got in their way how?" Corinne's eyebrow rose at his audacity.

"It doesn't even take much. I've been looking into it, just as a hobby. We could just throw a smoke bomb down in the River, hang something off a bridge that's long enough to make it even a little harder for a boat to pass underneath. You'd be amazed how easy it is to spook these big bad boats."

"Okay, now you really talking like a white boy. Won't we go to jail?"

"Yeah, I'm talking like a white boy whose daddy is a sheriff and whose granddaddy owns half of Shreveport and is in bed with the oil companies." His eyes twinkled. "We might go to jail, but one phone call and we're out."

Corinne knew what she'd just heard was crazy, but it felt like a new kind of crazy than the one where she saw visions no one else saw and wept for people who weren't even dead yet. This kind of crazy felt better, freer. But she knew deep down that just might be what made it more dangerous.

Corinne held her breath for a moment. "There's no way in hell I'm doing anything that crazy." She paused. "But I do want to do something . . . I just don't know what."

A million voices swirled in her head, but it didn't feel like a war. It felt like she was coming alive again. But she knew better than to put all her trust in Mercer immediately. She needed to give her emotions time to sort themselves out. In the meantime, she was getting the itch again to go down a research rabbit hole. *Is Mercer brilliant or a fool?* Corinne wondered if maybe he could be both.

PART TWO

The Ways of White Folks

February 12, 2014

Y ou think they gonna try it again?" Cleo asked, staring at a flyer for the Soul Session that would be happening at Afrikan Heritage House that weekend.

The Black students simply called it the House, and its semi-monthly Soul Sessions were their refuge, where they didn't have to code switch, explain, or apologize. There, they could holler, amen, and throw shoes at the best performers as they went through poetry, comedy, and so, so much music. At the last one, Cleo had sung "Someday We'll All Be Free," and Corinne thought he sounded just like Donny Hathaway, like his throat was lined with gold.

As she looked around at Ashley and the others in the TV lounge at Third World House, Corinne could see that they all knew what Cleo was really asking. The next Soul Session was the sacred Black History Month Soul Session. But after what happened on the heels of Black History Month last year—

when classes were canceled and Black students became the center of a national media firestorm, followed by a swift and fierce white backlash—it was especially weighted. Last year, Black students had watched in real time as the limits of white liberalism had revealed themselves and headline after headline made a mockery of their pain.

"Try what, Cleo?" Ashley asked, only halfway watching the drama and surreality of *Love & Hip Hop* playing in the background. None of them ever paid much attention to it. The TV was really just an excuse for them to pile into the lounge together with take-out Chinese food from The Mandarin. They stopped talking over the TV only when the cast started screaming. Corinne needed the escape from all the readings she needed to do for her classes. All her coursework seemed so frivolous since she'd gotten back from New Orleans.

"You know what I mean, Ashley. You think these dubs are gonna try the same mess they tried last year?"

"Dubs" was their unaffectionate name for white people. Cleo had coined it when they were freshmen still learning the meaning and value of a "safe space." They could use it right in front of their white classmates and teachers without setting off the minefield of their fragile feelings. It was the invisibility cloak they hadn't known they needed.

"Cleo, I think what she's asking is, which 'mess'?" Corinne hated how vague he could be. "A lot happened last year. Are you asking if some little white boys are going to scrawl 'nigger' over all the Black History Month flyers or carve *KKK* into a bench? Or if they're going to send rape threats to Black female students? Or are they going to wear Klan robes and parade across campus, and the police department will tell us it was somebody in a blanket? Exactly which thing are you talking about?"

"I'm talking about all of it, Corinne! Or any of it. Do you think we're up for a repeat of last year?"

"I don't think anybody would be crazy enough to do that again, Cleo." Faith tried to sound reassuring. "Think about how the administration responded. They canceled classes, and we had all those rallies and convocations and working groups. It changed the school forever. They had to remove those two white boys from campus altogether."

"Yeah, but it didn't stop after they left, did it?" Corinne asked. Faith was on the student senate and deeply involved with the president's office—of course *she* believed in the institution. But the memory still chafed Corinne. "Plus, it's not like it all started that night, so I don't know if I'd call what the administration did much of a response. We wrote them a letter last year when they defaced all those pictures at the House, and they didn't listen. They knew about all the hate speech on ObieTalk, and they didn't do anything. They said it was just 'trolling.' Then they got real for like a day before they let everyone say it was just a hoax. Joke or not, I'll never forget how terrifying it was."

Corinne's mind went back to 2:15 a.m. on March 4, 2013, when all of their phones had lit up with calls and texts from their friends across the way in Afrikan Heritage House. Shannon, a sophomore from Chicago, had seen a Klansman walking across campus. They hadn't wanted to believe it, but it had made almost too much sense in light of the recent vandalism and threats they'd been hearing about for weeks. Cleo, with his responsibilities as a residential assistant and instincts as the oldest of six, had made sure the doors were all closed tight and had corralled the nervous handful of them who'd woken up into the lounge so they could be nervous and angry together. They'd closed all the curtains and waited for a visit from campus security and had watched out of the corner of their eyes for a burning cross. They'd seen neither.

Her freshman year, when Corinne learned she had been placed in Third World House, she had been disappointed. She'd come to Oberlin to break out of her bubble and get exposed to other cultures. So she'd specifically requested to live on North Campus, away from the designated "safe spaces" like Third World and Afrikan Heritage House on South Campus. But by the end of her first semester, after she had realized just how white Oberlin actually was, she was grateful to have been placed where she was, especially after last March.

"Corinne is right; there were never any consequences. Just gaslighting." A teardrop glimmered in Ashley's eye. "They told us it was a joke and some fool was running around here wrapped up in a blanket. That we just *thought* it was a Klansman's robe because we're *so sensitive*. I don't care if they never found who did it; I believe Shannon. We live in a cradle of white supremacist hate groups, with all these backward white folks around here, so it's really not that unbelievable. Plus all the shit that led up to it? You wanna tell me that was a coincidence?"

"After the story broke in the news, my grandma nearly took me out of Oberlin." Corinne's head hurt as she remembered those panicked phone calls from home after Grandma had watched the story play out on MSNBC. She hadn't told her or Uncle Harold about the incidents that preceded it because she didn't want to hear their "I told you so" lectures. "She was ready to call the registrar and everything."

"Yeah, my parents were freaking out too," Cleo said with a groan.

They all knew that—Oberlin's liberal reputation be damned—the surrounding Lorain County was the same place that had produced Toni Morrison and had the same racial dynamics that jumped off the pages of her novels. They saw it when they drove to Elyria or Wellington or Lorain and saw the bumper stickers that said Barack Obama was a Muslim and Michelle Obama was a man.

"But at the same time, Ash, you can't rule out that somebody *was* really running around here in a blanket." Cleo's eyes grew wide, and Corinne knew he was thinking of the wilder things he'd seen as an RA. "We've seen these dubs literally dive into dumpsters and walk through the snow with no shoes. Walking around in a blanket is almost cute. Borderline normal!"

Corinne chuckled at the memory from their freshman year when she, Cleo, and Ashley had walked out of the dining hall at the House just in time to see a white kid in a cape leap into a dumpster to "liberate" the trash from that evening's dinner service: rolls, corn on the cob, green beans. If it had been packaged, they would have understood. If the dumpster diver had been arranging to take it to a shelter for people who didn't have enough to eat, they would have understood. But here was a child of probably one of the richest families in the country—who'd never known hunger a day in his life—choosing to eat trash and calling it activism.

"The ways of white folks," Ashley muttered under her breath.

"Is too much for me," they all said in unison. It was their paraphrased version of a Langston Hughes quote. Ashley had said it wrong their freshman year, but they kept repeating it that way.

"What really pisses me off, though, is that somebody could terrorize all the Black and brown students, all the gay students, and even the Jewish students, and it'll go down in history as a *joke*." Marcus finally spoke from the couch at the back of the room. "I mean, why do they get to define what is and isn't a joke? That shit wasn't funny! What the fuck is *trolling* anyway? And can you imagine one of *us* getting away with that? Let me go up to one of these white girls and threaten to rape her and then tell somebody it was a joke. They'd put me in jail and lynch me in the same media outlets that said we were too sensitive."

A palpable silence fell over the room as Ashley turned off the indiscriminate cussing and fighting of the rap-adjacent re-ality stars on the television. Corinne remembered their fresh-man year when seventeen-year-old Trayvon Martin was killed for the crime of walking through his father's neighborhood with Skittles and a can of AriZona Sweet Tea. They'd all worn hoodies and carried packs of Skittles to school for a week, but it all felt so futile, especially when the man who killed him was allowed to walk free. Corinne had seen a headline that week that DMX had challenged him to a boxing match. For the first time in her life, she'd been interested in a sport.

"To be fair, though," Corinne broke the silence, "the administration might have let us down, but a lot of the other students really showed up. If it had just been us, no way it would have gotten as much attention as it did. That's what made them cancel classes."

"You right, Cori," Cleo answered. "I still feel like we don't really know who did that. So how are we ever supposed to feel safe again?"

"Honestly, Cleo, I don't even think it matters if they do the same thing again." Faith broke the silence. "What's done is done. We're always going to be checking every flyer, every editorial, every message board to make sure it's not happening again. Walking around campus at night, I still half expect to see somebody draped in all white, or even in a Nazi uniform at this point. I was scared to death somebody was gonna do that shit on Halloween and call it a joke. And, honestly, I think that was their point the whole time."

"It's fine if it haunts us; we just can't let it stop us," Ashley said, nervously twirling the remote control in her hand. "We have to remember, there were Black people going to this school who had escaped actual slavery . . . And Marcus would know; he's old enough to have been right here with them."

And just like that, the silence was swallowed by laughter. Even though he was just one year older than the rest of them,

Marcus had the air of a senior citizen. He had a specific chair in the lounge that he always sat in, like a grandfather, and an unexplained affinity for butter pecan ice cream. He also walked so slow, it looked more like a saunter. Corinne could see him coming from across campus like a tortoise.

"You know what, *all* of y'all can kick rocks. You know Ashley is the real old one. She be running around here in *housecoats*!"

"That's fine. At least I ain't elderly." Ashley had been calling Marcus "elderly" ever since he sang a Nat King Cole song at her first Soul Session. "What was it like when Edmonia Lewis was here? Wasn't y'all classmates?"

"He probably was the model for her first sculpture!" Cleo joined in. "Marcus, I feel like we don't tell you enough how much we appreciate your sacrifices as one of the first Black students at Oberlin, before the Civil War was even over. I just"—he pretended to choke back tears—"I can't imagine what it must have been like for you when they kicked her out. What does it feel like to be a part of history like that?"

"First of all, I hate your guts. Second of all, *I was not here in the 1800s!*" Marcus sucked his teeth and turned to Corinne. "Cori, what happened at that polar bear protest you went to? Out there freezing with all the dubs?"

"Yeah, it was cold as all hell. And we marched from Tappan Square to the post office chanting all these corny slogans. I don't know . . . Like, I know they're trying, but it just felt so pointless. Sure, we're chanting about how the ice caps are melting and the polar bears are dying, but what are we really doing to stop it? We're screaming about a very specific place

that is very far away from here, and I don't even know if anyone who matters can hear us."

"But isn't that what they say when it comes to global
warming, though?" Faith was to be the voice of reason again.
"Think global, but act local?"

"Yeah, they do say that, but I'm not sure it makes any
sense. I feel like that's something that they started to keep us
confused and make us feel like we can't get to the root of the
problem. Like, it feels like I'm fighting the air itself. Because
nowadays local *is* global. Especially when it comes to the en-
vironment and global warming." Corinne had been to these
types of protests before and had made her peace with them as
her only resort, but after Cameron died, the futility of it was
overpowering. And now, with Mercer's words still ringing in
her ears from last month, they seemed almost harmful.

"Here she go." Ashley rolled her eyes.

"Go where? Sound like she don't wanna go local or
global," Marcus shot back. "What you wanna do, Cori? Fight
the *globe* for warming?"

"Think about it, Marcus: We know what the cause of global
warming is. It's fossil fuels. Oil and gas. Point-blank, period.
And that's big business. I don't just mean that it makes a lot
of money. I mean that it's big. It's everywhere, in everything.
That means here in Ohio we don't have to protest melting ice
sheets out in the Arctic. We can protest all the awful things the
industry is doing here in Ohio. You know those same oil boats
my brother died on? They go up the *Ohio* River too. They're
trying to build pipelines *here*. There's fracking *here*."

"So you want everyone to just fend for themselves? What about solidarity, Corinne?" Faith sounded disappointed. "In the civil rights era, you know New Yorkers protested lynchings in Alabama—"

"But that's kind of my point: my grandmother was actually *in* the civil rights movement, right? In Tennessee. It's something different to do it in the belly of the beast than from across the country." There was nothing Corinne hated more than a ham-fisted lecture on the civil rights movement from some chick from Oregon. "I think *that's* what actually changed things."

"I know, Cori." Faith seemed to realize she'd hit a nerve.

"I mean that we should make noise but make it in their face. If I'm making noise here in Ohio, I want it to be because of something happening to people here in Ohio because there's so much of it. If we're all focusing all our attention on the Arctic, it can make you feel like the whole reason we need to stop global warming is for the polar bears' sake, and it ain't. I've never even seen a polar bear—and I don't want to!"

"I got you, Corinne. So you gonna tell them that at the next little meeting?" Faith asked.

"No, I think I'm done with them. I'm thinking of doing something bigger. A lot bigger."

"Cori." Cleo put on his big brother voice. "You not about to go do something stupid, are you?"

"Maybe." She bit her tongue before she continued. "I had kind of an experience over winter term. There's something about being in a city so wracked by an oil spill on top of a hurricane and legit controlled by the oil and gas industry. You see their names everywhere. Concerts brought to you by Shell, Aquarium of the Americas brought to you by BP. Even the *Super Bowl* brought to you by Chevron! It's ridiculous! It's like a fucking company town!" Corinne could feel the sweat popping up along her brow.

"Okay, so what are you going to do about it?" Marcus was staring at her with concern.

Corinne took a breath and looked down. She hadn't talked to anyone except Mercer about what she was about to say, not even Ashley. She kept her eyes on the Soul Session flyer on the wall. "Well, also while I was in New Orleans, I got to thinking with one of my coworkers about doing something more direct and . . ."

"*And?*" Cleo was losing patience, and she realized she was being just as vague as he was earlier.

"Well, like I'm always saying, a lot of the oil and gas in this country goes up and down the Mississippi River from places way up north, even Canada, to the refineries down on the Gulf of Mexico. We're talking about staging something on one of the bridges that goes across the Mississippi River, maybe even the bridge outside of Vicksburg, close to where I'm from." Then her voice dropped. "My brother's boat used to pull in to work out of there."

"Oh, I see." Cleo's voice softened. "This is about your brother."

"That ain't no excuse to be acting foolish!" Ashley said, horrified. "What, exactly, are you talking about *staging*, Corinne? Please don't tell me you're about to bungee jump off the bridge or chain yourself to it."

"Well, I haven't decided yet, Ashley, but definitely not anything *that* crazy." The entire room seemed to breathe a sigh of relief. "But I do want to do something that would get the attention of all the boats that have to go underneath. We're talking about just breaking onto the bridge and hanging a banner or something like that."

"And where would you get the banner?" Marcus asked, his voice higher than normal. "What would it say? How would you get out on the bridge? Is all of this legal?"

"I don't know all of that yet. We're not talking about doing it until the summer, and like I said, I haven't decided yet." Corinne had known that when she told her friends, they would either shut her down immediately or ask a million questions. Of the two possibilities, she much preferred an interrogation.

"Girl, you gon' give your grandma a heart attack. I remember how she freaked out after that Klansman shit, then your brother. Now this? That poor woman!"

"Ashley, you don't get to tell *me* about *my* grandmama!" Corinne didn't realize she'd crossed her arms. "I'm doing this for my brother, and *out of love for her*, actually. Besides, if she could be brave enough to do what she did as a little girl, I can do this as an adult. It's better than running around Tappan Square screaming 'bout glaciers, I'll tell you that much."

"Calm down, Cori." Cleo's tone was patient. "We all know how you feel about your grandma, but tell us some more about this coworker."

Corinne breathed deep. "His name is Mercer. He's from Louisiana, but not New Orleans. He's from farther north near Shreveport, but I know y'all don't know where that is. He goes to Tulane in New Orleans, though."

"You trust him?" Cleo asked.

"Yeah, I mean he was my canvassing partner the whole time I was down there—"

"Which was just a month," Ashley reminded her.

"I know, but it was an intense month. And he always had my back."

"Cori." Cleo was serious. "This a white boy, ain't it?"

"Yes." She pursed her lips.

"I knew it." Ashley threw her hands in the air. "As soon as you started talking about breaking onto bridges. That's some dub shit—some *dumb* shit—if I've ever heard it."

"That's not exactly bad, though." Cleo sprang forward in his seat. "I'm almost glad to hear it, truth be told. If something does pop off, let him be the shield. Use him to your advantage. Why not? It's kinda smart."

"That's a good point." Faith looked genuinely surprised. "I hadn't thought about that part. Reparations, bitches!"

"But, Cori." Cleo was serious again. "You better not go out there with no other Black person at all. We won't be there, so you need to make sure somebody else with some sense *is*. It's one thing to be fool*ish*, but don't be a damn fool."

"I haven't even decided if I'm going to do it." Corinne finally lifted her eyes to meet Cleo's. She'd never been more grateful to share a smile with someone. "There's a lot more to think about, obviously. But I promise I'll be careful."

As soon as she said it, though, she made up her mind. That night, she called Mercer and told him she was ready to get serious.

DOWN THE RIVER

March 23, 2014

Miss Daphne and Corinne walked past a weeping willow with its green garlands bowed in devotion to the daffodils and irises that dotted the ground. Corinne couldn't look at those trees without remembering how Mama's heart had stopped every time she saw one. Sometimes Mama would go visit the cemetery in Natchez where she didn't know a soul, just to sit under the weeping willows and gingerly trace the leaves with her fingertips. Sometimes she took a book, and sometimes she took Corinne, and they'd listen for voices together.

Miss Daphne nudged Corinne. "If you think it's pretty now, you ought to come to the park around Christmas when all the lights are up."

They were strolling through the sculpture garden in City Park, right next to the New Orleans Museum of Art. The weather was so beautiful, Corinne almost didn't want to raise the subject that had brought them here. When Cleo had made her promise not to go breaking onto private property with some random white boy, Corinne had thought through all the potential people she could call. She didn't know anyone in Port Gibson who wouldn't either brush her off or try to tell her grandmother what she was up to. She even thought about approaching the one Black environmental studies professor at Oberlin but then remembered she had a job to keep. Then she remembered Miss Daphne, who always had been so calm and encouraging, and who also had her own history with a more radical strain of activism. After turning it around in her head for a few days, Corinne had called Miss Daphne and confessed to the crime she wanted to commit.

After Miss Daphne had listened, sighed, and sucked her teeth, she'd asked Corinne if she was sure. Corinne said she was. A week later, Miss Daphne had called with the offer to bring her to New Orleans for her spring break. She'd said she needed to lay eyes on her before she could believe her. Miss Daphne had made up some excuse about needing Corinne to edit the transcripts they'd collected in January and got her boss to approve just enough money in the budget to pay for her plane ticket and a twenty-dollar daily stipend.

Corinne followed Miss Daphne to a bench next to the lagoon, right across from a sculpture that looked like a giant black spider from a nightmare. It should have been frightening, but its gargantuan, gnarled limbs blended so perfectly with the curved branches of the oak trees behind it that she felt like she was intruding on its habitat. She had half a mind to apologize.

"I've seen the park at Christmas, just not since my mama died. And even then, we just drove around it; we didn't actually walk through it," Corinne said as they sat down. "I don't even think I could have appreciated all of this then. I was too little." The garden looked so different in the spring versus the winter: the flowers were newer, the grass was softer, and everything felt so much more innocent.

"Well, maybe you'll come back next Christmas and I'll come with you." Miss Daphne cradled her already bulging belly. "I'll be somebody's mama by then."

Corinne grinned at her. Usually when she thought about children and the future—or even of herself and the future—a dread fell on her like another, heavier, deader skin, but the way Miss Daphne talked about her impending motherhood gave her a sense of calm, even though she knew her optimism was all based on uncertainty, like the stock market. *We don't know for sure what's going to happen,* Miss Daphne would remind her, *so why assume the worst?*

"Does it hurt?"

"Does what hurt? The baby?" Miss Daphne rolled her eyes. "Yeah, sometimes it does. Morning sickness already ain't no joke, but I got a feeling it's just getting started. And then there's the lifetime after the baby's here. My auntie told me that the last time you sleep soundly is before your child is born, because after that you spend the rest of your life worrying about them. If that's true, I already had my last good night's sleep and didn't even know it. Ain't that a bitch?"

Corinne mustered a polite chuckle. She hadn't slept well since Cameron died and her nightmares became a climate-changed hellscape. But they weren't here to talk about Corinne's night terrors.

"I bet your mama still worrying about you beyond the grave, Corinne." Miss Daphne leaned toward her on the bench. The sun hit her cheekbones in a way that turned her pregnant glow into a full-fledged sparkle. "I know your grandma and your uncle done lost all kinds of sleep over you. You sure you wanna do this? To them?"

Corinne couldn't help rolling her eyes. "I'm not doing anything *to* them. I know they're going to see it your way, too, but I don't think it's fair to make me choose between their feelings today and my own life tomorrow. How is that fair to anybody?"

Miss Daphne let out a heavy sigh. "It's not fair, you're right. But you are proposing to take yourself onto private property, exposing yourself to some serious risks, quite possibly even death. And you can't pretend that your actions don't have consequences that go beyond you. I just wanted to make sure you'd thought about it, that's all. Sounds like you're sure you wanna do it then?"

"I'm sure. I told you over the phone." Corinne felt her throat tighten.

"I know you did, Corinne. I just wanted to hear it from you in person and to actually see the words fall out your mouth. But you know this isn't going to change anything long term, right? You know this isn't going to bring those oil boats to no screeching halt?"

"Yes, I know!" Corinne was trying hard to watch her tone. "Of course I know that! But I'm at the point where doing nothing is scarier than doing something, and even if this is futile, it's the least futile thing I can think to do. Besides, all those times you protested outside the courthouse and organized all those rallies, did that do away with police brutality? Did they empty the prisons? Or stop all evictions?"

"First of all, watch your mouth! We had a strategy—" Daphne stopped herself. "No, you're right. It didn't fix everything. But none of those things felt as big as 'global warming.' That's the whole world, and I just feel like I'm watching you take it all on your shoulders. And . . . you just turned twenty. Mercer too. I know that's grown on paper, but, Corinne, that is not *grown*. Y'all at that dangerous age where can't nobody tell you nothing—literally or legally."

"Are you trying to convince me not to do it?" Corinne braced herself for an answer she didn't want. She looked again at the spiderlike sculpture in front of her and thought of Edmonia Lewis and her *Forever Free* sculpture of a Black man and woman recently freed of the chains of slavery. She thought it would look so much more at home here in New Orleans—the city that was simultaneously the site of the country's biggest slave port and the most African city in America.

"No, I'm not. The opposite. I'm saying . . . I'm in. There's no way in hell I'mma let you do this by yourselves. Y'all don't know nothing about pulling no stunt like this on your own. You'll fool around and get yourselves killed for real. Since you trusted me enough to come with you, I'll come. But I'm not coming down there by myself. If y'all looking at this summer, I'mma be big-big by then. We need reinforcements."

Corinne felt a weight lift off her shoulders and was too relieved to ask what Miss Daphne meant by "reinforcements." She had a more important question. "Miss Daphne . . . Do you think I'm crazy for doing all this? Do you think I'm overreacting about nothing?"

"Girl, naw." Miss Daphne rubbed her shoulder the way Mama used to. "You not overreacting. You think I'm not scared about it too? You think I don't have nightmares living in this soup bowl? Everybody in New Orleans is just waiting on the next storm like a sitting duck. My college friend out in California been telling me all about the drought and the fires out there and how everybody's acting like it's normal. It's like the apocalypse is already here and we're the zombies. If anything, we're all underreacting."

"But you're having a baby still." Corinne didn't know what had gotten into her until the words were already out of her mouth. Once they were, she half expected to catch the back of Miss Daphne's hand to her mouth, but she just sighed.

"I am." Miss Daphne took her hand away from Corinne's back and put it on her belly bulge. "I'm choosing to be optimistic, but I only get to make that choice because there's people like you in the world."

Miss Daphne reached out and intertwined her fingers with Corinne's. Corinne let herself pretend they were Mama's fingers.

—

Miss Daphne had promised Corinne and Mercer some of the best Vietnamese food in all of New Orleans, but when they walked into Lilly's Café, Corinne was struck by how unremarkable the place looked. The aromas of ginger and lemongrass wafted by as the kitchen door opened and closed, and all the tables were covered with sharp plastic, and old jazz festival catalogs littered the doorway. Replace them with Claiborne County phone books and deer festival flyers, and the place would have fit right in in Port Gibson.

She and Mercer followed Miss Daphne to a small table all the way in the back, right by the bathroom entrance. Mercer pulled her chair out for her. The gesture made Corinne shudder, but she didn't feel like fighting him over it. Miss Daphne shot her a smile like she knew something Corinne didn't.

"So one thing I didn't tell you is that me and Mr. Stephens," she whispered as she leaned in, "used to date."

"The man who's gonna meet us here tonight?" Corinne asked, scandalized. Suddenly she felt like she was intruding.

"Yep! Obviously it was a while ago. I hadn't met Carlos yet. But this will be the first time he's seen me since I got pregnant."

"And you're still friends?" Mercer seemed impressed.

"You think I'd be bringing you to meet an enemy? Of course we're friends! I trust Alex with my life, which means

I'd trust him with your lives. I'm really happy he decided to come out to meet us today. He can be a little fatherly—even paternalistic—but I think you'll like him."

Corinne busied herself with looking at the menu, but in the back of her mind, she was preparing to defend her plan. She'd spent most of the week planting the seeds with Uncle Harold—hinting at the need to do something bigger, letting him know she was prepared to put her body on the line at some point—that arguing with a stranger felt like just the release she needed.

"Oh, you don't need to worry yourself too much with the menu, Corinne. I know just what to get us. See, you'll want the vegan pho. I want the chicken. Mercer probably does too. And Alex wants the beef, trust me. And I'll order the appetizers too."

Corinne was thrilled that someone else had done the work of figuring out her order for her. She dropped her menu as Miss Daphne waved the waitress over. She noticed the casual rapport the waitress had with Miss Daphne. It seemed like she already knew most of the items Miss Daphne was going to choose before she chose them. Miss Daphne had the same affect when she ordered coffee in the morning or lunch at the food truck outside of the office. She just seemed to know everyone. And something about the way the waitress stood close to Miss Daphne and brushed her shoulder with affection let Corinne know this was going to be one of the best meals she'd had in a long time.

"So Mr. Stephens has done things like what we're about to do?" Mercer's voice sounded hoarse and lower than usual.

"Oh yeah, he's done tons of them. Almost too many. It's like an addiction, so I honestly can't think of a better person to be out there with y'all. There's no such thing as a professional activist, but he's about the closest thing there could be."

"Why is there no such thing as a professional activist?" Mercer asked.

"Well, there are people who work on social justice professionally, but anybody you hear of making big money off actions like this, you need to be real wary. That's not an activist; that's an opportunist." She lifted her eyes toward the door and broke into a sudden smile. "And speak of the devil!"

Corinne and Mercer turned around to face the front door, where they saw a burly white man with a salt-and-pepper, barely-there beard and a battered brown T-shirt walking toward them. He was timidly smiling at Daphne. As he got closer, Corinne noticed he had that web of lines around his eyes that Grandma said meant someone smiled too much.

"Alex! I'm so glad you made it!" When he got to their table, Miss Daphne sprang from her seat faster than Corinne thought she should have been able to and was lifted off her feet as he hugged her tight.

"Of course I made it! I am a man of my word." He let her go to gaze at her belly. "And *you* are a woman with child!"

"I am! And this is just getting started!" She laughed and her eyes twinkled. "I want you to meet Mercer and Corinne. Get up and say hello, y'all!"

Corinne and Mercer whispered their hellos and extended their arms for handshakes, one after the other. Corinne noticed that Mr. Stephens's skin was rough, like a gardener's glove.

"I assumed you wanted your usual, so I already ordered for us," Miss Daphne announced as they sat down. "Corinne and Mercer, you want to tell Mr. Stephens why we're here? No use wasting time."

"I thought you already told him?" Corinne was horrified. She didn't realize she was going to have to tell the story from scratch.

"I want to hear it from you. If we're going to entertain the notion of putting our bodies on the line together, the least we can do is communicate with one another directly and not play telephone through Daphne here," Mr. Stephens said.

Corinne looked down and then nodded. "I guess you're right." She sighed and then looked up. "We want to stage a protest. Against all the oil boats that go up and down the Mississippi River. My brother died on one of them last May. And . . ." She looked down again.

"I'm sorry. That must really hurt," Mr. Stephens said in a softer tone.

"Thank you," she whispered.

Mercer picked the story back up. "One of the bridges Corinne's brother used to pass under is in Vicksburg, Mississippi, close to where she grew up. There's actually two bridges there. One for cars and one for cargo trains." He pulled out his phone to show Mr. Stephens pictures. There was the shiny silver bridge on the left. On the right, there was the older but still very functional black bridge.

"The black one used to be used for car traffic too?" Mr. Stephens asked.

"Yeah, it did," Corinne answered, collecting herself. She felt too raw to mask it. "Back before I was born, I think. I don't remember ever going out on it."

"Well, that couldn't have been very long ago!"

Corinne didn't appreciate the note of condescension in his joke. Miss Daphne turned toward the kitchen to hide her grimace. In an act of divine mercy, the waitress appeared with their appetizers: three different types of spring rolls and crab rangoons. Daphne handed Corinne the tofu spring rolls straightaway. Corinne could smell the seasoning in the food, and soon they were clanging their silverware and piling their plates high.

"Please, continue," Mr. Stephens said as the awkwardness lifted.

Corinne regathered her nerve. "Well, we want to stage a protest on the black bridge. We want to get out there—and I believe we can—to pause the barge traffic."

"Okay, I'm with you, but how do you plan to do that? To pause the traffic?"

"We think that if we can hang something from the bottom of the bridge, it would be enough to stall the boats. Even stalling them for a little bit will cost the industry money. So we want to hang a banner up there."

"And why do you think that's going to be effective?"

"We don't know if it will, to be honest with you." Mercer jumped in. "Our hope is that even if we don't get to stay out there long enough to slow traffic, we can send a message with the banner itself. Even if one person sees it and thinks about it, that's better than doing nothing."

Mr. Stephens smiled at Miss Daphne. "Actually, Mercer, that was the answer I was looking for. If y'all want me to join you—and Daphne here definitely does—I want to make sure you have realistic expectations. And the most unrealistic expectation you can have is that you will solve it all with just this one action. Now, Daphne told me neither of you have ever done an action like this. You do know there's a real risk of jail, right?"

"We know, but Mercer's daddy is a sheriff here in Louisiana, so he doesn't think it'll last too long. Even still, I'm willing to risk it."

"We're *not* going to jail," Mercer said decisively.

Corinne was tired of having this argument with him and promised herself that the next time it came up, she'd make sure it was the last.

"Okay, we can talk more about that later. I just wanted to make sure you knew that was really on the table. Now, Corinne, I understand why this is so serious for you. Mercer, what's your story? Why does this matter for you?"

Mercer looked back incredulously. "Because all that oil on those boats is lighting my future on fire? I mean, do I need a more personal reason than that?" He softened when Alex didn't respond. "Besides, Corinne is my friend, and I want to be there for her."

Mr. Stephens took a giant bite of crab rangoon and chewed for a little too long. He looked like he was floating away, and Corinne wanted to bring him back. "Mr. Stephens, we're going to do this with or without you."

"Okay. You got me."

The tension lifted from the table just as the waitress with the perfect timing removed their appetizer dishes and replaced them with bowls of steaming noodles and plates of bean sprouts and cilantro and lime. And just like that, Corinne's inner storm calmed and her appetite returned. She might have even smiled.

Mr. Stephens smiled back, deepening the creases around his blue eyes. "Now that I'm *in*, though, tell me more detail about exactly what I've gotten myself *into*."

Corinne was confused. "We just told you. We're going to climb onto the bridge and hang a banner to commemorate my brother."

"Okay, what's the banner going to say?"

She felt a wave of embarrassment when she realized she hadn't thought this far ahead.

"It's okay, Corinne," Miss Daphne said soothingly. "We're here to help you think it through."

"Well, I thought it could just be like a tombstone, with his name, birth date, and the day he died."

"That's meaningful," Mr. Stephens said as he took a slurp of his pho. He said it in a way that let her know that wasn't the end of his sentence. "But it's only powerful if you know the rest of the story. Not everyone who sees it is going to make the connection. They probably won't know your brother's name—may he rest in peace—and then it'll just seem random. No offense."

He was right. Corinne began to feel her youth in a way she hadn't before. As much as it made her ashamed of her own naivete, it made her even more grateful for their wisdom.

"Okay, can we make it say something more direct and keep Corinne's brother's name?" Mercer asked.

"I'm sure we can think of something," Mr. Stephens assured them.

"What about something like, 'People and Planet Against Big Oil,' and then an RIP to Corinne's brother—to Cameron," Miss Daphne offered as she gently tapped Corinne's foot with her own under the table.

Corinne knew she was trying to help, but she hated that for the banner. "Big oil" just sounded . . . old. Like something they'd say in those black-and-white movies from the 1950s with the smart-aleck detectives that Grandma liked to watch. Back in the days when a crime of this scale—what people were beginning to call "ecocide"—was the stuff of science fiction.

"No, I want something stronger."

"How about 'The Oil Industry Has Blood on Its Hands, and Some of It Belonged to My Brother'?" Mercer offered.

Corinne liked that a lot more but thought "industry" was too vague for the average person in Vicksburg to understand. They knew the boats, not the whole industry. "What if we go even stronger?" She leaned forward. "What if it's something like 'These Oil Boats Killed My Brother, Cameron Sterling, on May 5, 2013. You're Next.'"

"That's not half bad, Corinne!" Miss Daphne smiled in approval.

"I'd actually say that's damn good," Mr. Stephens followed. "I've heard people who've done this a long time come up with way worse."

"That's it," Corinne announced. "That's what the banner is going to say. We can hang it off the side that faces the other bridge so people in their cars can see it."

Mr. Stephens grinned at her. "I like your nerve, Corinne. I mean that. You might have a future as a bona fide hell-raiser. Another thing we're going to need to think about, that we don't have to decide on right now, is whether or not to have a manifesto."

Corinne bristled at the word. "A manifesto? Ain't that what white boys write right before they shoot up a post office?"

Miss Daphne laughed, but Mr. Stephens remained unmoved.

"It doesn't have to be that involved, and we don't have to call it that. It could just be a press release or a blog post. But, again, we don't have to decide right now, at this table. When do y'all want to do this?"

"It will have to be over the summer, when Corinne is back home," Miss Daphne answered. "We figure on the later side, around August, because she'll need to be able to get out there and scout the bridge out. She's even trying to get a summer job at the Mississippi River Museum out in Vicksburg. She might seem serious now, but she can get real charming when she wants to be."

Corinne was grateful that her skin was too dark for her blushes to show. Miss Daphne smiled back at her, revealing the dimple on the left side of her mouth that showed only when she smiled really big.

"Oh, are you now?" Mr. Stephens asked. "Does this all fall apart if you don't get the job?"

"No, but also I'm pretty sure I'll get it," Corinne answered. "I was part of this working group at school last year that made all these demands of the natural sciences to help Black students find internships and get them financial support. They helped pay for my internship back in January, in fact. Anyway, there's a really good chance I'll get the job at the museum 'cause Oberlin will likely pay for it. And then there's no reason not to hire me."

"Well, look at you!" Mr. Stephens looked impressed. "We can decide on an exact date after you get there, Corinne, but let's say it's August for now. You'll need to scout the area out very carefully. Send us pictures from every single angle you can get. As much as you can without drawing attention to yourself, get an idea for when the boats sail underneath and how guarded the bridge is and who owns it. But we can talk more about that once you're there. Have y'all decided how to deal with the police?"

"Well, I don't think we can call the police ahead of time," Miss Daphne said. "Then they'll just show up and ruin the whole thing. But we probably should have someone call as soon as y'all are out there and be the one who talks to the cops once they show up. I can do that."

"Daphne!" Mr. Stephens looked at her in horror. "You're going to be in no condition to come anywhere near this!"

"I'm coming, Alex. That's not up for debate. You might as well give me something to do."

Mr. Stephens sat back in his seat, staring down at what was left of his pho with half his beard wet with broth. He looked like he knew not to argue but still didn't know what to say, so he turned back to Corinne and Mercer. "If I'm going to do this with you, and I am, you have to make me one promise: you will go to an NVDA training."

"What's that?" Corinne asked.

"Oh, right, sorry. Nonviolent direct action. What you're planning is not so much a 'protest,' though I noticed you keep using that word. That's more like a march or something. This is what we call an 'action.' It has fewer people and higher stakes. An NVDA training will teach you all of that and how to interact with the police and what to expect in jail."

Mercer and Corinne looked at each other and nodded.

"I know where to get you a training here in New Orleans, Mercer. Corinne, I'm sure we can find somewhere for you once you're back in Ohio."

Corinne nodded. "Okay, I can do that."

WHIRLPOOL

May 5, 2013

Cora had been on her back porch for something like an hour, and she'd already sweated through her house-dress. Enough ice had melted in her glass that there was a layer of water floating atop her whiskey. Her bottle of George Dickel sat next to the vanilla candle on the plastic table beside her. She remembered all the times she'd sat out here with Grandma Cindy, Yvonne, and Corinne, listening to the frogs and thunder in the distance. Watching the weather was like a family sport. Tonight, though, she'd never felt more alone.

Cora had been watching the Weather Channel all day, so she'd known since morning that a fearsome storm was on its way before the air turned ominous and she got that feeling in her spine. According to the radar, the storm would hit Cameron in Lake Charles first, then her in Port Gibson, and then Harold in New Orleans. By now, the air felt the way it did when a tornado was on the hunt and the whole sky was about to fall. Even if it didn't, after the call she'd just gotten, she knew she wasn't likely to sleep that night. She picked up her whiskey and called Harold.

"Mama?" His voice was gravelly with sleep. "It's after eleven. Ain't it supposed to be storming there? You sure you should be on the phone?"

"Harold!" Her voice cracked.

She could hear rustling as he sat up. "What is it, Mama?"

"Harold . . ." She breathed deep. "It's Cameron. I got a call from his company . . ."

"And what they say, Mama?"

"They said there's been an accident. They're not sure if anybody died. But they said he was involved, and I don't know what that means."

"Yeah, me neither—"

"Does that mean he pushed somebody off the boat? Did somebody push him? Was he a witness?"

"Why would you go straight to a crime, Mama? Cameron ain't violent!"

"You know that's not where my mind went first, Harold! You *know*."

"I know, Mama, I know." Harold's voice became gentle again. "Do you know where they at?"

"They were out by Lake Charles tonight . . ."

"Mama, there was a big lightning storm out there . . ."

"That's what I know, Harold." She was suddenly overcome with the urge to get off the phone.

"Well, did they say anything about that storm, Mama?"

"They said to call them back in the morning if they hadn't called me yet. Can you call Corinne and let her know? My nerves . . ." Cora knew Corinne was worrying over her final exams and papers. She also knew that she could not bear having to tell another person. It was hard enough to call Harold.

"Okay, Mama. I'll call her now."

"Thank you, baby." Harold had been her rock ever since he was a little boy. She knew she could always count on him.

"And, Mama? You'll call me as soon as you hear something, right?"

"I promise. And I love you."

"Love you more."

As she hung up, there was a clap of thunder so loud she jumped. She thought about bringing her houseplants outside so something could grow from the storm, but she didn't have the strength. She'd just have to sit and watch God and wait for word. At the same time, her mind kept jumping through the hurdles of funeral planning or figuring out disability insurance for Cameron. What if he came back missing a limb? What if he lost motor control? What if she had to go back to caregiving in her old age?

She tried to remember this could all turn out to be nothing and Cameron could walk through her doorway tomorrow morning, grinning with that face full of features of people he'd never met. He had the wide nostrils of his grandfather. The man who'd run out on her before Yvonne was old enough for kindergarten ended up leaving his mark on his grandson anyway.

Cameron got his eyes from Grandma Cindy and his cheekbones from Mama, like her. He had the beginnings of Daddy's bottom lip, poking out in a perpetual pout. When she was a child, she'd made a religion out of watching gravity pull it out like a dresser drawer. She remembered that as Daddy had gotten older, it had looked more like a tongue than a lip, swinging low like a chariot. She wondered if that would happen to Cameron, too, but now she just prayed he'd make it that far.

Why did Cameron have to go off on that boat in the first place? He could have gone to college like Cora had planned for him. He'd had decent enough grades. She had wanted him to become a pharmacist or an accountant or a politician—something where he could work safely indoors and not on a barge with barrels of shit so toxic, the smell alone could kill him. Where he wouldn't come home with his skin burnt three shades deeper from the sun.

A hollowness began to radiate inside her, threatening to pull her under like a whirlpool. It was the same emptiness she'd tried so hard to fill for so many years, too familiar to mistake. Loneliness.

She surveyed the flashes of her life and tried to find the moment she'd gone wrong. First with her parents and then her lovers. Then with her own children—one who died and one who'd moved away—neither of whom finished college. Now, she felt like she was squandering the second chance she'd been given with her grandchildren. When they'd come to live with her, she'd thought maybe it was her last chance to finally get it right and lift her curse.

But with the worst-case scenario about Cameron swirling through her head, she felt afresh the hot glare of her father's disappointment after she'd told him she was pregnant and dropping out of Fisk. With that decision, she'd become the first person in her family *not* to finish college since slavery. For the first time in her life, she'd seen Daddy's chest cave in, only to rise moments later to let loose the most hurtful words anyone had ever said to her: *"Well, I guess all that sacrifice was for nothing."* Her teachers and classmates at the White Folks School had cut her skin and her flesh, but Daddy had cut into her bones, to her very core.

Decades later, she could still feel the pain like fire. Later, on his deathbed, he'd apologized for pushing her too hard and for giving up on her. When she'd looked down on him as a dying man, she'd promised to put the Sterling name back in the halls of higher education where he'd fought so hard to keep it. But deathbeds have a way of bringing out promises that don't hold. More than thirty years later, not a single new degree had made it onto Cora's walls.

She took a swig of her whiskey and welcomed the way it burned the walls of her empty stomach. Then the sky made good on its promise: the rain fell hard and violent. Angry wind made chaos out of the raindrops, and the frogs in the distance came to an immediate hush. Cora heard one of her hummingbird feeders crash in the yard and realized it was time to go inside.

After she blew out her candle, she stumbled into the house and locked the back door, making her way to her room. She didn't even turn on the light as she curled up in bed under the tattered hand-stitched quilt with green, red, and yellow squares that had once belonged to Grandma Cindy. Tonight, George Dickel would be the closest thing she'd have to a sleeping companion since Corinne had conquered her fear of the dark some fifteen years ago.

With the storm swirling outside and the whiskey spinning inside her belly, Cora wanted nothing more than to be held, cradled, rocked. Babied. And so began her all-too-familiar descent into that unforgiving cycle where she remembered her every lover—how they'd smelled, how they'd walked, how they'd failed. Then she remembered how their relationships and liaisons and "arrangements" had backfired and shot her in the heart.

She could always see it coming, even if she didn't want to admit it to herself. From her high school sweetheart to her children's father to the married deacon. They'd charmed her, courted her, hypnotized her—sometimes for weeks or months, and one time for *years*—and then, just like that, it was over. They'd push her away just as quickly and passionately as they'd pulled her in. Each time, it felt like she'd wandered across some invisible line that turned her from the object of their affection to one of scorn. And no matter how hard she tried, there was no way back. The paradise was lost.

When she'd dared to show them her wounds, they'd been aghast, disgusted. Not that she'd been hurt, but that she would dare suggest that her pain had anything at all to do with them. They'd looked at her like she was a heretic. And in the end, there was always a callous pseudo-apology. Like a chorus, they sang the same mealy-mouthed, foot-shuffling, eye-contactless song: "I'm sorry *if* I hurt you." Never mind the detailed, methodical, and entirely *not*-accidental way in which they had done so. And no matter what they said, Cora heard the part they never admitted: "I didn't know you could feel pain." So she'd slink away to lick the wounds she should have thwarted.

She remembered the last of her lovers—Randall, the deacon at her old church way out in the country. She'd known he was married, even knew his wife. But he'd assured her that for years the marriage had been as lifeless as the papers they'd signed years ago. He'd held her, and she'd melted as he molded her into what he wanted her to be. She'd worn his favorite colors, cooked his favorite foods, combed her hair the way he liked. She'd loved the secrecy almost as much as she had loved him. He'd said that was what made it special, and she had so badly wanted to be special. And then, with no warning, he stopped dropping by the house, stopped answering her calls, stopped making eye contact in church. Then she saw him in the cereal aisle at Piggly Wiggly with his arms around his wife, holding the small of her back the way he'd never held hers. They'd been in a world of their own, somewhere where she didn't exist. Cora had abandoned her cart full of groceries and walked as calmly as she could to her car and fell apart as quickly as she'd fallen in love.

Cora felt like she was always caught between two extremes—being either too much or not enough. Always conquered, never cherished. Fucked and never known. It was even harder to believe that she kept falling for it. So, finally, she'd stopped. She made her peace with the inescapable truth that she was not and never would be good enough. She hadn't been the pretty princess girl for whom princes slayed dragons, and she could never expect to be the beautiful queen whose honor must be defended. There was no concealer to cover it up. She'd still wake up the next morning and be herself.

It was liberating in a way, this realization. She stopped expecting it to stop, to get better. Instead, she set herself about the business of raising her children, and then her grandchildren, to be better than her.

This was usually where the cycle ended: with the memory of the boys she brought into the world and how they'd be better than the men she'd found. But tonight, there was no comfort there. Her spiral became a free fall, and she fell even deeper down the whiskey bottle.

By the time she heard her telephone ring, Cora couldn't tell if she'd slept at all or if she'd gone into a deep, deep daydream. All the whiskey had made her head ten pounds heavier, so she pressed the Answer button without sitting up.

"Mrs. Sterling?"

"Right, I forgot to say hello." Cora looked at the caller ID and recognized the 337 area code. Then she remembered the call from last night and her stomach sank.

"Ma'am, my name is Robert Finn. I hope I'm not waking you up?" He sounded somber.

"It's fine. I'm up now. Do you have news about Cameron?"

"Ma'am, these calls are never easy, but they don't get easier by beating around the bush." He heaved a sigh. "I'm calling to tell you that your son passed away this morning."

The sky fell. "What—what happened?"

"Ma'am, I could go into details, but I honestly don't think you'll want them. He fell off the boat during the electrical storm and . . . we got your son to the hospital as soon as we could . . ."

"Grandson." She tried to yell, but she could only whisper. She felt like the world was slipping through her fingers. College be damned, she'd had *one* job: to keep Cameron and Corinne safe. Now she'd failed her parents and her daughter.

"Ma'am?"

"He's my grandson," Cora said louder. She could feel her head start to spin, and that familiar cloak of guilt began to fall on her shoulders.

"Yes, I'm sorry, ma'am. Your grandson. I'm so sorry to have to call you with this news. Everyone on Cameron's boat is just devastated. I can't imagine what you must be going through. We'll call back soon to make whatever arrangements you want to make for the funeral, but I'm gonna let you go be with your family now."

"Th-thank you," Cora stammered before she even realized what was coming out of her mouth. The phone beeped, and she heard the sound ricochet through the empty house. Once the echo was gone, she felt her stomach push last night's whiskey into her throat and she ran to the toilet, where she sobbed and heaved until she passed out.

≈

Harold came home that night, Corinne three days later. They held the funeral—short, tasteful, and merciful—one week later. Cora stowed her tear-wrinkled program from the services in her top dresser drawer. Sometimes she got the courage to look at it, to press it against her heart the way she had held Cameron as an infant. She could still hear his cries and gurgles. His life span—1989 to 2013—looked so cruelly and criminally short printed out above his picture.

Neighbors from across four counties had brought plates and trays and deep dishes of fried chicken and fish, macaroni and cheese, freezer-safe jambalaya, chili, lasagna, and peach cobbler. It was a loving but futile gesture. There was nothing that could fill this emptiness. There were enough family recipes to cater a whole revival. *That's where the food should be going,* Cora thought. *Toward happy things.*

As the food piled up in the kitchen, Cora piled her bed with photo albums, tracing her fingers over the many faces of her beloved grandson. Baby Cameron in his white onesie on the way home from the hospital. Toddler Cameron squealing with joy as he realized Santa Claus was really his uncle Harold in a suit. Middle school Cameron in his basketball uniform, his features already starting to harden into manhood. Prom night Cameron with his bow tie and that grin he wore when he felt self-conscious. Then the one she'd gotten to know the least: grown man Cameron just last Thanksgiving.

As the weeks went by and her strength returned, she began to peel the pictures out of the albums and place them into the empty frames she kept in the closet. Then she would walk the new picture out into the living room and place it on the altar she'd made first for her parents and then for Yvonne. She pushed their pictures to the back and toward the ends of the table. It looked like they were surrounding him, protecting him. Sometimes when Cora walked by the altar, she thought she could hear him ask when dinner would be ready. Other times, she'd look at how crowded the table had become, but she knew there wasn't a single thing she'd take away.

Cameron had always been a moody child. As he'd grown older, he'd become like a tornado—too fast to predict, let alone to name. Cora had learned to weather his moods, never to argue with them. But his clouds just made his sunshine all the more precious. That's what she'd lived for.

Of course, Cora had wanted Cameron to go to college, but when he decided to go his own way and make a living on the oil boat, she'd been proud. She could still see his face the first time he came home after a month or so of working on the boat, his chest sticking out the way her father's used to. She remembered how he would saunter into Kroger all wide-legged with pride, pulling out his debit card like it was made of gold. *"Get whatever you want, Grandma."* And he'd wink. He'd talked about the work on the boat like he'd conquered the world—how narrowly he'd escaped an accident, how beautiful the sunsets were on the Ohio and Missouri Rivers and the Gulf of Mexico. And as the light grew in his eyes, Cora had shushed the part of her that had hated his job on the boat.

And now this.

For the rest of the summer, the house was too quiet. There was no sound, only echoes. She and Corinne retreated into their own private worlds of grief, walled off from each other with a thick fear of mutually assured destruction. In the first few weeks, Cora's grief had felt heavy all over and even the simplest tasks, like washing dishes or laundry, were excruciating, like she was moving through concrete. She'd once worked up a sweat just trying to get out of bed. She neglected her garden and her houseplants, and she found herself surrounded by even more death.

One day in July, when she was in the shower, she felt the heartache growing into a ball in the back of her throat so big she feared she might choke. It felt like she had glass in her lungs. She realized then that this grief was going to kill her if she let it. She stood as still as she could, held on to the shower wall, and chose life. As the water fell down, the fever broke. She could breathe normal and see color again. She knew the grief would never end; she learned that when she'd lost Yvonne. She didn't really want it to end either, because she didn't want to forget. But her grief was different now. It wasn't crushing her anymore. It had broken open. It was wider now, more airy. And so very, very lonely.

After that, she tried everything she could think of to reach her granddaughter, but no matter how hard Cora tried, Corinne stayed in her darkened room, hunched over her laptop like a goblin. She kept the curtains drawn and the lamps off, her face illuminated only by the dim, eerie light of her computer. It was like she was on another planet. When Cora cracked the door open, Corinne barely looked up, only grunted her responses. Some days, Corinne would call out "I love you" as Cora pulled the door closed behind her. Those merciful utterances were all that held Cora together that summer. She breathed them in deep and held them tight.

Rebuffed by Corinne, Cora took her grief to her hummingbird garden, the one place where she knew she'd never be alone. She'd planted it as a monument to her parents when she inherited the house from Grandma Cindy. There were petunias, impatiens, azaleas, and two different kinds of honeysuckle. And, of course, there was Mama's favorite: morning glories. Hummingbirds loved these flowers, and her daddy had loved hummingbirds. And Cora loved them both.

Every day, she sat for hours on her bench covered in vines from the pretty flowers. She didn't even mind the heat or the bugs. She told Mama and Daddy how much she tried, how proud they would have been of Cameron had they known him. How he stood tall like Daddy and was just as handsome. She told them he had Mama's poker face, and that he could have gotten a basketball scholarship if he'd focused harder.

She prayed that they were all together, with Yvonne, and she begged them to look after Cameron.

LOST SOULS

May 5, 2014

The air smelled sweet near the Oberlin Reservoir this time of year. The trees and wildflowers—drunk on mountains of melted snow—burst toward the sky with a new, audacious proclamation of life. Over the vibrant humming and buzzing, Corinne could hear the birds calling out for lovers. She picked their songs out one by one: the chirruping sparrow, the squawking blue jay, and the delirious robin.

She stopped when she heard the soft coo of the mourning dove cut through the cacophony. It was one of the most common birdsongs in the reservoir—and even across the country—but Corinne rarely heard it over the other birds. She knew that distinctive four-syllable melody meant that the bird was looking for the love of its life, but Grandma had told her that mourning doves sang the songs of those we have loved and lost. *"When you hear them,"* Grandma said, *"you should take the time to remember."*

Corinne wondered if the dove knew that that was exactly what she'd come to the reservoir to do. It was a year ago today that Cameron got caught in that awful lightning storm that took him away forever. Corinne would have known it was today even without a calendar. Everything reminded her. She remembered where she was the last time she saw spring flowers, studied for her spring finals, and watched the campus prepare itself for graduations and reunions. It was all the same as last year, but still so disorienting because nothing could ever be the same.

Corinne had always found it easier to commune with the dead away from the noise of other people. She liked to escape into nature and focus on a piece of it that reminded her of her lost loved one. For Mama, she focused on trees. For Cameron, she decided to focus on water, so she chose one of the only bodies of water she could get to on foot from campus: the reservoir.

Aside from the birds, it was quiet here. And she needed that silence because the hardest part of mourning Cameron was that her memories of him were cluttered with explosions. The two of them had fought constantly. They'd both known the quickest route to the other's last nerve. Sometimes Corinne found herself picking fights with other people just to feel that tension again, but nothing ever came close. But she was determined not to focus on that, not today. Today, she wanted to remember Cameron's sunshine more than his storms. The way he danced, never more than a two-step but decidedly his own. Or how good his memory was—he never forgot a birthday or a doctor's appointment in his life. Or his face and how the two of them only looked alike when they scowled. Sometimes she made that face in the mirror just to see him again. She remembered his smile and heard his laugh just as clearly as the birds that sang overhead right now.

As Corinne sat by the reservoir, she scrolled through the photos on her phone, creating an album full of Cameron's face. She put pictures of him in his Santa hat into sequential order so she could watch the hat go from way too big to just a little droopy to the perfect size. She had pictures of him playing chess with Uncle Harold and washing Grandma's car. And then there were the family portraits they'd taken at the mall when Mama had still been alive. Her favorites, though, were the ones Mama had taken of the two of them during bath time, splashing water at each other with their feet like they were pedaling a boat. Mama had hated the mess they'd made but loved how it had tired them out for bed. Now, they were Corinne's proof that there was tenderness and joy between them after all. She hated that he hadn't lived long enough for them to find their way back to that.

Corinne felt her temples tightening and her eyes begin to burn, but before the tears could come, her iPhone screen replaced Cameron's face with Miss Daphne's. She'd thought she wanted to be alone today, but this grief was too heavy. She slid her finger across the screen to take the call.

"Hello?"

"Hey, Corinne. I was just calling to check on you. I know today is a tough day."

"Yeah, it is." Corinne sighed. "But I'm making do. I was just looking through my pictures of him. I'm going to make an album to share with Grandma and Uncle Harold. And, looking at the bright side, at least I have so much to remember him by."

"Oh, that's sweet, I'm sure they'll like that. But, Corinne, take it easy on yourself. It can't be easy to look at all that. Especially today."

"Well, the way I see it, looking away is worse. The only way to keep his memory alive is to spend time with it. And with him."

"You might be right about that." Miss Daphne sighed lightly.

"I actually was thinking about you the other day." Corinne changed the subject. "Any news from the lawyers?"

Over the past two weeks, Miss Daphne had been talking with lawyers in both Mississippi and Louisiana about all the possible charges and penalties for breaking onto the bridge in Vicksburg.

"I have, but, Corinne, you sure you want to talk about this today? It can wait."

"No, no. I want to hear about this now. The only thing that's made losing my brother feel even a little bit bearable is knowing that we're going to hit back. Gives me something to look forward to."

"Oh, Corinne. We can throw a rock, but I don't know if it's gonna slay the dragon."

"I need to *do* something, Miss Daphne." Corinne hated all the reminders about the futility of it all. She knew she wasn't going to magically bring down every oil boat or every pipeline. But ever since she'd trained her mind on that bridge in Vicksburg, she had felt lighter. Even if it was a kamikaze mission, it was still a mission, and that was enough for her. "And this doesn't have to be the last thing I do."

"Well, amen to that." Miss Daphne laughed. "So it sounds like everyone thinks the most likely charges are trespassing, possibly criminal trespassing. And then there's this thing called 'obstructing a navigable waterway or railroad.'"

"Hmm, and we could potentially be doing both since that bridge is part of the railroad."

"Exactly," Miss Daphne confirmed. "And you don't have to actually interfere with either for them to charge you with it. The potential alone is enough. You'd also likely get disorderly conduct, which could turn into reckless endangerment, depending on how pissed off the cop is, and I think we can expect any cop who has to interrupt his morning routine to be pretty pissed. Which brings me to the next possible charge: obstructing an officer in the course of their duties."

"What does that mean?"

"It basically means that you stopped an officer from doing their job. They could claim that our action stopped them from helping someone in actual distress. Again, it all depends on how annoyed the cops are when they arrest us."

Corinne pursed her lips and sighed. "And what are the penalties for all these?"

"It depends. None of them have a mandatory jail sentence or even a mandatory fine. They're the type of charges that are almost completely up to the cop's whim—or the judge's, if it goes that far. It will be very important for all of you to cooperate with the police as much as possible. Do everything they say exactly when and how they say it. And it's going to be important that I call them before they find you on their own. You don't want to surprise them with something like this."

"Okay, I can do that."

"And, of course, Mercer has volunteered to use his connections in our favor, but that will only help after the fact. He seems to think there's a good chance y'all won't get arrested at all. But I don't know about that."

"Yeah, but he's a white boy." Corinne rolled her eyes. "If he did it alone, he probably wouldn't get arrested. If I do it with him, I think I'll still get arrested, but my odds of getting hurt or going to jail go way down. And those are odds I'm willing to take."

"And! Just in case, I have a lawyer in Jackson on standby. And Alex says he has up to $1,000 for bail money for each of us. Don't ask me where he gets his money. I don't want to know."

"Oh, that's not my business." Corinne sucked her teeth. "But tell him I said thank you."

"I will. I'm going to start looking for somebody to document this too. I thought I could do it all on Twitter, but now I think we need to do a little more. I'm gonna call on my friend from college. She's an actual photojournalist with a real deal camera. She's white, too, but that works."

"Yep, and I have my nonviolent training thing tomorrow too." Corinne was not looking forward to it. She just imagined a bunch of hippies who'd never really had to struggle for anything trying to teach her about resistance. But, as a child of Mississippi, she thought, this was in her blood, from her great-grandfather to her grandmother. How were they going to teach her about her own birthright?

"Oh right, I forgot about that! I think you'll enjoy it. You meet all sorts of interesting people. Never know what the cat's gonna drag in."

"Yeah, and I have a friend coming with me." She ignored Miss Daphne's optimism and focused on her gratitude that Cleo volunteered to come with her. He was even going to drive them to Cleveland.

"That's great, Corinne." Miss Daphne paused. "But I have to ask: Have you thought any more about how this is going to go over with your family? Especially your grandmother?"

"I have." Corinne sighed. "It's really all I think about. I even had a nightmare or two about it. It's funny 'cause my nightmares used to be all about Cameron or global warming, but I haven't had one of those in months."

"You know, there's still time to back out. We don't have to do this."

"No, no. I still want to do it. It was like once I made the decision to do it, I could breathe again, sleep again. I felt like a human being again. I might be scared to tell Grandma and Uncle Harold, but I'm still convinced it's the right thing to do."

"So what are you going to do then?"

"I'm gonna tell them. This summer. In person. I think Uncle Harold will be okay, but Grandma is gonna be the hard one. There's probably no way to break it to her easy, but I still am going to need to think long and hard about how to tell her. I'm so scared she's gonna flip out."

"Corinne, if she flipped out over you going to Oberlin, she's definitely going to flip out over this."

"I know. But I can't let that stop me." Corinne took a deep breath. "You know, this might sound crazy, but I feel like this is the only thing I can do to heal myself, and . . . maybe when Grandma sees that, she'll understand? And maybe she'll want to start looking for the thing that heals her."

"It doesn't sound that crazy to me, Corinne. It sounds idealistic. But you know what? Idealists have been right before."

"We'll see."

"Yes, indeed. Well, let me let you go, and I'll talk to you soon."

"Okay, Miss Daphne."

When Corinne looked up from her phone, she could see what looked like a giant dragonfly coming straight toward her from across the water. As it got closer, she realized it was a hummingbird flitting his little wings with all his might. It flew above her head and off into the clouds.

━━

Corinne's eyes followed the concrete staircase toward the dark redbrick arches that pierced the thick gray clouds gathered over downtown Cleveland. That perfect, holy blend of intimidation and invitation. Next to the door was one of those glass-encased signs with peel-off black letters. At the top it read: All God's Children Universalist Church.

Cleo looked up at the church like it was a mountain and exclaimed, "This looks just like my daddy's church!"

"Oh, I thought all your churches in New York were in old corner stores." Corinne laughed.

"Very funny, Cori." Cleo was not laughing. "But it's the same colors and everything. The doors and the windows are shaped the same too. I didn't think Universalist churches would look so much like Baptist churches. They don't even believe in hell."

"That's kind of a nice idea, right?" Corinne leaned against the handrail.

"Don't let my daddy hear you say that!"

"I promise I won't." Corinne shivered in the wind and pulled her scarf tighter. "But Cleo, they're about to get started, so can we get inside already?"

"Well, if this is anything else like my daddy's church, they don't start on time. But sure." Cleo bowed his six-foot frame and motioned for her to go up the stairs ahead of him. Corinne rushed up the stairs faster than her heels could touch the ground.

Once she was in the foyer, those classic church scents filled her nose: Pine-Sol, mothballs, and cough drops. She almost felt like she was back in Grandma's church in the woods. The air had that drafty feeling she knew so well. The only thing missing was that shroud of shame that enveloped her the minute she stepped into Grandma's holy house.

"Okay, well, it doesn't look so much like my daddy's church now," Cleo commented. The cherrywood on the floor and the chestnut wood on the wall all looked brand-new. "These white folks must be *tithing*."

They walked toward the murmur of voices in the main sanctuary. Underneath the high ceilings, there was a circle of white chairs, with more stacked along the walls. No pews, no benches. In the front sat a simple mic stand, no pulpit. Along the back wall, there was a table with two boxes of donuts and three boxes of coffee from Dunkin' Donuts, with plates and utensils, milk and sugar. Corinne looked closely and saw there was a small container of almond milk and thanked her stars. Even though it was five o'clock on a Tuesday afternoon, she was still groggy.

As she headed toward the coffee, a tall white woman with curly red hair walked up to her with crossed arms and a pursed smile. Corinne and Cleo shot each other a wary look.

"Are you all here for the training?" The woman asked this with enough warmth in her voice to bring their shoulders down from their ears.

"You mean the nonviolent direct action training, right?" Corinne wanted to be sure she was in the right place. "Yes, that's what we're here for. Is that okay?"

"Yes, yes, of course it's okay!" The woman looked incredulous. "I just have to make sure because the church gives away meals to the community in the afternoon, and if you were here for that, I wouldn't want you to be disappointed. My name is Madge, and I'll be the facilitator today. The sign-in sheet is right over on that chair, when you get a moment."

"Okay, we'll go sign in right now," Cleo said in his interview voice. He took Corinne by the shoulder and guided her toward the sign-in sheet. They didn't look at each other until Madge was back at the coffee table talking to a shaggy-haired white man in jeans.

"Um, did this bitch just ask us if we were here for free food?" Corinne asked through her teeth.

"First of all, don't be cussing in church," Cleo answered as he wrote his name on the sheet of printer paper attached to a clipboard. "Second of all, yes, yes, she did. You sure you still want to do this? We can walk out right now."

Corinne sighed. "No, I want to stay. I just can't believe that."

"Look, it's not an insult to need food. My daddy's church serves meals, too, and all sorts of people come, homeless and homeowners." He paused and looked over his glasses at her. "However, when that's the first thing a white woman asks you when she lays eyes on you, we should probably watch our backs. That's all I'm saying."

"No, I hear you. Let's just go ahead and get this done. It feels weird as hell to be learning about civil disobedience from a white lady in Ohio, but I'm sure I can get something out of today."

"Corinne!" Cleo was exasperated. "What did I tell you about cussing in church?"

"Hell is in the Bible!" Corinne was only half joking, but when Cleo didn't so much as smirk, she acquiesced. "Fine! Let me just get some coffee real quick."

"We're going to start soon, so please come take your seats." Madge stood in the middle of the circle of chairs and motioned to the others to come join her. With her long green dress and spectacles hanging from a bejeweled chain around her neck, she looked like a kindergarten teacher announcing story time.

Corinne took a giant gulp of her coffee before she followed Cleo toward the circle. As far she could tell, she and Cleo were the only Black people out of the dozen or so in the room. The worn and weary people around her would have looked entirely out of place at Grandma's church. For one thing, Corinne wasn't sure she'd ever seen a white person on a Sunday in Port Gibson, much less inside of a church. For another, no one was wearing church clothes. Madge's green dress and Cleo's khaki pants and polo shirt were the closest imitations, but everyone else was wearing jeans. Corinne wore them too—just to see if she could get away with it. Still, they didn't look like the comfortable hippies she'd expected. When she looked around the circle, she saw the worry worn into the creases of their foreheads. They looked desperate for some kind of healing or cleansing, like the lost souls every preacher dreamed about.

Once everyone was in their seats, Madge clapped loud enough to cut through the murmuring. "If you can hear me, clap one time." A collective clap bounced from the ceilings. "If you can hear me, clap two times." Two more claps came at once, and then a silence fell.

"Hello, everyone, I'm Madge. And I want to welcome you all to today's training." She even projected her voice like a kindergarten teacher. "First things first, I have to say that while we don't have anything to hide here, we do not welcome undercover informants or provocateurs. If such a person is here, we ask that you please identify yourself and leave." She paused a moment. Cleo and Corinne exchanged alarmed looks, but no one moved.

"Okay, let's get started. Before you leave here today, you're all going to get to know each other very well, and hopefully you'll learn even more about yourselves. We're going to talk about the principles and tactics of nonviolence, and what it really means to be 'nonviolent.'" She held out two fingers on both hands to imitate quotation marks. "Because it doesn't mean *passive*. It doesn't mean *cowardice*. We'll talk about how to communicate and cooperate with the police, the most common types of charges, and what to expect during arrest and in jail. Sound good, everyone?"

Everyone nodded. The shaggy-haired white man across from Corinne made eye contact with her and gestured at the name tags on the table in the middle of the circle. Corinne hadn't even noticed the table was there. He motioned to his own. It said Nathaniel. Corinne jumped up to pick up tags for herself and Cleo. As she slunk back to her seat, she mouthed,

"Thank you," to Nathaniel. He looked like he was in his thirties and, by her estimate, was the closest in age to her and Cleo out of everyone else there.

"Now, when you hear the term *nonviolent action*, what's the first thing that comes to your mind?"

Hands shot up across the room.

"Let's start with you." Madge motioned to a woman in a blue baseball cap.

"Martin Luther King!" Two other people put their hands down once she answered.

"Dr. Martin Luther King Jr., of course." Madge smiled. "A true legend. And you, sir?" She pointed to a man in a plaid shirt.

"Gandhi!"

"Yes, Mahatma Gandhi, another legend. Another great example would be Nelson Mandela. And so many others who committed to the philosophy of nonviolence to create change." Madge clasped her hands and looked around the circle. "I want to be clear that while this training is only about nonviolent resistance and does not encourage violence, I do recognize that it's not the only way to dismantle systems. I think it would just be silly not to acknowledge that. Now, for our first exercise, I want everybody to select a partner who is *not* the person you came with or the person sitting next to you."

Cleo nudged her with his elbow before he turned to the brown-haired white woman to his right. Corinne looked up to see Nathaniel motioning to her to be his partner. She nodded back.

"Now, I want you to take turns sharing what brought you here today. You'll each take about two minutes to tell your story while the other person listens. And you'll need to listen actively, because when the two minutes are up, the listening partner will need to repeat back what they learned about you before we switch speakers. You can ask clarifying questions, but keep them brief. I'll call you back when the time is up."

Corinne made her way to Nathaniel and realized she came up to his bicep. They smiled awkwardly at each other until the din of moving chairs quieted down.

"You go first," he said, crossing his arms and hunching over to hear her better.

"Sure. I'm Corinne. I'm a student at Oberlin, but I'm originally from Mississippi."

"Oh, from Mississippi!" Nathaniel's face lit up. "What part?"

Corinne looked him up and down and could tell that he didn't know the name of a single town in Mississippi. She decided to test her theory. "Memphis."

"Oh wow! Memphis! I've heard of that place."

"I bet you have." Corinne held her laughter. "Where are you from?"

"No, no, it's still your turn, remember? That was just my clarifying question."

"Oh right. The short story is that I'm here because my mentor's friend told me I had to come to one of these. The longer story is that I'm here because of global warming. My brother died on an oil boat last year, and the little protests at Oberlin about polar bears are really not doing it for me anymore."

"Oh my God!" Nathaniel covered his mouth. "First of all, I'm so sorry to hear about your loss. That's really painful, but I think it's powerful that you're turning that into action."

"Thank you." He was so earnest, it made Corinne sorry for the bomb she'd just dropped on him. "I've always been worried about climate change, ever since I could remember. Or at least as soon as I heard about it. And definitely since Katrina. It's even what I came to Oberlin to major in, but I'd always looked at it as this scientific question about molecules in the atmosphere. It wasn't until my brother died working on an oil boat that I realized it was so much bigger. It was just as institutional as racism. And that's when I decided I wanted to do more about it than recycle. So I went to New Orleans in January and worked with this organization doing oral histories around the BP oil spill, and that's where I met my mentor. She introduced me to a friend of hers who does a lot of these kinds of actions. He said he'd help me if I came to a training like this."

"Help you do what?"

"Well, we haven't worked out all the details." Corinne began to fidget. "But we're thinking about doing something back home, in remembrance of my brother, but also bigger. It might just be symbolic, but it would be a start."

"I see." Nathaniel nodded emphatically. "You know, I'm involved in a lot of different causes, but environmentalism is one I haven't really dipped a toe in."

"I think it's your turn now, actually."

"Right. I live here in Cleveland, but I'm from Kentucky. Now, most of my time is spent going to protests for marriage equality and gay rights, but I'm a regular at Palestinian rights and anti-imperialism protests. People think that because the Iraq War is over, the American war machine slowed down. It didn't."

"Oh, I know it didn't," Corinne interjected. She was starting to like this Nathaniel. She remembered learning about Israel-Palestine when she went to a program put on by the Not in Our Name students at Oberlin. The more she learned about it, the more helpless she felt. Anyone who could take that issue on gained her instant respect.

"You go to Oberlin, so I'm sure you know." His eyelashes fluttered over his light blue eyes as a smile crept across his face. "I'm sure you also know that wars are not unrelated to global warming. All the oil, the explosions. We don't talk about it that way often enough."

"So what about your work brought you here today?"

"I've been to one of these before, but it's been a while, so I thought I could use a refresher."

"You're not planning anything specific?" Corinne asked. She was starting to think she might have something to learn from him after all.

"I'm just looking at what we're up against and how much more extreme it's getting. I believe we're going to win on gay marriage, and probably on war too. You know what they say, 'The moral arc of the universe is long, but it bends toward justice.'"

"Yeah, and I know who said that." Corinne hated how that specific quote from Martin Luther King Jr. got worn out, but she wanted to see where he was going to take it.

"Of course you do, and I bet you know that it doesn't bend unless *we* bend it, and before it bends, it fights like hell. So I'm looking over at what's going on with the Tea Party and all these gun nuts, and they think their entire way of life is being threatened. They're getting bolder and crazier. I don't want anything to do with guns; they terrify me. I don't like violence. But I do think we might need to get more radical than mass marches to match the intensity on the other side. So I'm here."

Now this was the kind of radicalization Corinne was into. But she had one more question. "You really think we're going to win?"

"We have to, Corinne. The story can't end any other way."

Corinne could think of a few other endings, but she liked his version of the story better. She'd always thought hope was a useless emotion, that it put people back to sleep. But here, it was powering Nathaniel forward. *Maybe*, she thought, *hope isn't so dangerous after all.*

PART THREE

TROUBLED WATERS

June 24, 2014

Corinne didn't know she was laughing until the sound echoed off the water below her, wild and boisterous. She stared down in wonder as her belly and the Yazoo River shook with the same rhythm. It would have startled the fishermen who lingered here in the cool of the morning, but the heavy heat had already evicted them for the day. She pushed back and sank her heels deeper into the riverbank until the mud cloaked her feet like it wanted to suck her in for good. As the fresh, June-warm water splashed her ankles and tickled her calves, she closed her eyes and grinned until her cheeks ached.

She felt a tingle at her fingertips and knew that it was joy. She remembered the long months she'd spent estranged from this feeling, not knowing if it would ever be hers again. Now, she wanted to savor it and bottle it for the inevitable darkness. Like jam.

She was supposed to be at work, tending the exhibits at the Lower Mississippi River Museum, the state-of-the-art, insatiably air-conditioned building on Washington Street. At just two years old, the building gleamed with a newness that was nearly obscene in a town as historic as Vicksburg. Just like she'd planned, she'd finagled her way into a position as a docent for the summer. She spent her days patrolling the facilities, including the real-life, dry-docked tugboat affixed to the museum and the carved astroturf demonstration that looked like a golf course until you got closer and turned the water on to reveal a mini-rendition of the Mississippi River system from Memphis to New Orleans.

Her job was to make sure the exhibits stayed pristine, all the televisions turned on, and the interactive displays had the water they needed. Most of the time, she spent half the day buried in the archives, reading about the River she loved. Some days she led tours for summer youth programs or church groups or the occasional pack of wild tourists—some of them drawn to the town for its Civil War lore, some fumbling along the Blues Highway or lost on the way to Jackson. Earlier today, one of the Black old folks' homes had sent a group of ten over for a tour. She'd gotten to work two hours early, at eight, to greet them as the attendants gingerly helped them out of the little white van, some in wheelchairs, some with walkers.

Corinne had looked at their worn faces, lined with life, and wondered what they'd seen. These were the people who had grown up in and around Vicksburg, back before all the roads were paved and the River became a thing to be seen and never touched. Back when the color line was stronger than the power lines. They knew the River deep down in their bones. She'd wished she could cancel the tour altogether and just listen to their stories.

And they'd been more than happy to tell her. As Corinne pushed her wheelchair through the Orientation Theater, one lady had told her that on her wedding day on the banks of the River, her daddy had kept a shotgun trained on her groom's knee through the entire ceremony. Her soon-to-be husband had sweat so much, his ring kept slipping off. When they passed the Great Flood exhibit, an old man had interrupted Corinne's script to tell them all about his father's harrowing escape from the water in the Delta and how it turned into a lifelong compulsion to count his children to make sure he hadn't lost one.

Toward the end, they'd walked through the boat exhibit that showed models of every type of vessel that used to travel the Mississippi River. There was even a model of a Union submarine from the Civil War—without any mention of what the war was fought over. When they'd made it to the steamboats, a tiny brown-skinned lady with a walker waved Corinne over to whisper.

"*You ever hear about the boys from Waterproof, Louisiana, who died in the River in the fifties?*"

"*No, I don't think so,*" Corinne replied with a smile.

"*Well, they didn't drown,*" the woman whispered. "*They was lynched. And the next day, the headline in the paper said 'Two Waterproof Niggers Drowned.'*" And then she cackled.

Corinne had heard that story more times than she could count. When white people told it, they omitted the lynching and cited the headline as "Two Waterproof Boys Drowned." But no matter who told the story, they laughed with raucous abandon and Corinne pretended it was the first time she'd ever heard it.

After the group was on their way back to the nursing home, Corinne had told her boss she was going for a walk and would be back after lunch. She'd come out on Levee Street— just a few hundred feet away from where the Yazoo spilled its greedy mouth into the Mississippi River—and watched the barges, laden with crude oil and asphalt, make their pilgrimage to the refineries that marred Vicksburg's bucolic landscape. The barges didn't move much faster than the storied steamboats that had become tour boats, standstill casinos, and itty-bitty models in the museum behind her.

It was a strange sensation to stand on land that had been invisible during her senior year of high school. Had she tried to walk out on Levee Street that spring, she'd have washed away along with 183 years of recordkeeping. That knowledge made the ground she stood on all the more sacred.

Corinne wiggled her toes in the cool, gritty mud again. Grandma never would have let her be this backwater, this "country"—a word Grandma always said with a disdainful emphasis on the first syllable. She could practically see her now, hands on hips, her head cocked to the side. "Have you lost your damn mind? Do you know there's snakes in that water, girl?" Corinne knew she was standing near one of the most dangerous places on the entire Mississippi River, and not just because of the animals in the water. If she followed the Yazoo down closer to where it met the Mississippi, the current would be so strong that if she slipped on a rock and into the water, she was almost guaranteed to drown. But she was confident in her ability to stand upright. And so, she just laughed.

"Corinne?"

She jumped at the sound of her name and turned around to face the luscious bluffs of kudzu that made up Vicksburg's skyline. She had to shield her eyes from the sun to see Mark's wiry frame standing on the other side of Levee Street. Poor thing was so prone to sunburn, any time he came outside he had to wear a giant hat that made him look like a child on safari. If he wasn't her boss, Corinne would have laughed at him.

"Hey, Mark. I was just about to come back in. I thought I had a little more time."

"Oh, you do!" Mark looked apologetic. "I was just about to head over to the Welcome Center, and I wanted to see if you wanted to ride over with me. I think Miss Patti brought in a cake."

Mark never missed a chance to sample Miss Patti's baking, and Corinne never missed a chance to get closer to the bridge.

"I'll be right there!" She rushed back up the ridge and paused at the hose pipe next to the outdoor exhibit to rinse her feet before she put her sandals back on. Then she ran into the office to grab her purse, and off they went.

As Mark drove, Corinne stared out the window, counting the cannons left over from the Union Army's relentless, ruthless siege of Vicksburg. The city had been bombarded so heavily its population went subterranean—carving caves out of the earth and living in them. They stayed underground for weeks, bored and nervous. Now the town was home to an immaculate, federally maintained Civil War battleground with detailed placards and beautiful monuments for each battalion that had fought there—it seemed every state had at least one. Corinne couldn't look at it without imagining, again, those hundreds of refugees from the Great Flood who were held captive on a battleground that was supposed to have made them free. The field was a major tourism draw—and an open wound.

That forty-day siege was encoded in white Vicksburg's DNA. The town didn't even celebrate the Fourth of July until 1945, and even then they called it the Carnival of the Confederacy. They didn't deign to call it Independence Day until 1976, on the nation's bicentennial. By then, nearly all the caves that had once dotted its streets had collapsed.

Grandma had once told her about the time she'd gone to a bar in Vicksburg in the '70s—one of the historic ones downtown—and her drink had come with a Confederate flag attached to the straw. She whipped out her lighter and set it on fire without breaking eye contact with the waitress. Once the flag was all burnt up, Grandma had looked at her with a straight face and said, with the calmness of a killer, *"Ain't y'all lose that war?"* She finished her drink, paid her bill, and tipped with exactly one penny.

The Welcome Center sat in between the new and old River bridges, and across from a town in Louisiana so flat they named it Delta. As Mark and Corinne got closer to it, more and more cannons appeared, trained on the River like they expected the submarines to come back. In Vicksburg, it wasn't always clear whether the Civil War ever even ended. Instead, it felt like the past and the present remained locked in a never-ending uncivil war, where the future was the only casualty. Still, the cannons looked to be in better shape than the bridge. Corinne didn't see a single one with chipped paint. Mark pulled into the parking lot right next to Miss Patti's car.

"Looks like we made it here on a quiet day!"

"Of course it's quiet, Mark." Corinne laughed. "It's Tuesday in the middle of the day."

As they walked onto the porch, Mark reached from behind Corinne to open the door and bellowed, "If it ain't my three most favorite ladies in all of Vicksburg!"

The three sisters—Patti, Ella, and Debbie—stood up from behind the front desk and made their way into the lobby to hug them. They were all in their sixties, with silver hair that they'd teased up into a tizzy.

"Well, hello there!" Miss Ella cooed as she squeezed Corinne.

"Sorry for the sweat, Miss Ella," Corinne said as she tried to release herself.

"Oh, it's fine, honey. I know it's mighty hot out today."

"Well, it *is* hot," Mark said as he leaned into his hug from Miss Ella. "But little Miss Corinne over here is all sweaty 'cause she was standing out by the Yazoo in the middle of the day, basking in the sun like a lizard."

"On purpose?" Miss Patti put her hands on her hips. "Girl, I don't know how you stand all that sun!"

Mark had introduced Corinne to the "sweet old ladies" when she first started working at the museum. Right away, they'd become enamored with her and her fascination with the River and the bridges. They'd indulged her questions about the bridge's history and engineering, and even about its security. And she tolerated their whitewashed stories about Old Vicksburg. The ladies had that perplexing ability most Southern white folks had to tell local history without ever mentioning slavery, sharecropping, or Jim Crow, just like the museum itself. Sometimes Corinne tried to push them, but most of the time she let it go. With the Welcome Center's proximity to the bridge and the sisters' connections and knowledge of Vicksburg, Corinne needed to stay in their good graces if she wanted to be able to scope out the bridge.

"I hope y'all already ate lunch, 'cause all we got is dessert over here!" Miss Patti said with a great big smile as she pulled out a lemon bundt cake. Miss Patti's baking was legendary around the museum, but Corinne had never tasted any of her cakes. She didn't break her vegan vows for anybody but Grandma.

"Did anyone take a piece out to Steve?" Corinne was asking about the security guard on the old bridge. He sat all day in a tiny booth, watching videos on his phone and the occasional train that crossed the bridge.

"Not yet, but you can!"

Corinne cut two giant slices of cake and sandwiched them in between two paper plates. "I'll be back in a little bit."

Last week, the Welcome Center sisters had told Steve to give Corinne permission to walk out on the bridge. She got to spend all afternoon out there, watching the boats and barges that carried the world's most precious cargo from one economic nerve center to another. She'd brought her sketch pad with her and drawn barge after barge laden with crude oil. Some of it went down from North Dakota and Canada to be refined. Some of it went up from New Orleans and Houston to be burned. All of it went in the wrong direction. Corinne knew that some people died on those boats. Others came off them maimed and mutilated. Still others came off the boats with cancer they couldn't feel yet. The poison always caught them sooner or later.

Corinne was hoping that if she plied Steve with not one but two pieces of cake, he would let her go back out there today. She shuffled out the door and past another cannon to the bridge entrance, and there was Steve, buried in his iPhone like always. She knocked on the window.

"Hey there, girl!" Steve smiled big but didn't move. He wasn't the hugging type. "What you bring me?"

"Your favorite!" Corinne beamed. "Cake!"

He reached for the plate Corinne held toward him, but she pulled it back. "If," she teased, "you let me go back on the bridge."

"Again? Girl, ain't you seen it all?" Even in his air-conditioned booth, he wasn't safe from the heat. Corinne could see beads of sweat popping out of his golden-brown skin.

"It's just so peaceful out there! Just let me go out for a half hour?"

"Okay, okay, just a half hour." He took the cake out of her hand and pressed the button to lift the gate. "You drive a hard bargain, Miss Corinne."

She winked and skipped through the gate. She walked about a third of the way out on the bridge, studying every metal beam and bolt, trying to plot out how she and Mercer and Mr. Stephens would hang the banner when they came out here in August. She opened the ruler app on her phone to take measurements, being careful to make it look like she was taking pictures instead.

Once she had the measurements she needed, she put her phone away and gazed down over the water. It was almost like she could see the slave ships that had traveled this same route. Even if the museum couldn't face it, she could see her ancestors—bewildered, enraged, and terrified—shipped from port to port. The bad niggers coming south, the new niggers heading north. She thought about the ones who had jumped to their deaths in these waters in a radical declaration of selfhood. Each plunge a revolution.

She felt the sun blazing on her skin, and it occurred to her how hot it must have been for the slaves forced to travel this river by way of steamboats: cramped and shadeless above deck, cramped and damp below. Heavy metal shackles on their arms and legs and necks. She wondered how hot their chains must have gotten in the sunlight and whether they burned their skin. There was no electricity and therefore no air-conditioning and no fans. Given the angle, they probably couldn't even fan themselves with their own hands. Precious little water and no mercy. They must have held on to every breeze like it was the breath of an angel.

Back then, her ancestors—their flesh and their blood—had been the most precious, most lucrative commodity in the world. With their bodies, and against their will, they had charted the course for the crude barges Corinne watched so closely now. Black bodies replaced by black oil.

Cameron had told her how dangerous the current was in Vicksburg because of the gush of water out of the Yazoo into the Mississippi. He'd said that when the water got to a certain height, all the barges had to cross single file—like a chain gang. He said that from underneath, the bridge looked like the underbelly of a giant mechanical caterpillar. You felt like it would fall on you, and it was even worse when it rained. She imagined it must have been very different from Huck Finn's bullshit raft ride.

She saw a barge coming toward her from the other side of the shiny new bridge with all the cars, and she could tell it was either carrying crude or asphalt because the barrels were covered with tarps. Cameron had taught her that those were the two types of cargo that were too dangerous to leave uncovered. Soon, it would pull into a dock and the men in the tugboat would climb out and do their dirty work. She would have given anything to see Cameron among them, cursing and grunting.

Corinne could feel Cameron out here with her, petulant and pouting but alive. She tried to breathe him in, to take another small piece of him back with her. *Soon*, she thought, *I won't be the only one living with his ghost.* At the very least, the people who took his life would know his name.

"Corinne!" She heard Mark calling her again. "It's time to head back now!"

She jumped to her feet. "I'll be back," she whispered to no one in particular.

COME HELL OR HIGH WATER

July 8, 2014

"H ey there! How you doing, Miss Louise?" Harold shouted to the elderly woman standing on her front porch.

"Oh, hey, Harold!" She took her hand away from shielding her eyes to wave back at him. "How you been? *Where* you been?"

"Now you know it's been way too hot for just about anybody with sense to be outside. If you need me, I'mma be in the truck or in the house!" He had already sweated through his shirt just walking the three blocks from his house so far.

"I know that's right! I only came out here 'cause I thought I heard my son's car. He supposed to be coming out here to cut this grass."

"Well, if he ain't make it out here before the weekend, just knock on my door. I'll come cut it."

"Don't worry, he'll be out here." She smiled wide and winked. "You get on out of this sun now. Mess around and burn your face off."

"Don't you worry about me." Harold laughed. "Skin or no skin, I'mma still be Black."

Miss Louise laughed big-big and waved him off down Bienville. If he'd tried to walk down this same block a few months ago, he'd have had to stop and speak at every other porch, especially at this time in the afternoon. But today, the humidity made ninety degrees feel like one hundred, so Harold wasn't at all surprised to find himself virtually alone outside. No one else would come out until closer to dusk when the sun had fallen off its throne.

Harold wanted to walk today just to see if he could stand the heat. If Corinne was right, ninety degrees in the summer would feel like heaven soon enough. She saw a world he didn't want to see, where Katrina conditions were permanent and places like New Orleans would fall into the sea without so much as a second line. He had no doubt Corinne was smarter than him, especially book smart—it was one of the things he loved about her. And, after her visit over the winter, he knew she truly was haunted by all the horror she saw on the horizon. But, try as he might, he could not see the world the way she saw it.

As he looked from one historic house to another, it was hard for Harold to imagine a day when they wouldn't be here. All these houses had been built precariously, surrounded by water on all sides, and yet they'd been built to last. And here they stood. They looked just as natural as the oak trees. They lasted because of the people in them, the descendants of the people who built them. Every time the city got knocked down, those same people, like Miss Louise and her son, loved it back to life. As long as they were around, Harold couldn't see the city fading, come hell or high water.

But Corinne was so convinced of the coming catastrophe, she'd set herself up to do something drastic. On his last visit back home, she'd told him her plan to invade the old bridge in Vicksburg and, she hoped, send a message to the oil barges below. He'd tried to reason with her while they sat on Mama's back porch.

"Niecey." He spoke gently. "You think this is going to change somebody? You really think you doing something?"

Corinne sighed hard, sweating like a devil in the heat and looking like a ghost in the moonlight. "I don't really think about that, Uncle. I think about whether or not it's the right thing to do. And it *feels* right. I can't handle doing nothing. If it reaches one person, even indirectly, it's worth it to me. Plus, it's not like I'm doing this by myself."

"And who's doing it with you?"

"You remember Mercer? From my internship in New Orleans?"

Harold almost spit out his beer. "You cooked this up with that skinny little white boy from Tulane? Cori, that boy *breathes* money! You can't do the same thing he do—"

"It's not *just* him! *Gah!* Let me finish!" Corinne's forehead glistened with fresh beads of sweat. "Miss Daphne will be there too. You liked *her*, right?"

"Miss Daphne? *She* ain't try to talk you outta this?" Harold remembered how happy he'd been when Corinne came back to work with Daphne during her spring break. "Is this why you really came back to New Orleans in March?"

"It was part of it, Uncle, but I didn't lie to you. And, yeah, she did try to talk me out of it, but . . . I wound up talking her into it."

"Ain't you tell me she was pregnant? Cori, you done dragged a *pregnant lady* into this? What on earth has gotten *into* you?" His mind was already racing with images of Corinne with her face in the gravel and her hands cuffed behind her back—or worse—and Mama wailing herself into a coma. But now he could see Miss Daphne going into early labor in the back of a police car.

"Ain't nobody got no gun to her head, Uncle." Corinne gave him that exasperated look he hated, but she softened when he met her gaze. "Plus, she's not coming out on the bridge with us. She's just coming along."

"Then it's just you and Mercer going out there? I oughta have you committed!"

"No." Corinne sighed and looked at her feet. "Daphne brought in a friend of hers to go out with us. He's older too. He's been through a whole lot of actions like this, so he has a lot of experience."

"He white, ain't he?" For once, Harold was actually hoping the answer was yes. If she was actually going to do this, having a Black man with her would just make her a bigger target.

"Well, yes. He is."

Harold let out a breath. "Cori, this sounds dangerous as all get out." He took another sip of his beer. He knew how stubborn Corinne could be and how she could shut down if you pressed too hard. So he chose his words carefully. "Are you sure this is worth it?"

"You said you'd have my back, Uncle . . ." He could see a tear in the corner of her eye, and the betrayal on her face was enough to knock his knees out.

"Then I'mma need to talk to this new fella. Tonight. Or I'll call the cops on you my damn self."

By the end of that night, the two men had agreed to get a drink together when Harold made it back to New Orleans. That was tonight.

Once he crossed Broad Street, Harold walked over to Bell, where the massive oak trees broke the sidewalk into bits, to shade himself from the sun. Over here in Bayou St. John, even on the most pleasant of evenings, there was rarely a soul outside. *Such a shame*, Harold thought, *with so many extravagant porches*. Most of the houses had stately yards and beautiful flower beds that would have made Mama jealous. If she were here, she'd probably make him go ask if she could take a cutting of the more exotic flowers.

By the time Harold made it to Bayou Bar, he was lightheaded from all the sweat he'd lost. He could all but see steam lift off his skin as he stepped into the air-conditioning. The last thing he wanted was a beer, and it must have shown. The bartender took one look at him and poured him a glass of ice water.

"Thanks, Jean," Harold said after his first blessed sip. "How you been?"

"I would say hot, but looks like you know enough about that."

"I do indeed." His temples finally stopped throbbing. "I'll holler at you in a minute for something stronger."

"Take your time. I ain't going nowhere."

Bayou was one of those no-frills bars that both Black and white folks came to, but absolutely no tourists. The wall was covered with old Polaroid photos and random signatures and sayings in Sharpie. It reminded him of the Under-the-Hill Saloon in Natchez, the centuries-old bar so close to the River you could wade right into it. He used to go there with Yvonne on his "surprise" visits back to Mississippi that only she knew about. She'd leave work early to meet him there, and they'd sit in the bar that was crawling with treasure from Natchez's pirate era and talk about all the things they couldn't in front of Mama or the kids. After she'd died, he still stopped there on his way home. He'd order a beer for himself and a shot of bourbon in his sister's honor—"*A spirit for the spirit*," he'd say. He'd drink them both, while he imagined her there, lighting a cigarette, laughing at his jokes, and telling her stories. One day, maybe when Corinne finished college, he planned to take her there with him and tell her all her mother's secrets.

"You must be Harold?"

Harold shot off the barstool and onto his feet, turning to see a stocky white man with graying hair and curious blue eyes. "And you must be Alex?"

Alex nodded and motioned toward an embrace, but Harold hardened his gaze and extended his arm for a firm handshake. He made a point not to break eye contact and watched as the curiosity in Alex's eyes gave way to alarm.

"Thank you for meeting me." Harold motioned toward the green leather barstool next to his. "You been here before?"

"Yeah, a couple of times. A friend of mine has a food truck that comes by here every month or so, and I come out to support him. It's really good food actually. Brazilian."

"Sounds exotic."

"I don't know about exotic. It's really good, though. Especially if you like beef. You should come someti—"

"So you the one gonna go out on that bridge with my little niece?" Harold wanted to get to the point.

"I— Well, I couldn't let them go out there by themselves." The lines spilled out like he'd practiced them. "Corinne and Mercer don't know what they're doing, but Daphne made it clear that they were going to do this with or without me, so I decided to do it."

"Did you try to talk them out of it?" Harold's shoulders fell down from his ears.

Alex laughed. "Well, Daphne tried. I'm sure you already met her." Harold nodded. "Yeah, so she's the whole reason I got involved. She told me some of the kids she was working with had this bright idea in their heads and they weren't going to change it for anybody, so she asked if I could help them. To be honest with you, I thought about trying to talk them out of it the first time I met them back in March, but I was worried that if I tried, they wouldn't trust me, and then they really *would* do it on their own. That Corinne of yours is really something."

"Something *else*!"

"I'll drink to that!" Alex waved Jean back over.

"Y'all got any Bluff City Blondes?" Harold asked before Jean or Alex could get a word out.

"Harold, you know good and damn well we ain't got none of that Natchez-ass beer in here!" He let out a sigh and tossed his bar rag over his shoulder. "I'mma get y'all some Abitas, and you're gonna drink 'em."

"What's a Bluff City Blonde?" Alex asked.

"He come in here every other week and ask for that shit!" Jean yelled as he poured Abita Purple Haze from the tap.

"Which mean you done had plenty of time to get it!" Harold yelled back. Then he turned back to Alex. "It's a beer from Natchez. I just be fucking with him. I know they not gon' ever have it here."

"No," Jean said with a smile as he put the two beers down in front of them. "We're not. Now drink up."

"Well, maybe I'll try some when I come out to Vicksburg." Alex smiled slyly at Harold.

"Maybe you will." Harold smiled back. "Cheers!"

They lifted their glasses in the air and drank.

"I tried to talk her out of it too," Harold continued after his first sip. "I know global warming is important to her and it feels like the most important thing in the world, but everything feels that way *when you're twenty*."

"Well," Alex started slowly. "Climate change really is the most important thing in the world, because it *is* the world. If we let the planet turn into a living hell, I won't say nothing else matters, but everything else is going to get a whole lot worse."

"But how soon, though?" Harold asked. "Mind you, Corinne is the same child that's been running around here fretting about a flood that happened in the 1920s. Before her own grandma was even born. I don't exactly trust her gauge of time." Part of him was hoping that Alex would tell him that Corinne was overreacting, and all the doom and gloom Corinne was worried about wouldn't happen until long after they'd both died. He was desperate to have one less thing to worry about.

"Thing is . . . it's happening now. Katrina was part of it," Alex said in a measured tone. "So is the drought out in California. It's not that subtle when you think about it. And it's definitely getting worse. Corinne isn't wrong to be freaked out."

Harold bit his lip and then said, "I know. Trust me, I know it's important. I know it's real. I ain't one of them Republican fools. Them *your* people," Harold said, gesturing to the paleness of Alex's forearm. "I used to be a fisherman, you know. I saw the climate change with my own two eyes. I had quit before the oil spill, but when I went back out for fun, I saw them fish start coming up with three and four eyes. But what I don't understand is why *my* niece needs to be the one risking *her* life for it. If it's so hellfire important, why can't white people be the ones putting their lives on the line this time? Ain't we done enough for y'all?"

"You know, I don't disagree with you there. That's why I'm going with them."

"When I talked to her about it, she said she knew this thing on the bridge wasn't going to fix everything. And I can think of a lot of things it could break, starting with my mama." He paused. "But I want to hear from you, since you have some experience with these things. Do *you* think it's worth it?"

"Well, that depends on how you define 'worth' and 'it,'" Alex said, half chuckling. "No one thing is going to turn this around, just like no one thing got us into this situation. But I do think it's a worthy cause to register dissent and try to influence public opinion."

"It's a bridge in Vicksburg, y'all. Not exactly a huge public platform." Harold sighed and then turned on his stool to face Alex. "Look, I didn't come here to argue with you about this. I invited you here because I want you to understand something, Mr. Alex. That little girl is important to me. She might be a little dramatic and more than a little stubborn, but she's all I got left of my sister and all I got left of my nephew—the one y'all going out there to 'honor.' I wanted to meet you in person because I wanted to make sure you understand that she's precious to us."

"Of course I understand that."

"I hope you do. We've had a lot of loss in our family. We can't take another one. Her brother's barely been gone a year. Her mother just about ten years. And who knows where her daddy's at."

"Oh my god! I'm so sorry!" Alex turned red. "She told me about Cameron but not about everyone else."

"It's okay. You didn't know 'cause it wasn't exactly your business." Harold quickly switched back to his point. "As much as I hate this, as much as I wish she wasn't doing it and was just focused on finishing school and minding her business, I'm coming to accept that this is who she is and this is what she's doing."

"I hear you." Alex took a sip of his beer. "I've had a lot of loss in my life, too, though most of it was my own doing, but I think I can understand."

Harold smiled at him slyly. "I got a feeling I don't want to know all the details behind that, but yeah, everybody knows loss. I just wanted to lay eyes on you myself and tell you about ours." He paused another moment. "It's just . . . I hope you understand that there's something different about you and that Mercer boy walking out on that bridge in *Mississippi*, and Corinne walking out there. You understand what I'm saying to you?"

"I do." Alex was blushing only on his cheeks now. "But I'm prepared to do everything I can to protect her. We've thought about everything as carefully as possible. If she needs bail, I will pay it. If she gets fined, I'll pay that too. I'll treat her like she was my own daughter."

His sincerity calmed Harold's nerves and piqued his curiosity. "You got a daughter, Alex? Any kids?"

"No," he said bashfully. Right at that moment, Jean came back with two fresh beers for them.

"Me neither." Harold raised his glass. "And as much as people told me I would regret it, I been on this earth forty-two years and ain't regretted it yet. I'm of the mind, personally, that you don't need to have kids of your own to love them. And you definitely don't need to have them to be responsible for them. Being an uncle is enough work for me."

"Thank you!" Alex shouted a bit too loud.

"I decided a long time ago I didn't want no kids, and I didn't want no wife. I didn't want nobody following up behind me. But I do love my little niece. More than anything in this world." Harold twisted on his stool to look Alex directly in the eye again. "Alex, I like you. But if anything happens to *my* niece on *your* watch, I want you to know that I *will* kill you."

Alex's eyes went wide and he turned red anew. "Y-yes, sir," he stammered like the beer had gotten stuck in his throat.

"I know that girl thinks she's grown. And she's fearless up to and through the point of foolish, but that's my baby girl. My Niecey. I couldn't take it if anything happened to her. And it'd kill my mama. And as much as I like being left alone, I don't want to be *all* alone. So it means a lot to me that you're gonna be there with her, and I have your word that you're gonna take care of her. To you, Alex." Harold raised his glass again.

"To you, Harold. The world's best uncle!" Alex raised his glass too.

As he took a swig, Harold recognized Sam Cooke's voice, "Wait, wait, you hear that song?"

"Yeah, I think I've heard it before."

"You *think*? Alex, that's 'Having a Party' by the legendary Sam Cooke. Best soul singer to ever live. And you know where he was from, don't you?"

"Chicago, right?"

Harold slammed his beer down on the counter and hunched over. "No, no, not at all. He moved to Chicago. He was from Mississippi, the Delta."

"But didn't he move to Chicago as a kid or something?"

"Sure," Harold hissed. "But the thing about being from Mississippi is that you never stop being from there. You can hear it in his voice. That grit? It's like he has the Mississippi River in his throat."

"Doesn't the Mississippi go to Chicago?"

He might know global warming, Harold thought. *But he don't know shit about rivers.* "Alex"—Harold glared at him in disappointment—"I hope you know you 'bout to buy these beers."

Alex nodded and chuckled. In another world, Harold could see them all becoming friends, but not until Corinne was off that bridge.

Soon and Very Soon

July 19, 2014

The smell of Grandma's county-famous fried whiting wafted from the kitchen and into the living room, coating everything it touched with the salty scent of Tony Chachere's seasoning salt. The aroma found Corinne splayed across the couch with one leg up the backrest and one arm grazing the ground. Her mouth began to water, more with nostalgia for the fish she'd eaten before than hunger for it now.

"Grandma!" she called to the kitchen. "You need help?"

"No, girl. You stay out there and play with your little phone," Grandma said with amusement. Then, with overt sarcasm, she added, "I'd *hate* to make you touch one of these poor dead fish. You know they probably all had families and had planned vacations and everything. Now, they're not going anywhere but in this oil."

Corinne heard the oil sizzle as Grandma added another fish to the skillet. She went into the kitchen to fix herself a

glass of the sun tea she and Grandma had made yesterday—
and to get a closer smell.

She had given up on trying to make Grandma understand
that she hadn't gone vegan because she thought animals were
people but because of the greenhouse gases and cruelty of factory farming. Except she took one look at the fish in the skillet
and decided tonight might be as good a night as any to steal a
piece of fish when Grandma wasn't looking.

"Ha. Ha. Ha." Corinne returned the sarcasm. She looked
over to the pile of uncooked fish that sat uncoated in a colan-
der in the sink. "You sure you don't need no help, Grandma?
That's a lot of fish."

"No, it's fine, girl. After I'm done you can get in here and
fry your little tofu," she teased.

"You're hilarious." Corinne picked up her glass of sweet
tea and headed back to the couch. "Maybe I *will* go back to
my phone, then."

"Go on!" Grandma shooed her out of the way as she pulled
the first few pieces of fish from the oil. They were golden and
perfect.

Just then, the house phone rang and Grandma rushed to
answer it. Even though Grandma made fun of Corinne's iPhone,
she was just as addicted to her landline and had been for
much longer. At least Corinne could multitask and do work
on hers—once she even wrote the outline for her midterm paper
on it.

Corinne would have gone out to the back porch, but it had
stormed just a few hours ago, which meant the mosquitoes

would be lying in wait. But at least today, those obnoxious little creatures would just suck her blood. One day, she knew they could leave her with West Nile or dengue or Zika or something they didn't have a name for yet. She knew that would change one day, probably soon.

As she collapsed back onto the couch, she felt her brother's eyes on her from the altar. Her eyes fixed on a picture from Cameron's birthday two years ago. It was of him standing over the blackberry lemon cake Corinne and Grandma baked for him. He was smiling like a toddler. The untrained eye wouldn't be able to tell that just a few hours before, he'd exploded at Corinne because he'd lost his phone and was convinced Corinne must have moved it. He'd learned how to find the perfect volume so that Grandma couldn't hear him from her side of the house. She hated how the pictures on the altar could force her to remember the darker, stormier parts of Cameron that she wanted to forget.

Corinne had been home for almost two months now and had yet to make her peace with this shrine that lived in the living room, that Grandma dusted daily like a prayer. Corinne didn't need a specific place to remember Cameron. He was with her all the time, brooding in the background, even when she didn't want him to be. But it took her a while to look at the photos without shuddering.

Her phone vibrated in her hand. It was another text from Cleo.

Cleo: They're saying he had asthma.

"He" was a man named Eric Garner. Corinne couldn't bring herself to watch The Video, but there was no way to avoid talking about it. It was being played on every news channel, plastered across every news site, and posted all over social media. Her Twitter feed had become a minefield, her Instagram a trove of obituaries and outrage.

She texted back.

Corinne: Asthma? Is that what police officers are calling their arms these days?

Immediately, three gray dots appeared, lingered, disappeared and reappeared, for what felt like an eternity but couldn't have been longer than a minute. Maybe Cleo was just as tired as she was of talking about it. What more was there even to say? She put the phone on airplane mode, set it on the table, and turned on the television. She didn't want to think right now. She wanted to get lost in a bad reality show. Maybe *The Real Housewives of Atlanta*. But before she could find one, Grandma shoved the phone into her face.

"Your uncle want you," she said casually and turned back to the kitchen.

Corinne's stomach sank. She'd been ignoring Uncle Harold's increasingly irate texts for the past week. She knew what he was going to ask her. "Hello?"

"Niecey!" His voice sounded gruff. "You can't call your uncle back?"

"Hey!" She tried to sound cheerful. "I . . . ," she started, but the words got stuck in her throat.

"Did you tell her, Corinne?"

No, she hadn't told her grandmother about her grand plans for the bridge in Vicksburg. She hadn't told her grandmother that she was going to risk jail—maybe even prison or death—by willingly getting arrested.

"Did I . . ." She choked on her own shame. She didn't want to admit to him that she was still keeping secrets.

"What are you? A parrot?" Uncle Harold snapped.

Corinne sat up straight. She had only ever heard him angry a handful of times.

"Corinne, I know you haven't told Mama about your little plan for next month. Now, you can keep playing these little bald-headed-ass games if you want to, but if you ain't told her by Monday, I'm telling her, and I won't help you if she tries to lock you away somewhere."

"Okay, Uncle," Corinne whispered. She knew he was serious, and he was right. "Okay."

"She deserves to know, Corinne. If you dead set on doing this, somebody is gonna have to come bail you out, and you know it's going to be her. And you ain't even had the decency to tell her? How trifling can you get?" He didn't wait for an answer. "You got two days, Niecey. Including today."

He hung up. No "goodbye." No "I love you." It was eerie. Corinne sighed, turned off the television, and went into the kitchen to put the phone back on its base.

There was now a plate piled high with perfectly seasoned, perfectly fried whiting fillets. Grandma was flipping the last few pieces over on the stove. Corinne wished she didn't have to ruin such a perfect, peaceful scene.

"Grandma?"

"Yeah, Cori?" She didn't look up from her cast iron skillet.

"I need to tell you something."

"Okay, I'm listening." She still didn't turn around.

"Grandma, it's serious. I think you should sit down."

Corinne watched as Grandma's whole body seemingly braced for impact. When she finally looked at her over her shoulder, Corinne could see the trepidation in her eyes. "Fix me a drink, Cori," she said firmly.

The dread in the pit of Corinne's stomach grew as she mixed Grandma's favorite cocktail: whiskey and sweet tea with enough ice to reach the brim of the glass. She sat it on the table just behind Grandma.

"Bring me that plate," Grandma ordered without looking at her.

Corinne did as she was told, and Grandma pulled each piece of fish out of the oil and placed it on top of the others. Then they both sat down.

Grandma picked up her glass and sighed as she took a long sip. "Now, what is it, child?"

Corinne lifted her eyes to meet her grandmother's. Her throat felt dry. "Grandma . . ." She swallowed. "You have to promise not to get mad."

"How did you get pregnant?!" Grandma shrieked, slamming her glass back on the table so hard it spilled.

"What? I'm not pregnant!" The shock lifted the weight from Corinne's shoulders. *Maybe this won't be so hard after all*, she thought. "I'm going to be part of a protest next month. In Vicksburg."

"What kind of a *protest*, girl?" She sounded suspicious. *No*, Corinne thought again, *this is not going to be easy.*

"It's on the River . . ."

"What? You got a boat? What did the River do to you?" She took another sip of her drink. "You're not making sense, Cori."

Corinne took a deep breath. "You know how those boats that Cameron used to work on go up and down the River? And he used to talk about how they'd stop in Vicksburg and go up the Yazoo River?" Grandma nodded. "Well, I'm going to protest his murder by hanging a banner off the side of the Old Vicksburg Bridge so that the boats that go under it have to see it."

"Murder? What mur—" Grandma stopped herself. She stared at Corinne for at least a full minute, though it felt much, much longer. Then she leaned back in her seat and crossed her legs, the bottom one bouncing up and down. Finally, she spoke. "How are you gonna get out on this bridge?"

"We're going to climb underneath the gate at the security station. I know the guard, and I know he's always late in the morning."

Grandma's face twisted in disgust. "Corinne Jewel Sterling, do you know who owns that bridge?"

Corinne's skin tingled at the invocation of her full name. "The Mississippi Department of Transportation. I researched it."

"Oh *good*! You *researched* it! So that means you know it ain't yours. And you just gon' traipse your ass out there and trespass on government property? You know what you are proposing to do is illegal? They'll Daughters-of-the-Confederacy your Black ass so damn fast!" She said the last sentence through her teeth.

"Yes, I know." Corinne lowered her eyes. This was the reaction Corinne had been afraid of—more than the bridge, more than the police, almost as much as global warming itself.

"Then, little girl, why in the *hell* are you doing it?" Grandma hissed.

Corinne's heart was beating at a breakneck speed, but she found the courage to look her grandma in the eyes. "Because it's the right thing to do."

"Oh, is it?" Grandma tilted her head to one side. "How is you going to jail—if you're lucky enough to even make it there—the right thing to do for your brother, Corinne? How is it the *right thing* for anyone?"

"Because they don't get to just get away with that, Grandma!" Corinne didn't realize she'd raised her voice until she heard the words come out of her mouth. "They don't get to just murder my brother, *your grandson*, and then keep on doing business as usual. I won't let them!"

"Nobody *murdered* Cameron, you silly, *silly* girl! It was a freak accident! Do you know what that means? It could have happened to anyone! Nobody pushed him out of that boat!

Next you'll be out here protesting the *sky* for Katrina! Do you know how *insane* you sound?"

"That's not true! He worked for a company that is part of an industry that killed him quick and is killing us slow. So no, it's not just about Cameron; it's about so much more than him. It just started with him."

Grandma rolled her eyes. "Even if that's true—and it's not—but even if it was, you think your little banner is going to stop something? You think that boat is gonna see your little banner and then turn around because you said so? Have you lost your damn mind?"

"No, I don't think it's going to stop everything." Corinne could feel tears burning at the backs of her eyes. It was hard to stand up for herself and walk on Grandma's eggshells at the same time. "But it could bring them to a pause, even just for a moment. It could make someone on the boat think for a second, or somebody driving across on the other bridge. The point isn't stopping them. The point is not letting them get away with it."

Grandma sighed. "What day are you even doing this? How do you know Cameron's old boat is going to be the one to come through there?"

"August 5." Corinne turned her spine into steel when she remembered the date and the plans she'd already committed to. "And we don't know if his boat is going to be the one to come under the bridge, but it's not about his specific boat. It's about the whole industry."

"Oh, well look at you!" Grandma mocked. "Gon' huff and puff and take on a whole industry! And who is this 'we' you keep talking about?"

Corinne didn't realize she'd said "we." She thought she'd save that detail for later. But now that it had slipped, she thought maybe it would calm Grandma down to know that at least she wasn't reckless enough to do this all alone.

"Well, I'm not doing it by myself. I have some people coming up from New Orleans to help me. Two of them are even going out on the bridge with me. And they're white, so the police won't—"

"Oh! They're *white*? So that oughta fix everything then! Nothing bad ever happened to a Black person while a white person was around! Girl, have you even heard of Philadelphia?"

Corinne felt a flush come over her face. Yes, she had heard of Philadelphia: the town on the other side of Mississippi made famous for the murders of Chaney, Schwerner, and Goodman. A Black man and two Jewish white men. When she was ten, Grandma had sat her in front of the TV to watch *Mississippi Burning* because she'd asked Grandma too many questions about her childhood.

"Grandma, listen! Two of them are coming on the bridge with me so that when the police come, I won't be the main focus. They'll be focused on the two white men, and one of them has a daddy who's a sheriff, so they won't lay a hand on us. And then we have this white lady who's going to tape the whole thing."

"Do you know how stupid you sound, girl? In what world would your Black ass not be the focus of the police? What in the hell makes you think you even gonna make it to the precinct so your little friend can call his daddy? *He'll* probably make it. But *you*?"

Corinne's throat tightened again. She knew Grandma had a point, but when her mind was made up, sometimes she couldn't even change it herself. She didn't answer her grandmother, but she didn't break eye contact either.

"How the hell you know? Seriously, Corinne, what do you *actually* know? About *anything*? You all of twenty years old! What have you even been through that wasn't in a book? When you were a little girl, you was scared of ghosts. When I was a little girl, I was afraid of grown men dressed up as ghosts! With guns and nooses and burning crosses!"

Corinne bristled. To Grandma, if you were born after 1970, you'd never known suffering or sacrifice, and certainly not oppression. Your life had been handed to you, all wrapped up in a pretty little bow, dyed with the blood of the generations that came before you and soaked with Grandma's own personal tears. It didn't matter how much you appreciated her, because you could never *understand*. And you'd better not try to understand because that would mean asking and that would make her remember and that was cruel.

Corinne bit her lip and muttered, "I'm sorry I wasn't there in the fifties." As soon as the words left her mouth, she regretted them.

"What did you say to me, girl? WHAT did you just fix your mouth to say? To *me*?"

As much as she wanted to take back her words, she knew she couldn't swallow them. "Grandma, I'm sorry I wasn't there in the fifties, but I'm here now. And I hate to be the one to tell you, but y'all didn't solve everything. Why can't I pick up where you left off? Don't I owe you that?"

"We didn't *solve* everything?" Grandma spat back at her. "Well, I'm so sorry we didn't do enough for you, Corinne. But I did not risk my life so my *granddaughter* could be a *damn fool*! You think those white folks can protect you? Better yet, you think they even gonna try? If it comes down to your life or theirs, you think they *won't* use you as a human shield? Then you got less sense than I even gave you credit for. I knew I shouldn't have let you go to them white folks' school!"

Corinne paused. Every nightmare she'd had about this moment came flooding back to her. She'd known Grandma would be angry, hurt, confused. And she knew most of it wasn't about her at all but about things that happened long before she was born. She remembered that Uncle Harold said your pain is the only type of pain there is because you can't feel anyone else's. She knew that meant she couldn't heal anyone else's pain either. She knew she had to do this to heal herself, no matter if it hurt someone she loved so much. Now that she was at this fork in the road, what would be the point of bringing Grandma to the brink if she was just going to turn around?

"I don't know," she said. "But I have to try."

"If these white folks are so damn trustworthy, what they even need you for? Hmm?" Grandma asked as she pulled out a cigarette. "Why can't they just do this on their own?"

"Because he was *my* brother. I have to be there. It was *my* idea."

"He was *my grandson*! Corinne, I'm *so sick* of you acting like *you're* the only one that lost somebody! Like all of this only happened to *you*! I've never seen somebody this stingy about a death before. Now, what am I supposed to do if something were to happen to you? What do I have left then?"

Corinne breathed deep. She wanted to soften what she said next, to temper it, but there was only one way to say it. "Grandma, I can't live my life in fear just 'cause you want me to!"

At that, Grandma gulped what was left of her drink and slammed the glass back on the table hard enough that it spilled over. She stomped to her bedroom and turned on the television. Corinne thought that might have been the end of the conversation until she heard, "Get in here, Corinne Jewel!"

Corinne could already hear the mumble of cable news talking heads, none of whom ever aspired to make a point, only to score them. By the time she'd walked into the room, the talking heads had been replaced by a lone anchor reminding the audience that the video they were about to see, which had been played again and again over the last few days, contained distressing images and should not be shown to children.

It was the video Corinne had been avoiding, the one Cleo and Ashley and Mercer had been texting her about. The video of Eric Garner's state-sanctioned, cold-blooded murder in broad daylight.

"I want you to see this!" Grandma commanded as Corinne came into the doorway of her bedroom. Grandma was rocking back and forth as she sat on the bed, practically inhaling her cigarette. Corinne worried she would burn her lips.

The footage lasted all of one minute, but long enough to have two distinct acts. In Act I, two white plainclothes police officers stood on either side of Garner, a large Black man. You could see and hear bystanders (soon-to-be witnesses) in the background. Everyone in the video looked hot and very, very bothered. Garner insisted that he'd done nothing wrong, that all he'd done was break up a fight. But his protests were merely verbal. Physically, he was a statue. It was almost like you could see him trying his hardest to become smaller.

In an instant, though, something changed, and Act II began. The officers leapt onto Garner and were joined by an entourage of uniformed officers who'd just arrived. A plain-clothes officer who'd been there the whole time, but mostly out of the frame, put Garner in a choke hold as the uniformed officers cuffed him. After the cuffs were on, though, the plain-clothes officer kept his hold on his neck. When he finally did let go, he held Garner's face into the concrete. Over and over, you could hear Garner saying, "I can't breathe." They would be his last words. Maybe he knew it.

Corinne felt sick. Hearing about the video was one thing, and reading about it was another. Seeing it was beyond believing it. Corinne knew that as much as she would never unhear

George Zimmerman's 911 call before he killed Trayvon Martin, she would never unsee this video.

"That"—Grandma took a long drag of her cigarette—"is New York City. If they'll do that *there*—choke a man to death in front of all those witnesses *on tape*—what do you think they'll do to you in *Mississippi*? I don't care how many white people you got on the bridge with you. I don't care who you got filming it. I don't give a shit if you're out there with the Grand Dragons of Mississippi *and* Louisiana. To the state of Mississippi, you still are and will always be not just a nigger but a *negress*."

Corinne felt her knees weaken underneath her. She reached to hold on to the foot of Grandma's bed. She knew the man holding the camera was Garner's friend and that he probably thought that his footage would save his friend's life. She realized that it wasn't just one police officer's aggression that killed him. It was the negligence and complicity of all the other officers and emergency responders around him. She wasn't sure, but she could have sworn she saw a Black woman in the sea of blue.

For a moment, she wondered if her grandmother was right. What if, soon and very soon, she'd come to regret her brashness—and what if that regret came in her last breathing moment? She was beginning to feel like a character in a Richard Wright story: trapped and making all the wrong choices in some sort of condemned rebellion. *No*, she told herself. *Life is not a short story.* And even if it was, she was writing this one. She asked herself again, for maybe the thousandth time, if this was worth dying for. The answer that came back, again, was yes. She felt it deep in her bones, in her soul. Her stomach began to settle, her knees unbuckled. She stood up straight and looked back at her grandmother.

"Please don't do this, Corinne," Grandma pleaded.

"I have to," she whispered.

"*No, you don't!*" Grandma's voice became a wounded shriek. "You think I want to watch a video of *you* dying? You think I can survive that? Leave it to you to take something so damn foolish and make yourself sound like a motherfucking martyr. You ain't Gandhi!" Grandma was sobbing now.

Corinne steeled herself for what she was about to say. "Grandma, I know you want me to be scared, but I'm more afraid of doing nothing than I am of doing something."

"How can you do this to me?" Grandma threw her ashtray across the room, just barely missing Corinne's head.

Corinne wiped the ashes away from her cheek. When Grandma was scared, it looked like anger. And the best way to deal with it was to stay calm. "I'm not doing anything *to* you! I'm doing this *for* you!"

"No, you're not, Corinne," Grandma sobbed. "You're doing it for yourself. And you're too selfish to see it. This isn't about Cameron. It sure the fuck isn't about me. It's about you. You always want to be the supreme victim."

"No, I don't! And I'm doing this not just for you and Cameron. It's bigger than all of us. You realize what happens when they burn the oil that's on all of those boats? You realize how many people die? Not just now, not just tomorrow, but forever? And that one day, yes, it *will* be you and me and Uncle Harold and everyone else any one of us has ever loved? You realize how much poison they're carrying around? That bright future you want me to have? They are setting it on *literal* fire! If I can do something about that—if I can do anything at all—that's not much of a choice, is it? I would think you, of all people, would understand that!"

"There you go with that shit again. What's that really supposed to mean, Corinne?" Grandma turned her back to her. She was crying softer, angrier tears now. "'Me of all people'?"

"I know how much you sacrificed, Grandma." Corinne tried to soften her voice. "And I'm grateful. It feels like the best way to honor that sacrifice is with one of my own."

Grandma dragged on her cigarette again. "You don't know shit, Cori. It's not just you that you're sacrificing. And you don't know what you're up against. I know you think you do, but you don't."

"But I'm a strong Black woman, Grandma, just like you."

Now Grandma turned around. Apoplectic. "So you just a mule *and* a fool, huh? You actually believe that shit? Girl, there is no such thing as a 'strong Black woman,'" she mocked. "That's some bullshit white folks made up to forgive themselves for treating us like dirt and working us like dogs. If you'll believe that, you'll believe anything, and I . . . I . . . just might have failed you."

"Grandma, you didn't—"

Grandma cut her off. "Corinne, you don't know what the fuck I did or didn't do. But I know what you're doing. You're killing me. If you die doing this stupid-ass stunt, I'll plan your funeral. I'll be there, and I'll cry for you just like I did for my daddy and my mama and your mama and your brother. But if you live longer than me, Corinne Jewel—like you're fucking *supposed* to—don't come to my funeral 'cause you'll be the one who put me in the casket. I don't want my murderer mourning me."

Corinne felt a sharp pain in her gut. The wall she'd spent so much time building to prepare herself for this moment came tumbling down, and she ran to her room and slammed the door shut before Grandma could see her cry. She half expected Grandma to follow her to open the door behind her and re-slam it herself. But she didn't. By the time she made it to the bed, Corinne was crying and sweating so hard her clothes were drenched.

Desperate for a distraction, she took her phone off airplane mode and saw that the group text with Ashley and Cleo had more than fifty unread messages. She started to read them, but she couldn't take anymore talk about Staten Island. She curled into a ball on the bed and lay in the dark until there were no more tears left to cry.

EDUCATED FOOL

July 19, 2014

C ora sat on the edge of her bed and drew on her cigarette with all her might. Her angry shaking had slowed
into a rock—back and forth, back and forth—but her
heart was still racing. The television was still blaring with
non-updates about the non-arrest in Staten Island, and she
was convinced that if she looked at the screen, Eric Garner's
large body would be replaced by Corinne's slight frame. She
closed her eyes and rooted around her bed in search of the
remote control to turn it off. But that didn't stop the images
flashing through her mind of Corinne falling off the bridge,
Corinne bloodied by the police, Corinne in the visitation room
at Parchman. Or worse. Even as she sat on the edge of her
bed, she had the overwhelming sensation that she was falling,
falling, falling.

She felt crazy, and she needed someone to tell her she
wasn't, so she grabbed the phone and dialed the only person

she could talk to right now. He answered on the first ring, like he'd been waiting for her call.

"Mama?"

"Harold, you know what your little fool of a niece has got herself into?"

Harold sighed hard. "So she finally told you?"

"*Finally?* What the fuck you mean *fine-uh-lee*?" Cora saw red again. "You knew about this?"

"Mama, it wasn't for me to tell you. I've been telling her to tell you herself the whole summer. You may not like it, but that girl is grown."

"Oh, I'm real sick of everybody telling me how old that girl is, like I wasn't there the day she was born. She might be legally grown, she might be off in that white folks' schoolhouse, but that don't make her nothing but an educated fool."

"I tried to talk her out of it . . ."

"Well, you shoulda tried harder! You know you're the only one she listens to anymore!" she screamed. "And you damn sure shoulda told *me* before now. I can't fucking believe you. *Either of you!*"

"Mama . . ."

"Harold, I need to get this fish down to the church while it's still worth eating, before I've wasted even more of my time. There's nothing you can say that's gonna make any of this okay anyway, so I think we need to just get off this phone."

"I'm sor—"

"Bye, Harold."

She slammed the phone down, finished her cigarette, and headed over to the church fish fry to keep her promise to the fundraising committee. She dropped her Tupperware of fish off with the ladies in the kitchen, told them she'd see them at service in the morning, and came back home.

───

The next morning, Cora woke up to a spinning ceiling. When she saw that it wasn't even seven o'clock yet, she relaxed knowing that she could still make it to church on time. But when she attempted to sit up and felt her brain slide around in her skull, she decided that no matter what she'd said to anyone last night, nobody needed to see her today. She could thank the empty whiskey bottle next to her bed for that.

She had been looking forward to the annual church Fish Fry Off all year. When she'd woken up yesterday, winning first place felt like the most important thing in the world. She could finally take bragging rights back from Gloria Scott. She had even been debating whether she had enough time to fry some okra for Corinne before she went to church. But then Corinne had announced herself as a fool and a brat, and just like that, the ground had dropped out from underneath her.

Her own words were still echoing through her head, growing louder with every repetition: *"I don't want my murderer mourning me."* She wanted to take it back, but how do you take back something you didn't even know you had in you?

Cora wished she could take all of it back. The whole night, even the whole year. Maybe even farther back, if she could just find the wrong turn that brought her here. If she could stop Cameron from dying, but what if that meant stopping him from taking the job on the boat, which would have meant getting him more interested in college? Then again, maybe he needed his mother for that, and maybe that meant Cora should have picked Corinne up from school that day instead of Yvonne. What if Yvonne was supposed to be somebody's boss and not somebody's secretary, and to do that she needed to have finished college, and maybe that meant Cora should have finished college before she had her. Maybe she'd done it all wrong.

Now her thoughts just hung in the air, threatening to choke her. She told herself it was the alcohol that pushed her too far. That it wasn't really her talking. But the first drink she had that night was the one that Corinne had poured her, before ashtrays and silences and hearts had been broken. Things she didn't know how to put back together again.

When Corinne had first come into the kitchen and told her to sit down, Cora had been almost certain that she was about to be a great-grandmother. All her dreams for Corinne had crumbled in the same instant that Cora realized that her life-long opposition to abortion wasn't as firm as she'd thought it was. She had decided in that split second that Corinne should at least consider terminating the pregnancy, and Cora would have driven her to whatever clinic, no matter how many states away. Even if she didn't want to go through with an abortion, Corinne could've transferred to Alcorn or Jackson State or even a school down in New Orleans, and Cora could've raised the baby while she got her degree.

Instead, Corinne was out on a wild vigilante fantasy to get a villain that didn't exist. After she heard that, Cora wished Corinne *was* having a baby. She'd known that Corinne thought there was some grand industrial conspiracy to murder her brother. Cora had thought before that it was just her way of making meaning out of chaos, so she didn't argue with her. If it was easier for Corinne to believe her brother died by conspiracy instead of fate, why take that from her? But now it had gone too far.

She kept replaying Corinne's self-righteous rant about the world being on fire and how she had to do something, any-thing, about it. How she thought her sacrifice was in honor of Cora's own sacrifice. Cora didn't know whether she should be more insulted or terrified.

Cora's head began to thump loud, loud, loud. She hated herself for letting her granddaughter go to Ohio. Now look at how she'd come back: loud, proud, and wrong as hell. She knew Corinne was just on the other side of the house, but to her mind she was already dead. She might as well start work-ing on the funeral arrangements. What kind of flowers do you use for a girl who cut her own self down on the cusp of her womanhood? Tulips, probably. Or lilies. Something with soft petals that came half-bloomed.

Corinne said that she refused to live in fear just because

Cora "wanted her to." But that wasn't what Cora wanted. She wanted her to live in sense, but most importantly, she wanted her to *live*.

Cora's mind went back to the angry mobs that had shouted and spat at her on her way to the first grade. To the crosses that had burned across Nashville at night. To the teenagers who had thrown rocks at their house at night so often that Daddy and the neighbors had taken to sitting in the living room all night with guns. What had been the point of that if Corinne was just going to walk into a fire she didn't have to?

Cora wanted to get up and escape her swirling ceiling and her tangled, twisted thoughts, to make eggs and coffee and toast, to tend to her garden. To stomp and holler. Most of all, she just wanted to drink some water. But she couldn't move. She just lay there and spun without moving for hours. *Maybe this will be what kills me*, she thought.

Cora didn't go to her hummingbird garden for a full week. She was too embarrassed. She wasn't ready to tell her parents that she'd failed their great-granddaughter, like all the times she'd failed before. She wasn't sure she could carry their disappointment on top of her own shame. That could break her.

After their giant, hellish fight, there were three long, icy days of silence that turned into four more of eggshell-walking and hint-dropping. Neither of them was willing to give an inch, so the miles between them kept multiplying.

After a week, Cora broke down and called Pastor Dixon. She told him the short version of the story, and he told her to meet him at the church the next afternoon. He promised her that no one would be there. They sat together in the echoey pews, and she noticed how much smaller he looked now that he wasn't behind the pulpit. So much humbler. He listened to her story as it echoed across the sanctuary, only punctuating it occasionally with a "hmm" or "aah." She told him about all her plans for her granddaughter and how Corinne was throwing them all away without so much as a thought for what that would do to her and how much she'd suffered.

"Cora, you really think she didn't think about you at all?"

Cora was taken aback. "Does it sound like it?"

"Well, to me, it does, just not as much as you want her to. And not as much as you're thinking of her. But our children never do." He was speaking slower than she was used to. "Look, I understand why you're worried. I can't say I wouldn't be in your place. Have you thought about calling the police?"

"On my own grandbaby?" Cora looked at him like he had three heads but then calmed herself. "Of course I have, but I can't do it. That's out."

"Then, Cora, I hate to tell you, but all you can do now is pray."

She picked up her purse as slowly as she could, turned to Pastor Dixon, and said, "Well, I guess you can't help me with this. I thank you for taking the time to try, though."

"Cora!" He stood up as she hurried down the aisle, but she didn't stop.

The next morning, Cora knew it was time to tell Mama and Daddy. She went to her garden just after sunrise. She waited for the first hummingbird, light and colorful, before she spoke. Then it came out like a flood: Corinne's scheme, Cora's near certainty that she would either be killed or put in prison, how hard she'd tried to stop her, all the things she wished she hadn't said, all the things she wished she had. She sobbed until her throat went raw. She could feel them breathing near her, but they said nothing. She hadn't expected an answer exactly, but she had expected judgment. Questions. Something. There was nothing.

She came back the next day at the same time and waited for the first hummingbird. Again, she confessed. Again, there was no answer. The same the next day and the next until, finally, Cora whispered, "Well, aren't you going to say something?"

Just as the words escaped her lips, two new hummingbirds came to the garden. That's when she felt it: her mother's hands on her shoulders, heavy, and her father's hand on top of her own, gentle. She heard a raspy voice that belonged to neither of them say, *Hush now.* And she obeyed. She closed her eyes.

Her father told her things that she'd wanted to hear and that she needed to hear, but not with words. It was like she could feel them: that he loved her, he was proud of her, she was doing everything right because she was doing everything she could. But there were some things she couldn't do. She couldn't live Corinne's life for her. She had to let go.

He told her that he'd tried to do that with her. And that he was so, so sorry. He was sorry that he'd stolen her childhood, when she should have been able to run and play and be safe and protected like her brothers and cousins and Jackie Faye. Back then, he'd reasoned that there was no safety under Jim Crow. He hadn't wanted her to grow up with the same sort of fear that he saw all around him, the same internalized inferiority that segregation forced down Black folks' throats. He'd wanted his daughter to shatter those walls. Part of him had wondered then if he was pushing her too far. Now he knew.

Now that it was much too late, he realized the difference between having the world shatter your childhood and having your father do it. He wished he could take it back. But, he told his daughter, just because she was robbed of her childhood didn't give her the right to rob Corinne of her adulthood. That was hers to squander. If Cora didn't want to lose what he had lost, she had to let go.

Even as the knots in her stomach loosened and her breathing eased, Cora struggled to take it all in. Was that really Mama and Daddy, or had she lost her mind?

So she came out again and again at daybreak, and she heard the same thing again and again. So clear it made the hairs on her arms stand up straight. From that day on, she spent more time listening than talking in the hummingbird garden. It felt like a wall had come crumbling down, and not just the one between the living and the dead.

She began to feel lighter than she had in years—probably since before Yvonne died. She wanted to tell everyone what had happened in the garden, but she couldn't tell a soul. She knew how unbelievable it sounded. She had too much pride to tell Corinne, so they both floated through the house like living ghosts, only chancing to glance at one another. She didn't tell Harold either. She was too scared he'd start looking for assisted living facilities.

But just because she'd made her peace, that didn't mean she had found ease. Each day, as soon as she woke up, her first conscious thought came with a wave of dread. She had nightmares every night about every possible scenario: Corinne in a casket; Corinne in prison; Corinne kicked out of college with a criminal record, never able to reenroll or get a job. When she worried too much, Mama and Daddy were there to remind her to control only what she could control. Her mother reminded her that she could have a stroke, and then Corinne would have to come home to take care of her, and wouldn't that stifle her future in a whole other way?

So instead of fretting about the future, she decided to face the past. At least she knew how that story turned out. She pulled her dusty, ragged old photo albums out of the closet. She'd all but hidden them from herself in boxes underneath boxes, but she didn't dare to throw them out. The plastic edges of the pages were so frayed they'd become sharp to the touch. The covers—which she remembered as bright red with orange flowers and blue with yellow flowers—were now a faded pink and brown and a faded green and beige.

The first day she took them out, she took them to the garden. She didn't want to be alone with them. With the hummingbirds behind her, she took a deep breath and opened the pink one. The first photo was from picture day in the second grade. Her sixty-two-year-old eyes met her seven-year-old eyes, and she cried all the tears she couldn't then. There she was: so small and so vulnerable and so alone. She was wearing white. Mama, whose breath she could feel on her neck even now, had thought the white would signal purity and innocence. But Mama hadn't been there for the moments right before they took the picture, when Cora's teacher had pulled at her ponytail so hard it had made a sore spot.

She'd been the last child in her class to get her picture taken, just like she had been the last to do everything, sometimes by choice, sometimes by force, and sometimes by stale habit. She remembered the nose of the photographer as he stood over her. His voice had gone from soft and friendly with the other students to harsh and menacing with Cora. With the girl before her it was *"Smile for the camera, sweetie!"* and *"What a pretty smile you have!"* Cora couldn't remember what he'd said to her, but she remembered it hadn't felt good.

When the other children had finished with their pictures, they had gotten a piece of candy. When Cora finished, her throat had been dry and achy from holding in her tears. And she hadn't dared ask for candy.

It was strange to look back, after she had borne and raised her own children and taught classrooms full of kindergartners. She couldn't understand how anyone could have treated a child the way those people had treated her. How could a tiny little girl with pigtails and Mary Jane shoes have scared big giant men and women to the point that they had wanted to kill her?

Just then, the wind ruffled Cora's hair in exactly the spot Mama used to fix it just before she went into the White Folks School. She remembered the look in her mother's eyes then—that pained, fervent glimmer that said, *If I could fix it, I would.* Now she knew what a special, impotent kind of pain Mama must have felt, because it was how she felt when she looked at Corinne.

She flipped to another page and saw little Cora in her Sunday best, seated on the piano bench with her brothers. While they had big, wide smiles, hers looked restrained, performed. She looked sheepishly up at the camera through hunched shoulders. She remembered Daddy yelling at her to look up, to pull her shoulders back. What he called "sitting proud." She kept trying to comply, but every time she'd looked at the camera lens, she'd felt herself start to cry, and she knew that would make him angrier, so she hunched again. They'd gone back and forth until finally Grandma Cindy snapped at him, *"Just take the picture, George!"*

The picture had turned out to be just as unflattering as the one she'd taken at school, and it didn't take her long to believe that she was just bad at taking pictures. She avoided cameras for the rest of her life.

"Daddy, why?" she whispered.

There was a long pause before she got an answer. So long she almost went back indoors. But then she felt a breeze strong enough to push the swing she was sitting on. She felt her father's breath.

There were so many reasons, he told her. Almost too many. Every day, he'd worked at the post office, routing and bundling mail all over the city. He'd developed little formulas and schemas to make it go easier. Gerald and Harvey used to help him with it. But he'd always said, *"You don't need but an eighth-grade education to do this."* And Daddy had a college degree. Daddy left Mississippi and came to Nashville, to Fisk, because he'd wanted to do something bigger than pick cotton. Daddy was a World War II veteran. He'd come back from the war damned if he was going to let his children grow up in the world he grew up in. When he'd gotten the call about the NAACP planning to make the city comply with the *Brown v. Board of Education* decision, he'd all but run to the meeting.

He'd just so happened to have a child about to enter first grade, and that child had just so happened to be Cora. He'd thought about what it would do to his daughter, but he'd also thought about what life under Jim Crow could do to her. One was more dangerous in the short term, the other more dangerous in the long term. He chose the path that could end Jim Crow altogether. It wasn't that he wanted her around white folks. He wanted her to have what white folks had, because she deserved it. Mama fought him in the beginning, but it was hard to argue with that logic.

Mama had never liked it, though. Cora had known that then, but she felt it even more now, as she turned the page to another picture of the two of them together on the porch the morning before Cora's first day of third grade. By this point, Cora no longer tried to smile in pictures. She hardly ever smiled at all. She just looked straight ahead at the camera before she dropped her head again to stare at her shoelaces. It had seemed like the only safe place to rest her eyes. Cora looked closer at the photo and noticed that the bones of Mama's knuckles were protruding so sharply it looked like they were going to come out of her skin. She could see the anguish in her face as Mama looked past the camera to the man holding it.

From the pink and purple morning glory vines behind her, Mama told Cora that she could see the toll it all was taking on her only daughter, and she was becoming less and less assured by her husband's insistence that children were resilient. He had seemed so convinced that Cora would bounce back, that there was nothing those white folks could throw at her that she couldn't handle. She was tough, he reasoned, because she was his. But he wasn't in the halls of that schoolhouse. Cora was. All alone.

Mama had seen Cora becoming more and more withdrawn and nervous. Scared of everything that moved. She'd noticed Cora trying to shrink herself: in chairs, in conversations, and into backgrounds. She'd floated around the house like a skeleton, doing her best not to touch anything, never speaking much over a whisper. The sound of Cora's laughter had become so rare, Mama had jumped whenever she heard it. Mama had made a practice of asking Cora questions she knew Cora knew the answer to, and she had become increasingly horrified when Cora had hung her head, shuffled her feet, and mumbled that she didn't know.

When Cora finished the fourth grade, Mama had put her foot down: she was not sending her baby girl back to that school. The plan with the city, after all, had been that they would integrate the schools citywide for every year of elementary school that Cora finished, and this was the last year of elementary school. That was enough. It was time for Cora to go to school with her brothers. This time, Daddy didn't argue.

Cora felt a strong sense of protectiveness over the little girl in the pictures. She wanted to reach through the decades that divided them, down into the photographs, and apologize to her. She was sorry that she had left her alone all these years—never remembered, never celebrated, never healed. She wanted her to know that if no one else knew how scared, how lonely she felt, she did.

Cora spent every morning looking back at pictures that brought back the memories she'd long buried, talking to her father and her mother and even the little girl in the photos. As they talked, the picture became fuller. Finally, it was so full that the woman Cora had become and the little girl she'd left behind could stand in the same frame together.

The day before Corinne was supposed to haul off and take over a bridge in Vicksburg, Cora looked down at her elementary-school self and asked, "How'd you like to meet your granddaughter?"

WOMAN TROUBLES

September 4, 2002

Mrs. Rankin believed the Bible when it said, "Spare the rod and spoil the child," and made it the cornerstone of her teaching philosophy. So every time a student in Corinne's fourth-grade class got an answer wrong at her chalkboard, Mrs. Rankin made them hold out their hands so she could give them "licks" with her ruler. Sometimes five. Sometimes as many as ten. The exact number depended on her mood and what she thought the student was capable of.

Corinne had always been the "smartest" student in her class. The teacher's favorite. The one who helped the other kids with their homework and rebuffed help with her own. While some of her classmates quietly resented her, they were all happy to have her on their side when it was time for group work.

But now, she was locked in a struggle with multiplication that threatened her very identity. This wasn't like addition or subtraction where she could use an abacus or make up her own stories about the relationships between the numbers. She'd tell herself that the five went to the two's house for dinner and they invited their cousin seven. The stories didn't make sense to anyone else, but they didn't have to. But with multiplication, she couldn't, for the life of her, understand why the numbers changed the way they did. Four times four equaled sixteen because Mrs. Rankin said so. Corinne was just supposed to remember it and not question it. She would be well into middle school before she realized four *times* four really meant four plus four, four times.

The last time it had been Corinne's turn at the board, Mrs. Rankin had said, *"Mrs. Scott said such nice things about you as a second grader, and here you are making her a liar!"* She counted out eight sharp taps across her open palm. And for the past few weeks, Corinne had small bruises on her hand and red marks all over her homework. So far, she'd been able to hide it from Mama, but today might be the last day for that.

"I've tried everything, and some of y'all just still refuse to learn," Mrs. Rankin said at the end of class. "I used the ruler, I used the yardstick, but neither of them is working. Even the ones of y'all supposed to have sense can't get it right." She looked directly at Corinne, who'd moved from her usual seat at the front of the room all the way to the back corner. She dropped her head onto the wooden desktop until the pregnant pause was over. "We *having* this test tomorrow. And I'm bringing in a belt. If you fail it, if you get more than five answers wrong, I'mma take you in that baffroom down the hall with that belt . . . and the only way you getting out is gon' be through that window, you hear me? And that's not a threat. It's a promise."

On the bus after school, Corinne stared at her sheet of multiplication tables the entire way home, but she couldn't find a pattern. Eventually, the numbers all ran together. As soon as she got home, she followed Cameron into his room and groveled for his help.

"Can you teach me my times tables? Please?" she begged. "Mrs. Rankin is gonna kill me tomorrow! And if Mama finds out, she's gonna tell Grandma!" Corinne couldn't stand the thought of Grandma being disappointed in her.

At first Cameron was too stunned to speak. Corinne had never asked for help with her homework before. "Okay, Cori," he finally sputtered. "Bring me your times table sheet."

She handed him the paper and sat at the end of his bed. He quizzed her on her times tables until dinnertime, and Corinne gave one wrong answer after another.

"Corinne, are you being serious right now?" he asked in exasperation. "Are you trying?"

While memorization was a struggle for Corinne, Cameron was a master of it. He had the highest *Tetris* score of anyone else in their school because he'd learned the patterns in which the shapes appeared at different speeds. In the third grade, he'd memorized all the states and their capitals and never forgot. One of Corinne's favorite games was to dare anyone to ask him, unprompted, for the capital of any state.

She didn't know how to tell him that she was just as intimidated by her teacher as she was by the fact that he didn't need a book or a calculator to quiz her. All he needed was his brain. She didn't want to tell him how unbearable it was to see the pity in her classmates' eyes. Luckily, she didn't have to say anything because Mama opened the door, and the smell of pork chops wafted in behind her. She was still dressed from work in her blue dress and clangy earrings, but her feet were bare.

"Oh! You're *both* in here?" Mama smiled big, her lips lined with traces of lipstick. Corinne loved it when Mama wore lipstick and her mouth looked like those kissy-face stickers they sold at Walmart. "Well, dinner's ready if y'all wanna eat."

Mama was one of the best cooks in the family. She'd learned from Grandma, who'd learned from Grandma Cindy. But Mama also watched cooking shows and collected cookbooks from all over, constantly learning and trying new recipes. Cameron and Corinne fantasized about her opening a restaurant but never suggested it because then they'd have to share her cooking with strangers.

"You don't have to tell me twice!" Cameron nearly knocked Mama over in his haste to get to the kitchen and stack a plate with three pork chops, mashed potatoes, and the tiniest pile of green beans he could get away with. Corinne picked up one pork chop and a mountain of green beans and potatoes. Before they finished making their plates, Cameron asked if they could eat in his room. Corinne was relieved to hear he wasn't tired of her yet.

"Uh, sure!" Mama was thrilled to see them bonding instead of bickering. Corinne thanked Cameron with her eyes before they went back to his room. By the time he was done quizzing her, it was bedtime and she was finally starting to get some of the answers right.

They were waiting in their driveway for the bus to go to school. And Cameron was doing his best to pass his gift for memorization on to his sister. And Corinne could tell he thought she was faking the whole thing for attention. *He ought to know that this is the last thing I would want attention for.*

"What's five times five?" Cameron asked, this time with genuine concern.

"Twenty-five?" Corinne winced.

"Yes! See? You do know your times tables!"

Corinne knew she wasn't exactly smarter than her brother; she just cared about her grades and the accolades more than he did. When she got her first B in the second grade, she'd cried the whole weekend. It was one of Cameron's favorite things to taunt her with. At random, he'd break out his impression of her breakdown at the kitchen table, snot bubbles and all, when she told Mama she got a B. She didn't ever want him to see her like that again.

By the time Corinne made it to school, her stomach was full of rocks and knots. She had Mrs. Rankin's class at fifth period, right after lunch, and it hung over her like the stench from the paper factory on the other side of town. During her morning classes, she kept sneaking glances at her sheet of times tables. She'd cover the equal sign with her pinky finger and try to guess the answer. Every time she got one wrong, it felt like her stomach was trying to fall out beneath her.

By third period, her clothes had become so tight, she felt like she was going to tear them at the seams. She might even bust out of her skin. If someone had poked her with a fork, a torrent of air would have rushed out like a balloon. When she sat, she felt invisible daggers stabbing her through her groin, but standing made her knees want to give way.

When Corinne went to the bathroom just before her fourth period English class, she found herself staring at a vibrant pool of red in her underwear, and that was how she learned she had much bigger problems than a math test. She went straight up to Mrs. Sanders, her home room teacher, beckoned her to bend down, and whispered through cupped hands, "I'm bleeding."

When Mrs. Sanders pulled back from her, Corinne saw a look of shock plastered across her face. Mrs. Sanders placed her hand gently on Corinne's shoulder and told the rest of Corinne's classmates milling about the hallway to wait for her. She assigned Angelique to take names if anyone acted out while she walked Corinne to the guidance counselor's office. Mrs. Sanders told Corinne to go sit on the couch while she talked to Mrs. Sampson. Corinne watched as the two women whispered to each other. When Mrs. Sampson finally came over to Corinne, she was beaming.

"I know it's blood, sweetie, but you don't need to be scared. This is part of becoming a woman."

Once the halls had cleared, Mrs. Sampson took Corinne back to the bathroom and taught her how to attach a maxi pad to her underwear to catch the blood. Then she took her back to the office, where Corinne took a nap on the couch and waited.

"Your mama's on her way. She'll explain more when she gets here. You just go to sleep."

When she woke up, Cameron was sitting in the corner across from her, his face red and covered with what she thought was sweat, but as she came to, she realized it was tears. She sat up expecting to see her mother but found Grandma instead, holding on to Corinne's toes. As soon as she made eye contact, she realized that Grandma had been crying too.

Before Corinne could ask, Grandma pulled her into her bosom and whispered, "I'm so sorry, baby. I'm so sorry." As Grandma rocked her and Cameron's sobs grew louder, Corinne began to wonder if maybe the wound she discovered in the bathroom was fatal.

She pulled back from her grandmother with a jerk.

"Grandma! What is it?" She noticed that the three of them had Mrs. Sampson's narrow office all to themselves.

Grandma reached for Corinne's hand and took a massive sigh before she said gently, "Baby . . ."

"Mama's dead!" Cameron shouted, like he wanted it to hurt.

"What?" Corinne craned her head from her brother to her grandmother. "Grandma?"

"I'm sorry, baby," she whispered. "She's gone."

"Grandma?" This time her voice broke and she buried her face into their grandmother's lap and sobbed so hard her whole body shook.

It took months before she understood what had happened. Her mother had been at work in the dean's office at Alcorn when she got the call to come pick up her daughter. About thirty minutes later, a state trooper found her dead on Highway 61. She'd been driving behind one of those giant, menacing logging trucks, piled high with pine tree carcasses, one of which broke loose and came crashing through her front window. She'd died on impact.

Cameron had been the first one to point out that Mama didn't usually take Highway 61 between Alcorn and Natchez. She preferred to take the much prettier, calmer Natchez Trace, where you had to drive slower and no trucks were allowed. Sometimes when they weren't in a rush, she'd even make odd stops to look at the historical markers and Indian mounds and creeks. She must have taken 61 because she had been in a rush to get to Corinne.

"If you coulda just learned your damn times tables, Mama would still be here!" Cameron shouted at his sister when they got home.

It wasn't until the wake, a full week later, when Corinne finally told her brother that she hadn't faked being sick to avoid a test. She'd hit puberty.

He shifted away from her. "Well, congratulations!"

She felt herself disappear in his eyes, and it made her feel hollow inside. She retreated to the other end of the row to Uncle Harold and curled into his lap and sobbed until she slept, hoping to end the nightmare. She knew Cameron blamed her, and Grandma blamed herself, but Corinne wondered why no one blamed the person who cut the tree, or the person who let it hang off the back of his truck and fly into Mama's windshield.

Their father had been too busy with his new wife and his new stepchildren in Georgia to come to the funeral. Cameron only vaguely remembered him, Corinne not at all. Neither of them had thought about him enough to miss him. His absence probably wouldn't have registered if Uncle Harold hadn't mentioned what a son of a bitch he was at dinner after the wake. He called him by his first name: Walter. Corinne tried to picture his face but could only muster a question mark. Walter called once. They didn't answer, he didn't leave a message, and he never called back. And he didn't protest at all when Grandma announced that she wanted the children to move in with her in Port Gibson. He just rerouted his meager child support checks to her address.

Corinne and Cameron moved into the bedrooms their mother and uncle had grown up in, the ones they used whenever they stayed the night at their grandmother's house. They changed from the Adams County school system to the Claiborne County system. Cameron left his basketball team behind. Corinne left Angelique and her clique. Now, Cameron kept his door closed and never invited his sister in again.

PART FOUR

DAYBREAK

August 5, 2014

Cora watched the light from her window change from hazy gray to lazy yellow. The brighter it got, the more the lump in her throat climbed higher and higher. She pulled herself up and rocked back and forth, savoring these last sweet moments before her granddaughter became a criminal. She wasn't sure if she was sweating from the heat or the trepidation, but she knew it didn't matter.

As she lumbered out of bed, she tried to swallow the ball in her throat, but it wouldn't budge. *Coffee. Maybe that will help.* As she stood, her bones felt heavier, like they'd turned into logs. She dragged herself to the kitchen and reminded herself that Harold was coming this morning. He'd promised again, just last night.

When she put the coffee beans in the grinder, she couldn't smell them at all. She wasn't confident there would be a taste, but she needed the ritual more than the caffeine at this point.

She packed the grounds into the filter nearly to the top and poured water in the back of the machine. She listened to the coffee brewer gurgle and the linoleum floor crackling under her feet and tried to ignore the bubbles in her stomach.

While the machine whirred, she walked across the living room to Corinne's room and paused with her ear to the door. It was so quiet that—as Grandma Cindy would say—you could hear a rat piss on cotton. *This must be the calm before the storm*, she thought. She went back to the kitchen and fixed her coffee the way Mama taught her: a tiny bit of condensed milk and one scant spoon of sugar. Mama had learned how to proportion it when she worked for the PET Milk Company, but of course the entire family had switched to Carnation when Mama had gotten fired.

Cora took her mug out to her hummingbird garden. If ever there was a day she needed her parents, it was today. She felt the dew squish underneath her bare feet as she walked past her vegetable garden to take her seat in her swing. The morning glories were wide open and the hummingbirds were already there, as if they'd been waiting for her.

"Morning, Daddy," she whispered.

Cora felt her father ask her, in that gruff way of his, if she was ready. She wasn't, as much as she wanted to be. She knew she couldn't stop it, and she wasn't going to try. She knew that to keep what was precious to her she would have to risk it in one of the most grotesque ways she could imagine. She'd prayed and fasted, tossed and turned, but she wasn't "ready." She was tortured and numb. Mama told her that they knew that feeling well. They hadn't been "ready" when they'd taken her to Glenn, when they'd gotten the death threats, when Mama had gotten fired. "Ready" is an illusion. The only thing you can be is "willing."

Since her fight with Corinne, Cora had taken it upon herself to try to learn more about global warming. She had found a few articles on the internet, but they were so full of science jargon and conjecture she couldn't figure out if they had a point. When she looked at MSNBC, nobody said a word about global warming.

The only place she ever saw anyone talk about it was on Fox News, and there it was all snark and denial. Cora thought that the people who denied global warming were a special kind of idiot—not just stupid but evil too. They were the dangerous idiots who watched Fox News and listened to Rush Limbaugh and hung President Obama's effigy at Tea Party rallies. Every time she saw them on TV, they had the same menacing glint in their eyes that she'd seen in her third- and fourth-grade teachers' when they suggested to Daddy that Cora needed remedial classes. Their faces had gone from gleeful to fearful in seconds, as soon as they saw the rage on Daddy's face. He'd snatched Cora's hand and walked her out of the building so fast her feet didn't have time to touch the ground.

But as evil as those people were, Cora still didn't understand how global warming was worth Corinne's life.

But—Mama reminded her—that wasn't for her to decide. Daddy reminded her that Grandma Cindy didn't understand why he'd taken the risks he took.

Still, this was not the life Cora had imagined for her grand-daughter. Cora was supposed to have been part of a generation making another world where their children and their grandchildren could live, like Nina Simone said, with no fear. If she had faced those mobs and walked that tightrope just to watch her granddaughter—*two generations later*—do the exact same thing, what had been the point, really? If Cora had learned anything in all her years on this earth, it was that Black tears were never going to save this country. That they'd only run themselves silly trying to free these fools from their own chains. They were the ones with the keys.

She felt her father grip her hand. He reminded her, again, that Corinne couldn't know what no one told her. Cora knew that she owed her granddaughter the whole story, not just the basics: that she had integrated the schools and it had been in the newspaper. Cora knew that she had never told her what it had been like—how big the mobs had been, what they'd said, how cold the other students had been. She'd never told Corinne about the terror or how much it had hurt then and still hurt now. She'd never told her that she didn't want to do it or about the beatings at home when she wasn't "smarter than them white kids," how it created a chasm between her and her brothers that she still couldn't cross. She didn't tell her even how old she had been when it happened or how long it lasted. Cora had figured that what Corinne didn't know couldn't haunt her. But the ghosts had found her anyway. She'd been born with them at her back. Corinne deserved to know why.

There'd been so many times she almost told her, but she couldn't find the words. It was one thing to talk about it with her parents, or even to whisper to photographs of her eight-year-old self. It was another thing entirely to say it out loud to another person who'd never even seen a "whites only" water fountain outside of a museum. It was like explaining a whole different planet, with different ecosystems and physics. So Cora had bided her time until it had run out. What if Corinne went off today and never came back and never knew? She couldn't let herself think about that. Not now.

Just as she took her last sip of coffee, the heavy screen door creaked and Corinne stepped out, looking like an angel. She was wearing the nightgown with a bunched neck at the top and sleeves that flowed down like a church robe that Cora had sewn for her when she was in the tenth grade. Cora used to sew her one every year based on the same pattern Grandma Cindy had used.

They looked at each other from across the lawn, both holding their coffee cups. Instead of smiling, their mouths twisted into looks of half embarrassment and half apology. Without a word, Cora got up and went to the kitchen, and Corinne followed behind her like there was a rope tied to her waist.

They set about making biscuits in instinctive unison. Cora knew it was Corinne's favorite breakfast, and she'd heard more than she ever cared to about small-town, Southern jails. She knew that you never know how long you'll be in there, and that biscuits are a stick-to-your-bones kind of food. The kind that doesn't melt off easy, even in the August Mississippi heat. There was a reason sharecroppers carried them in their buckets day in and day out.

Grandmother and granddaughter worked together in harmony and silence. Corinne reached for the baking powder and salt and sugar before she turned on the oven and pulled out the biggest bowl from under the cabinet. Cora got the flour and milk and butter out of the refrigerator. Now was the time to do what worked.

Cora wanted to tell Corinne that she was proud of her, but she wasn't so sure her granddaughter could even hear her. She looked like she had already put on the same unassailable, invisible armor Mama had worn when she took Cora's hand and marched down to Glenn, head held high, ears closed. *Probably best to leave it for later*, she told herself. She didn't want to break her concentration. She threw the chunks of butter into the mound of flour and baking soda and salt and sugar that Corinne had mixed together.

She saw a little smile come over Corinne's face. This had been her favorite part of their biscuit-making ritual ever since she was a little girl: getting her hands dirty and oily as she kneaded the butter into the flour until it turned into sand, like the silt on the banks of the Mississippi. Cora tried to shake off the feeling that she was fattening her granddaughter up for the slaughter.

Cora poured the milk straight from the carton into the bowl as Corinne made circles with her spatula. There was no need for measuring cups. Grandma Cindy never measured anything. Cora had learned at her elbow, and she'd taught Corinne the same way. Corinne's smile had faded into a more pensive concentration. Cora noticed a tear drop from Corinne's cheek into the biscuit mixture. *A little extra salt might make the biscuits even better*, she thought.

A hurricane swirled in Cora's stomach. At its center, there was a calm, peaceful eye that looked at her granddaughter with pride.

Corinne took the baking sheet out of the just-right oven and dropped a chunk of butter that exploded on contact. Cora remembered the first time Yvonne had done that as a little girl and how she'd howled in pain when the butter splashed back and burned her. Cora wished she could go back to that moment and comfort her daughter instead of scolding her for her carelessness.

Now, she scooped the biscuits into palm-sized dollops and dropped them onto the buttery sheet while Corinne watched in silence. When she was done, Cora put the sheet in the oven and spoke for the first time.

"Go on and get dressed now. I'll keep watch." She meant over both the oven and the driveway. Corinne's people from New Orleans should be arriving any minute.

"Yes, ma'am," Corinne whispered. She sounded grateful, though Cora couldn't imagine for what.

Cora watched the biscuits bake like she was watching a movie. Grandma Cindy would have had a fit to see her idle like this. But this could be her grandbaby's last meal.

Her mind began to race again. Those white folks could go get arrested and expect to come home the same day. But when you had skin like hers, Corinne's, and Grandma Cindy's, all you had to do to wind up in prison was mind your business. She thought again of Eric Garner all the way in New York City, where the mayor had a Black wife and Black children. Now, anytime she turned on the news, there was so much attention on police violence and Black men but never Black women. Like Black women weren't raped and murdered by the very same officers. *No one takes our pain seriously*, Cora thought. *Not even us.*

Cora didn't want to watch Corinne become one of those Black women destroyed by their own pain because they refused to admit that it hurt—or, even worse, tried to convince themselves that they'd deserved it. She knew it was a trick because she'd lived it, which was exactly how she knew it wasn't something she could tell Corinne. She had to let her find it out herself. And that was the agony.

The smell of golden biscuits wafted from the oven and straight into Cora's nose. For a moment, she was a little girl again visiting Grandma Cindy. Then she remembered that *she* was the grandma now, and the biscuits would burn if she kept daydreaming. She pulled the tray out and started another pot of coffee, this time actually taking care to measure the water and the coffee correctly.

When Corinne showed up in the kitchen doorframe still fussing her curly hair into a bun, Cora was struck by her resemblance to Mama. Both Corinne and Yvonne had looked a lot like her mother. She could even see it when Corinne was a baby, so when Yvonne told her she could choose her granddaughter's middle name, she'd chosen Jewel. Today, Corinne was a little shorter and a little darker than Mama had been, but she had the same deep-set eyes and high cheekbones. When Corinne smiled, her eyes disappeared, just like Mama's did. She was wearing camouflage pants and sneakers with one of Cameron's old shirts. She looked like she was going to burn up. Cora sighed deeply and thought about how much Corinne was going to sweat today and how it would ruin her hair. And then she imagined the police dragging her off by her bun.

Cora took four biscuits out of the oven and put them on a plate for her granddaughter. She pulled the blackberry preserves and honey out of the cabinet and set them in front of Corinne. Then she went to fix them both another cup of coffee. They were going to need it.

Corinne groaned when she saw the fullness of her plate. "Grandmama . . ." But Cora gave her that look that let her know she best not argue.

Cora didn't fix a plate for herself. She had only the coffee and her cigarette. In the past week, she'd cut back on smoking. She'd even made it all the way through Thursday without a single puff. But not today.

The air felt ominous, the way it had in the days right after the four little girls were bombed in Sunday school in Birmingham. Or the day President Kennedy was shot, or the day Martin Luther King Jr. was shot, or the day Bobby Kennedy was shot. The way it had felt when she'd woken up and all the adults were whispering about the bomb that ripped through Hattie Cotton School on the other side of the parkway and debating whether to send their kids back to the White Folks School. Cora's pastor came to their house to beseech them to take her to school. To-day of all days, he'd said, they couldn't give up.

Just as Cora took her third long sip of coffee and Corinne finished her second biscuit, she heard the engine in the driveway. Cora and Corinne looked at each other, and both tried to force a smile. Cora jumped up to wrap up the two biscuits left on Corinne's plate and pack them into a plastic bag with the other eight biscuits. *They may be young and foolish*, she thought, *but at least they won't be hungry.* Not if she had anything to do with it. She shoved the plastic bag into her granddaughter's hands. Corinne leaned in to kiss her grandmother, but Cora waved away the kiss and yanked her granddaughter into an embrace so tight their cheeks touched.

Cora placed her hands on Corinne's shoulders as she followed her out to the driveway. As they walked out, an extremely beautiful, extremely pregnant woman climbed out of the car.

"You must be Mrs. Sterling! I'm Daphne. Corinne worked with me down in New Orleans back in January." She came forward to shake Cora's hand.

"Oh, hello! Corinne's told me some about you, but she didn't tell me you were . . ." Cora trailed off as she stared at the woman's belly.

"This pregnant? Ha, I know. Corinne hasn't seen me since I got quite this big, and it's kinda something you have to see to believe. But she's told me so much about you!" Daphne grinned and put her hands on her hips. "'My grandmama makes the best gumbo on *earth*!' 'My grandmama integrated the schools in Nashville!'"

Cora laughed. It was a pretty good impression of Corinne, but Cora never knew that she talked to people about her, let alone that Corinne *bragged* about her. She looked over to Corinne, who was grinning down at her shoes. Cora promised herself right then and there that they were going to have that talk tonight, even if it was through a jail phone.

"Y'all be careful out there today." Cora turned back to Daphne. "What y'all are doing might be half brave—"

"And half crazy?" Daphne finished her sentence for her. "It might, but, Mrs. Sterling, I don't want you to worry. I'm gonna take care of your grandbaby. We all are."

Cora looked in the car to see two white men and a white woman waving back at her.

"Obviously, *I'm* not going out on that bridge, but I'll be right there the whole time. Now, I got your son's phone number and I'll be texting him, but I wanted to give you mine so you can call whenever you just get a feeling. It's on this card." Daphne handed her two business cards and a pen. "Can you write yours down on the back of this other one so I can call you when it's time for you to come to Vicksburg?"

After Cora wrote down her number, she looked back down at Daphne's belly. "And you can call me, too, if . . . your water breaks or something. I know the folks at the hospital over there."

Daphne smiled. "Well, I thank you, but I'm sure hoping that doesn't happen. I'm not due for another four weeks."

"Then you must be having a full-grown man and not a baby!"

Daphne laughed. "It's a girl, actually. But speaking of this child, though, can I use your restroom before we head out?"

"Oh, of course! It's just right through the kitchen on your left." Cora thought about walking her in to show her, but she wanted to stay out here with Corinne a little longer. She had a sense that Daphne could find her way out of anything. Her confidence was contagious.

"Y'all come say hi to my grandmama," Corinne said with a big beaming smile, taking Cora's hand and walking her closer to the car.

Everyone got out of the car. A tall, jumpy white boy with sandy hair bent down toward her. "Hey, Mrs. Sterling, I'm Mercer. I'm friends with Corinne."

She shook his hand and found it was already sweaty. "Well, I would hope you're all friends, right?"

"We are, Grandma." Corinne walked Cora over to the other side of the car where a white man, probably in his fifties, and a white woman, probably in her thirties, were standing.

"I'm Alex. It's a pleasure to meet you. I met your son down in New Orleans."

"Oh, did you?" Cora said as she shook his hand. She wondered why Harold never mentioned that.

"I'm Kathleen, and it's an honor to meet you, Mrs. Sterling." She then lowered her voice like they were about to share a secret. "I'm very sorry about your grandson."

Cora jerked back from her, and Kathleen looked embarrassed. "I'm sorry, I shouldn't have said that."

"It's okay." Cora was still taken aback by her over-familiarity, but she could tell she meant well. "No one knows what to say in these situations. It's nice to meet you."

"Thank you, Mrs. Sterling," Daphne said as she floated out of the house. "All right, y'all, let's get this show on the road." She put her hand on Cora's shoulder before she got back in the car herself. "I promise I'll call you as soon as we get to Vicksburg, and if you call me, I promise I'll pick up."

"Okay, thank you." Cora sighed. She turned back to Corinne and pulled her in for another long, hot embrace. She smelled of honeysuckle and salty sweat.

"You're never going to know if it's enough," Cora whispered. "And that's never the point." She pulled back and looked her granddaughter in the eye. "You hear me?"

"Yes, ma'am," Corinne mumbled as tears welled in her eyes.

"You call me the minute you need me, okay, girl?" She hadn't told her that Harold was on his way at that very moment.

"Yes, ma'am," Corinne said as she reached to hug Cora one more time. "I want you to be proud, Grandmama. I want you to be so proud."

Cora wiped away her granddaughter's tears and tried to choke back her own. "I am, Corinne," she whispered. "You will never know how proud I am. So proud I could bust." She reached down to stroke her hair. "You be careful out there, you hear me?"

Corinne nodded.

"Go on if you going."

Once the car had pulled out of the driveway, Cora went back to the kitchen to refill her coffee mug before she headed back out to her hummingbird garden to wait for Harold.

TAKE ME TO THE WATER

August 5, 2014

Once they pulled out of the driveway, Corinne passed out Grandma's biscuits like they were a sacrament. The eagerness with which everyone took them made Corinne worry that they'd forgotten to eat breakfast that morning.

"By the way, Corinne, it's nice to meet you," Miss Kathleen said. "I didn't want to say that in front of your grandmother and make her think you were riding off with a stranger. Besides, I've heard so much about you from Daphne that I feel like I know you already."

"Thank you for that!" Corinne hadn't even thought about it. "It's nice to meet you too. You're a photographer, right?"

"Yeah, but more journalist than photographer these days. I'm not, like, an artist or anything."

"Corinne?" Mercer asked through a mouthful of biscuit. "What's all this business about Port Gibson being too beautiful to burn?"

Corinne chuckled. She forgot how jarring and audacious that must sound to an outsider. "Oh, that's from the Civil War. When the Union passed through Port Gibson, they said it was too beautiful to burn. So they left it standing."

"It *is* a cute little town," Miss Daphne said from the passenger seat. "Kinda wish they had burned they Confederate asses up, though."

After that, they rode in complete silence. No talking, no music, no nothing. The silence hung so heavy it felt like if any of them punctured it, even with a grunt, steam would come hissing out and none of them would be able to see again. The road outside was just as quiet.

Mercer had insisted that he sit in the back seat, in the middle. It was an odd choice for the tallest person in the car, but his to make. Even though the space was limited between them, Corinne suspected it was more than accidental that Mercer's leg leaned into hers so heavily for the entire ride. She thought of saying something but instead leaned into the comfort of human warmth.

Corinne turned her attention away from the car and devoted it to the patches of woods that punctuated the highway. Mississippi had the type of beauty you had to leave to appreciate. The things she'd seen her entire life—in all their gore and glory—took a whole new hold on her now that she'd left and come back. The trees, the swamps, even the simple kudzu arrested her. She'd never noticed before how, in the summer, all the colors came alive and seemed to throb. She knew that she would want to protect this glory for the rest of her life. She tried to memorize the tree bark, the blades of grass, the cows, the vultures. She focused like she'd never seen them before, or like she'd never see them again.

She thought about the Natchez and Choctaw people who'd been forced off this land, and maybe others that history had written into the wrong places. So many never to return, their hearts broken to the core. They'd known this place so intimately it was part of their bones, their spirits, and they had to leave it with people who'd showed them only brutality. That's a heartbreak that becomes part of your bloodline.

Back when Grandma was a child, these same trees Corinne adored now had borne strange, hideous, castrated fruit. They'd muffled the shouts of lynch mobs and silenced the screams of the suffering. She knew that if she searched for images of Black people and trees, she'd see trees just like these with Black men, women, and children hanging from them, and white men, women, and children smiling and handing out severed toes and thumbs as souvenirs. But she knew that wasn't the whole story either. She knew a slave woman named Rose had guided Union soldiers through these woods to lay siege to Vicksburg, to bring the Confederacy to its knees. During the Great Flood, these same trees had been a solace and a shelter for the Black folks who'd refused to become refugees in Vicksburg. She thought if she looked closely enough, she could see their eyes, teeth, and torches. It was all she needed to light her way forward.

She'd expected to be nervous today, but she couldn't quite figure out how she felt. She'd woken up with butterflies in her stomach, but they'd flown away with Grandma's embrace.

She remembered the "centering" exercise that she'd learned in her direct action training in Cleveland. She closed her eyes and breathed into her stomach, slow and deliberate. With each breath, a new emotion appeared. Anticipation. Excitement. Defiance. Resentment. Anger. Resolve.

By the time she opened her eyes, they'd made it to the traffic light near the Vicksburg Walmart. When she was a little girl—back when she thought New Orleans and Memphis were megacities—she'd thought Vicksburg was a throbbing metropolis. By now, though, she knew that Vicksburg was a sleepy little town. Right now, it was sound asleep. She wondered if this was what it had looked like when the Union forces had crept up on it a century and a half ago.

Before she knew it, they'd pulled into the parking lot at the Welcome Center, and the River was staring her in the face. The Welcome Center wouldn't open for another hour and a half, when the three sisters would tumble out of their silver Camry. For a moment, they sat there staring at the two bridges just ahead. Everyone except Corinne was seeing them with their own eyes for the very first time. Even to her, though, the bridges had never looked this imposing before. For one fleeting moment, she thought they might come alive and run away.

"We're here." Miss Daphne broke the silence, and they filed out of the car like they'd been released from a trance.

Corinne knew that Steve showed up closer to eight than seven thirty. The night guard, for whatever reason, couldn't be bothered to wait for him. So this was their blessed window of opportunity. She looked over to the security post to confirm.

"Told you he'd be gone." She winked at Miss Daphne in the rearview mirror. "The car isn't there."

Corinne looked past Mercer and smiled at Miss Kathleen. "Let me show you where to set up your camera. I found the perfect spot for you."

Miss Kathleen swung her camera bag over her shoulder and followed Corinne up to the pedestrian overpass. From there, she'd be able to see both bridges, the Welcome Center, and the police arrival, no matter which direction they came from.

"Is that cannon trained on the bridge?" Miss Kathleen looked horrified.

"It does look that way," Corinne said with a chuckle. "But that cannon is from the Civil War. The bridge wasn't here then."

Mercer, Mr. Stephens, and Miss Daphne walked up. They'd all dressed in black, but looking at them now, Corinne wished she'd told them to dress in green or blue to blend in with the rolling hills or the river. Corinne hurried back down the stairs to meet them.

"Y'all be careful, now!" Miss Daphne whispered, her hand on her belly, before she waddled back to the parking lot. They wanted to post the banner before Steve got there so Miss Daphne could call the police before he could. Since she would see it from the same angle as the people driving on the shiny bridge, Miss Daphne was also tasked with taking cell phone pictures and videos of the banner.

Corinne led Mercer and Mr. Stephens toward the gate to get onto the black bridge, down the concrete slope that cars used to drive down to cross into Louisiana. As they passed the bronze plaque with the bridge's history and then the narrow, empty security guard station, Corinne felt like she was walking in slow motion, weighed down by the history and the humidity. Finally, they got to the silver wire fence that blocked the entryway. A bright orange sign warned "No Pedestrians Past This Point." But Corinne had measured the gap at the bottom of the gate and knew that it was a little more than a foot high, just high enough for them to squeeze underneath.

"This is your last chance to turn back, you know?" Mr. Stephens sounded more patriarchal than patronizing. Still, something about the way he said "*your* last chance" gave Corinne a twinge of indignation. Before she knew what had come over her, she let out a whoop, sprinted ahead of Mercer and Mr. Stephens, and slid underneath the fence like a football player.

"Well, that answers that question!" Mr. Stephens chuckled.

When Corinne jumped back up on the other side, she found them both staring, mouths open and eyes smiling. When she made eye contact, they busted out laughing. Mercer slid the backpack under the fence before he made his way underneath as well.

"If you scared"—Corinne yelled—"say you scared!"

Corinne grabbed the backpack and ran as fast as she could to the middle of the bridge. It wasn't until she stopped running that she realized how heavy her bag was. She threw it to the ground, and they pulled out the banner Miss Daphne had ordered from a friend of hers who owned a printing press in New Orleans. Corinne walked her half of the fabric toward

Louisiana while Mercer backed up toward Mississippi. The banner was made of heavy canvas cloth and was big enough to read from the other bridge. Once it was open, Corinne read it for the first time, taking in the bold words in even bolder red print on a cream background:

> *An Oil Boat Killed My Brother.*
> *You're Next.*
> *R.I.P. Cameron Sterling*
> *April 11, 1989–May 5, 2013*

There was no breeze, but Corinne felt something light on her forearm, and she knew Cameron was out here with her. And for a very short moment, she wondered where she would be if her brother was still here. Maybe they'd be fishing on the River or taking a road trip to Memphis. *Maybe*, she thought, *this is a blessing in disguise.* If Cameron were here, maybe she wouldn't care about oil boats and pipelines, and maybe she wouldn't know her future was on fire until it really was too late. But then she heard a voice that might have been Cameron's say, *Blessings don't wear disguises.*

"What time is it?" she asked.

"It's seven forty-one," Mr. Stephens said as he pulled the ligatures out of the bag. "We got twenty minutes if this guard stays on schedule, Corinne. Everybody feeling okay?"

Corinne and Mercer nodded and carried the banner over to the giant metal beams that made up the bridge's guardrail. They were arranged like a series of Roman numerals: IXIXIXI.

Corinne and Mercer stopped at one of the X's and Corinne shuddered to notice how much it looked like the Confederate flag. She slid a piece of rope through one of the metal rings at the top of the banner and tied it to the bottom of the beam on one side of the X while Mercer tied his to the other side. The rope felt rough on her hands, but a smoother material would have slipped through her sweaty palms.

Once upon a time, the guardrail had been a precaution to keep cars from falling over into the River. Grandma used to tell her how scary it was to get caught on the bridge while a train was crossing. Even though the train was on the tracks and she was on the road, she could feel the wind from the train as it sped by. There was nowhere to run and nothing to do. She said it always felt like the train was going to hit you, but it never did.

Once they'd finished affixing the corners, Corinne looked down to see the banner hang over the River and felt her brother's breath on her neck. She felt like her heart, now unbroken, could burst out of her chest. She didn't know if she wanted to laugh or cry or both all at once, like when it rained while the sun was shining.

"I'm fine!" She saw the looks on Mercer's and Mr. Stephens's faces and waved them off before they could ask what was wrong. She knew they meant well, but sometimes their abundance of concern was infantilizing. It was the earnestness that made it doubly obnoxious, though. She knew she couldn't have pulled this off without them, and they wouldn't have done it if they didn't actually care about her. And while she'd come to genuinely care about them, too, she was still using them for their experience, access, and privilege. She wondered if she should feel bad about that, but she knew she didn't.

The sound of a car horn on the other bridge brought her back to the moment.

"You think they're with us or against us?" Mercer asked.

"Doesn't matter," Corinne answered. "They noticed."

"They might be calling the police," Mr. Stephens added. "Good thing Daphne already did."

Corinne knew how much of a spectacle they must be. She'd been traveling back and forth on that bridge her whole life, and she'd never seen anything like this. When she'd asked the Welcome Center ladies and the security guard and the museum staff if they'd ever heard of anyone breaking onto the bridge, no sooner had she asked than they'd shrugged her off and assured her that they'd have been arrested before they ever made it. But here she was.

She looked below her at her raging, beloved River, surrounded on both sides by a lush green. So much life: above the River, below it, all around. The closer she looked, the more the bridges felt *wrong*, like it was the metal and concrete that actually trespassed on the River. It felt even more wrong when she remembered that the bridge was built the year after the Great Flood, the River's big rebellion against human tampering.

"We did it, y'all!" Mercer reached down and hugged Corinne tight.

"It's not time to celebrate just yet, Mercer," Mr. Stephens said, giving him a tepid embrace. "The cops will be here any minute now, and that's when it really starts."

Corinne knew he was right. But she couldn't deny her joy. She'd earned it. When she and Mercer first started talking about doing this, she'd hoped one of the oil boat captains would see it, maybe the rest of the crew too. She'd hoped they'd ask questions of themselves and the people they worked for about what their boats were carrying, to where, and for whom and why. She'd fantasized about passersby seeing the banner, going home to google the oil industry and how it could kill a person, seeing themselves in the crosshairs, and finally understanding the trouble they were in.

But now that she was here, she didn't care. She didn't care if the banner stayed up for just another minute, for the rest of the day, or forever. She didn't care if it never touched another soul. Grandma was right: Corinne *had* done this for herself. But there was nothing wrong with that.

Then she heard the police sirens. First one, then two, then three. Her heart jumped into her throat and, on instinct, she raised her hands high above her head.

"Stay still," Mr. Stephens warned them. "Don't move until they tell us to."

Corinne watched as one police car stopped at the Welcome Center and the officer got out and walked toward Miss Daphne with a notepad. She saw two more cars drive into the entryway underneath Miss Kathleen. The sirens stopped. She saw the other four officers coming toward them with their hands on their hips, not far from their holsters. When they got to the wire fence they'd slithered under, a short, sweaty, and visibly annoyed officer emerged as the leader.

"What the hell y'all think you doing?" They were close enough that he didn't need a megaphone, but he still had to holler.

"We're exercising our right to free speech and assembly, Officer!" Mr. Stephens shouted firmly.

"You need to be on private property to do that?" the officer shot back. His skin was turning red and Corinne wasn't sure if it was because the sun was rising or because his temper was. He looked around at the other officers, including a Black one, to see if they were equally as livid. They were.

"Are we being arrested, Officer?" Mr. Stephens asked with a calm that was almost menacing.

"Hell yeah, you being arrested! You think you just gon' traipse off into the sunset after breaking onto a bridge in broad daylight?" His skin got redder. He seemed disoriented by the sheer gall of the question. "Come on out from in there. Right now. Keep your hands up where I can see them too."

She wondered if they should take the banner with them but thought it was probably better not to make any moves or ask any questions now. They walked toward the gate in a single file with their hands up—Mr. Stephens at the front, Corinne in the middle, and Mercer at the back. She watched a mosquito land on Mr. Stephens's neck and worried that he might flinch to swat it away. He didn't, and she felt a wave of relief. Their shuffle came to a halt when they made it to the gate.

"Well?" The lead officer glared at them. "You the ones got yourselves in there. Get yourselves out!"

Corinne was terrified of the prospect of lying down on her stomach and turning her back to four armed and irritated men with bureaucratic immunity to crawl underneath the gate. Even though their guns weren't out, she knew they were there and loaded. She closed her eyes for a moment, and when she opened them, she saw another car coming toward the entryway, just as Mr. Stephens was stooping to start his descent underneath the gate.

It was the same baby-blue Thunderbird she'd checked for when they pulled up to the Welcome Center. The door swung open, and all eyes turned to Steve as the prodigal morning guard tumbled out, tall and wide. A bit too much for his car. Like every morning, he had his customary coffee and bag of donuts. As he walked toward the officers, he looked bewildered, until he recognized Corinne. Then he looked betrayed. The guilt that came over her quelled her fear. Steve had trusted her. They'd become friends, sharing fried okra and hush puppies and laughing at the sisters behind their backs.

"What's the problem, Officer?" Steve was using the voice that Corinne knew he'd cultivated to talk to white folks. Since he'd gotten out of his car, though, he hadn't taken his eyes off her.

"Steve, can you come on and open this gate? Look like we got a couple of clowns on our hands."

Steve sat his coffee and sweets on the window ledge of his security guard post just to the right and came over to oblige. As Corinne looked into his eyes, she realized that she'd likely put his job in jeopardy.

"Corinne." Steve greeted her dryly. As he held the gate open, he stood close enough that she could only barely walk by without touching him, and she could feel his breath on the top of her head.

"Oh, so you know this one?" the lead officer asked. Corinne could read "Officer Garrett" on the metal nameplate on his shirt.

"Used to." Steve looked at her like he wanted to spit. She wanted to disappear. "She from Port Gibson."

She didn't stop staring at Steve until one of the white cops who hadn't spoken yet grabbed her arms out of the sky and pulled them behind her hard enough to make her shoulders crack. He held her hands together with one hand as he pulled his cuffs out with the other. The metal felt sharp against her skin. She made a fist so he couldn't fasten them too tight, just like they'd taught her at her training.

"Interesting she didn't know no better then." Officer Garrett scowled at her before turning to Mercer and Mr. Stephens. "Where you two from?"

"Shreveport!" Mercer shouted defiantly. "And my father's a sheriff!"

"Okay, well, we'll just see about that," the other white officer said as he cuffed him.

Mr. Stephens refused to answer the question. Corinne followed his eyes up to the pedestrian bridge overhead to

Miss Kathleen, who was still recording. Corinne wasn't sure the police had even seen her up there.

Corinne's officer marched her to his car. He had one hand on her head and the other holding her already-cuffed wrists. She could feel his knuckles digging into the small of her back and his breath on her neck. His touch was chilling, ominous, and she hoped he didn't notice her shudder. As he pushed her into the back seat of the car, she still had not heard his voice. He didn't read her her rights. He didn't tell her she was under arrest or what the charges would be. He didn't even call her names or ask what her real name was. It was nothing like the TV shows promised.

From the window, Corinne saw Mercer and Mr. Stephens being herded into the other car with the Black officer and the other white one. Officer Garrett walked over to the driver's side of her car. The officer who cuffed her took the passenger's seat. He was average height, average build, average face. Brown hair. Brown eyes. The only thing remarkable about him was how indistinguishable he was. He looked like a stock photo. She marveled at how difficult it would be to pick him out of a lineup. Then she thought about how, if he were to harm her, she'd never get that chance.

Officer Garrett climbed into the car and slammed the door shut. Before he turned the ignition on, he looked at her from the rearview mirror.

"You know you got the right to remain silent, right?"

SHADOWS OF DOUBT

August 5, 2014

Corinne had never been a good crier. Her rhythm was always off—it was always too much or too little. As a little girl, she'd cried at every scratch, every slight. At her mother's funeral, she'd cried so much that the ushers had to bring her an entire roll of toilet paper from the ladies' room. Charmin. Double-ply. After that, though, came the Great Drought. For years she couldn't cry more than a sniffle, even if she huffed and puffed and tried her hardest. Until Cameron died. That released the Great Deluge for months.

When she caught a glimpse of herself in the rearview mirror between Officer Garrett and Officer No Name, she saw a stream of tears running down her face. Her cheeks looked like glass. This wasn't the violent, breathless, desperate crying she was used to. The kind that left her throat raw and her temples throbbing. This was steady, staid. Even dignified. It felt like a cleansing.

But she didn't feel at peace. Back on the bridge, she'd felt firm, solid. Now, in the back of the police car, she felt like she was floating away from herself. She saw herself burst into two, then four, then even more versions of herself. The many Corinnes stared back at her from different angles of the car, each asking, in unison, *What have you done?*

As they pulled into the parking lot for the Warren County Jail, Corinne's many selves came back together long enough for her to feel all their panic in her stomach. Then just as quickly, they split back out. *Poof.*

"All right, Cain," Officer Garrett said. "Can you take care of this on your own? I'll be back to pick you up in a minute."

Officer Cain. Of course. Like sugar cane. The thing that sweetened her coffee, conquered swamps, and severed limbs.

"Yeah, I got it," Cain answered. His voice, like everything else about him, was nondescript. Average. Like a human boilerplate.

He opened Corinne's door and motioned for her to make her way out. As she scooted toward the car door, she realized how hard it was to balance without her arms and hands.

"Come on, now!" Officer Cain sighed. She couldn't tell if he was angry or exasperated. He was just as menacing either way. She didn't want to give him a reason to touch her again, so she thrust herself out of the car to face the redbrick building that looked like a medieval fortress. She half expected to see a moat.

When she stepped out of the car, her legs disappeared from underneath her like smoke in the wind. As the entrance of the building drew closer and closer, she wasn't sure if she was moving toward it or if it was moving toward her. She could barely feel her own skin, much less the cuffs that dug into her wrists.

Once they were inside, the blast of the air conditioner blew right through her. Officer Cain walked ahead of her to greet the small uniformed woman who sat at the wide desk at the cross-section of two grand linoleum hallways.

"Got one already?" she asked, her eyebrows raised.

"I'll tell you later. You won't believe how stupid this shit is."

The woman looked at Corinne and nodded toward the gated hallway behind her. There was a loud *buzz* as it opened. Officer Cain ushered her through the gate until they came to a metal bench in a long, empty corridor. He gestured for her to sit before he released the handcuff on her left wrist and affixed it to the metal bars behind her. He placed his hands on his hips and looked down to admire his handiwork. "That oughta hold you!" As he walked away, his laughter reverberated against the walls and the windows and the all-metal everything. It seemed that every noise in the jail was magnified and echoed into infinity.

The Shadows of herself had followed her from the car into the jail. Now they filled the emptiness around her. They sat on all sides of her, across from her, above her. One even sat on her shoulder. She had herself surrounded. They didn't say a word; they only stared in righteous disdain. She didn't dare to look back at them for fear that their eyes would draw blood. She tried to look down and made a game, perhaps a dangerous one, out of holding her breath to avoid the subtle but unmistakable smell of off-brand bleach, urine, and body odor.

She went so deep in her head that she wasn't in her body at all anymore. Now, she was curled up watching late-night TV with Grandma because she couldn't sleep. She was back at Oberlin watching herself stumble from the library to the cafeteria to her dorm, exhausted from an all-nighter and shaking from caffeine. She was at Alcorn's homecoming, and the band was playing, and everyone was singing: *"Glad to see you again, I haven't seen you since I don't know when."* She was swimming with Cameron at the beach in Ocean Springs. She was anywhere but here.

It felt like she'd been gone for hours before she heard Officer Cain's footsteps again. She didn't open her eyes until he'd uncuffed her from the bars. When she heard the *thud* from her arm falling down, she realized she'd lost all feeling in her right hand. As it tingled back to life, she looked around and all her Shadows were still scattered around the room, still staring.

Finally, her eyes fell on Officer Cain, who looked back at her in disgust. "Come on," he grunted.

She followed him down the corridor, and her Shadows trailed behind her like a wary army. The Shadows didn't have to state their name and get their fingerprints taken. They didn't have to have the inside of their mouths examined or their shoelaces taken away. They didn't have to change into a jumpsuit and "pose for the camera," from the front, the side, and the other side. She did all of that alone.

Officer Cain rattled off the list of charges—not to her but to a Black officer who had brought him a cup of coffee. She saw the words come out but could hear only their echoes.

" 'Reckless endangerment.' 'Trespassing.' 'Disorderly conduct.' 'Obstructing a navigable waterway.' 'Vandalism.' 'Obstructing an officer in the course of their duties.' Maybe 'Resisting arrest'?" That last one sounded like he was throwing it in just for fun. All the words overlapped and blended with the clacking keyboards and clanging doors around her. She couldn't tell which one came before the other.

"What you do all that for?" the Black officer asked her when Officer Cain finished. She could still hear the echoes from the cells down the corridor just behind him. So many voices ricocheting off the cinderblock.

She looked the Black officer in the eye. He had a baby face, like he'd probably just graduated from high school. She wanted to answer him calmly, righteously. Eloquently. But all that came out was a meager mumble: "Global warming."

"That's what you worried 'bout?" The officer's voice rose two decibels. "People ain't got food on the table *today*, people can't pay rent *today*, and you out here going to jail behind some shit that ain't happening *tomorrow* or even *this year*?"

Corinne looked at the floor.

The two officers exchanged a bewildered but knowing look that turned into a sigh.

"We got anybody in the tank?" Officer Cain asked.

"On a Tuesday morning? Shit, naw!"

He turned back to Corinne. "Well, it's your lucky day, missy! You get to have the drunk tank all to yourself!"

She followed him back down the corridor where she'd waited for him before, away from the cells where all the voices vibrated into a roar. She thought about asking for water or the phone call she thought she was entitled to—the whole reason she'd memorized Daphne's cell phone number—but decided that could take him from indifferent to irate. At the end of the hall, Officer Cain opened the door to a large L-shaped room with a toilet in the middle and built-in benches lining all sides. The entire room was plastered with many coats of dark blue paint—a sharp contrast to the bright beige of the rest of the jail. She wondered what was in that paint and what was underneath it.

Officer Cain slammed the door behind her no sooner than she'd set foot in the room.

"Get comfortable!" The echo of the turning lock stung in her ears.

She fought through the stench of stale alcohol, vomit, and dead bugs and moved toward one of the two small barred windows next to the toilet. They were too high for her to look out of them, even if she stood on one of the benches. Still, the extra sunlight was a welcome addition to the overhead fluorescent lights with covers so full of bugs, they produced more noise than light. She thought the orange would make a pretty nail polish color. Like a field of marigolds.

Corinne slumped down onto the bench below the window closest to the door. One by one, all the Shadows that had followed her into the room burrowed back into her. She went from feeling like she was made of air to feeling like she was made of concrete, harder than the metal slab she was sitting on. It was such a heavy thing to be whole again.

And it was so hot. If there was air-conditioning, it wasn't working. There were only two puny fans in the top corners of the room. With so little ventilation, the smell of the room became tangible, almost animate. She regretted the heavy camouflage pants she'd put on that morning. She wanted to throw up, but her biscuit breakfast stayed down. *God bless Grandma.*

She imagined Grandma waiting for her outside of the station. In her Sunday best, hands on her hips. Or maybe the next time she saw her, it would be in a courtroom. Corinne would be in chains, the judge in a robe, Grandma in a fit of rage. Maybe she would see her again in prison, on the other side of one of those thick plates of plastic. Grandma would bring her cookies and ask her if it was worth it, and Corinne wouldn't be able to answer.

When she'd left home this morning, it had all felt worth it. On the bridge too. But now, her nostrils full of vomit and her body drenched with sweat, she wasn't sure of anything anymore, much less herself. She thought back to all that plotting and planning with Mercer and Miss Daphne and Mr. Stephens. What had felt so meticulous then felt so naive now.

She was especially annoyed with Mercer. To him, going to jail was a big *if*. He thought the cops might even think it was just some silly prank. Boys will be boys, after all. She wondered where he was now. Why didn't she see him in the booking area? What if he'd called his father already and they'd let him out? What if he didn't even mention her to his father?

What if she was alone? Maybe Mississippi was, like Grandma had said Corinne's whole life, *different*, and

Miss Daphne really didn't know how things worked across state lines. Even though she was sweating through it, she lifted the collar of Cameron's shirt to her nose to try to smell the traces of him, to remind herself why she'd done it.

Corinne thought about Martin Luther King Jr.'s "Letter from a Birmingham Jail." When she'd first read it, she marveled at its beauty, but now she had more practical questions. How did he get the paper? How did he get the pen? Did he have a table to write at? Didn't his neck hurt? What did he do when he needed to edit it? Did he write with a pen or pencil? Did they even have Wite-Out in the '60s? Or did he write a perfect draft on the very first try?

She remembered Fannie Lou Hamer, the sharecropper who hadn't even finished middle school but had rocked the world. How she'd been beaten in prison—beyond recognition and almost to death. How they'd been desperate to shut her down and shut her up, but she had a voice that boomed through time. How she could rile a crowd with her singing as much as her speaking. When Corinne was in the fourth grade, she'd heard Fannie sing "Keep Your Eyes on the Prize" in a documentary, and she'd wanted to follow her into the screen. She thought about all the autobiographies she'd read on those nights she couldn't sleep: Anne Moody, Ethel Waters, John Lewis. The bomb threats and death threats and lynch mobs and prison sentences. All the times they'd said their final prayers. All the times those prayers had turned into song.

Corinne had never been a good singer, just passable. But right now, even as the walls echoed her voice back to her, she didn't care how she sounded. Just how she felt. And it felt good.

"This little light of mine, I'm gonna let it shine!
Let it shine, let it shine, let it shine!"

It occurred to her that there were so many stories she'd never get to read because no one had lived to tell them. Her sweat ran cold and got colder when she thought about how many of them had never even made it to her age. Her mind crowded with all the images from all the documentaries she'd watched in school or at home when Grandma had grown tired of her questions. She saw again the children who had packed the jails in Birmingham and in Mississippi. There was one little boy she saw again and again: he had stood in the front of a cell in the Jackson jail packed so full of children that there had only been room to stand. As the door shut to lock them in the dark, he had leaned back and folded his arms in stone-cold rebellion. The first time Corinne saw him, he had looked so brave, so fierce, that he barely looked like a child at all. She could see him so clearly now, she wished she had her sketch pad to draw him.

Now that she knew what a jail cell felt like, she realized there was no way those children weren't scared. "Fearlessness" was a myth. She wondered what happened when they got as thirsty as she was right now. She knew the guards didn't give them any water. Their cell didn't even have a fan. In this same Mississippi heat. She was grateful to be in a cell alone, with a toilet to herself, a buzzy light overhead, and a fan that barely worked. She wondered how long those children had stayed in jail, how they took care of each other, and whether their parents had understood. Or their grandparents.

Grandma hadn't gone to jail, but she had been one of those children too. She'd risked her life—braved mobs and death threats—to integrate the schools in Nashville. Grandma could write a book, but Corinne knew she never would. She barely even talked about it beyond mumbles and whispers and the occasional outburst. Corinne didn't remember how she'd found out about Grandma and the White Folks School. At times, it was like an open, guarded secret. At other times, it was like an open, festering wound.

When she was really little, Corinne had tried to ask about what it was like to live in the segregated South, but her questions were always clumsy: *"What's the difference between white and Black people?"* *"What did you think of your second-grade teacher?"* or *"Why did y'all go to different schools?"* Or the even more pedantic *"What was it* like?" Her questions had sent Grandma's shoulders straight up to her ears, and Mama had to rush to hush Corinne up and send her out of the room to play with her dolls. Now that she'd had people in Ohio asking her that same question about the South today, she was embarrassed she'd ever asked it that way.

When she'd gotten a bit older, after Mama had died and she'd moved in with Grandma, she'd crafted more careful, better questions: *"How scary was it to integrate the school?"* and *"What were you thinking when you walked through the mob?"* Most of the time, Grandma would deflect with a funny story from her childhood, like the time her cousin's dog married a duck or when her brother Gerald would steal all the pencils in the house to make an imaginary army. But other times Grandma would mutter a one-word answer and make her watch another documentary. The one time Corinne begged her to watch the movie with her, Grandma had hissed, *"I don't have to watch it! I lived it!"*

When Corinne won an award from the Mississippi Chapter of the NAACP for her essay about the 16th Street Baptist Church bombing in Birmingham, Grandma had asked her, *"You know they bombed a school in Nashville, don't you?"* No, Corinne hadn't known. *"Well, you never asked,"* Grandma had scolded.

She wondered if Grandma ever sang on her way to school the way those marching children did. Sometimes Corinne would catch her humming while she cooked or worked in her garden or sat alone on the back porch with her whiskey. She always assumed it was the Temptations or Roberta Flack or the Supremes or Sam Cooke, but maybe it wasn't. Corinne promised herself that the next time she heard her, she'd listen a little harder.

The bench became too hard for her bones, so Corinne got up to pace. The air felt a little freer at this height—less heavy, less putrid. She could tell that the sun had moved, but not exactly how far. Between the heat and the brightness, though, she figured it couldn't be any later than 2:00 p.m. She stood on the bench and tried to jump to see outside.

She almost fell down when the door behind her clattered open and there stood Officer Cain in a flood of light with a Black female officer beside him.

Undertow

August 5, 2014

When Harold woke up, his mouth tasted like he'd just thrown up, but when he looked around, he saw only beer cans. There was no time to tidy them, no time even for a proper breakfast. He was going to have to make do with the bag of peanuts he kept in the car.

All summer, he'd kept hoping Corinne would come to her senses. For the life of him, he couldn't understand how she figured her little act of defiance would be worth it. Best-case scenario, she'd torment the people closest to her. He couldn't even bring himself to think about the worst-case scenario. Either way, she was making a mess. It was like she went off to Ohio and forgot common sense. But when his alarm woke him up at 5:00 a.m. and there was no last-minute "never mind" text waiting on his phone, he knew he'd better hit the road.

He hurried out of the house like it was on fire and was on I-55 before the sun had finished rising. There would be no scenic routes today. No Highway 61, 19, or 33. He needed to get to Port Gibson quick, fast, and in a hurry. He didn't know who he was more worried about: Corinne and her foolish head or Mama with her foolish heart.

After a little more than an hour on the road, he saw the exit for Magnolia, Mississippi, and decided to stop for gas and a Gatorade. On his way down the exit ramp, he noticed the sign for the Confederate Cemetery. Harold rolled down his window to spit in the cemetery's general direction just to piss off the ghosts.

He wondered what would happen if one of them were to come back to life today. How all the roads and buildings and cars and technology would scare the holy hell out of them. How the mere sight of Harold driving a truck that he owned, to go wherever he wanted, would send them into a hissy fit. He imagined a Confederate general in his stiff, gray coat and long, ridiculous whiskers, scandalized into a seizure. In his head, the general would sound like Foghorn Leghorn: *"I say, I say, I do declare!"* Harold laughed aloud as he pulled into the Chevron station.

Inside the gas station, it smelled like fried chicken and potato logs. The blast of cold air from the refrigerator felt like the sweetest mercy. Harold lingered over the Gatorade choices: purple, red, green, yellow, blue, and light blue. He decided to choose blind. He closed his eyes and let his hand rest on Fruit Punch. Just as well.

When he went to pay for it, the short, dark-skinned woman with finger waves gave him a warm smile that revealed a gold tooth at the front. He started to smile back, but then he remembered he'd forgotten to brush his teeth. He picked up a pack of gum instead.

"You have a good one, now!" she sang as he walked out the door.

"You, too, baby!"

As he walked back to his truck, he tried to smile at the tall, portly white man pumping gas into a beat-up red Chevrolet Impala. But the man looked past Harold, out to the road, almost like he had X-ray vision. Harold looked a little closer and saw a Confederate flag sticker on his back window. This guy, Harold decided, was probably the great-great-grandson of the Confederate general he'd just imagined. The thought made his whole fantasy far less amusing. He pumped his gas and got back on the interstate as fast as he could.

For the rest of the drive, he kept expecting his phone to ring. Every ten minutes or so, he'd glance over at it, praying it would make a sound, vibrate—something. He'd promised Mama last night that he'd be there in the morning. If everything had gone to plan, Corinne would have left by now with her little ragtag crew and their half-baked scheme.

He had half a mind to call home, but what if they'd slept so soundly that neither had noticed when the car from New Orleans had come to pick Corinne up this morning? What if they hadn't heard the doorbell or the knocking? What if the New Orleans crew had been forced to go to Vicksburg without his niece? What if they were all rotting in jail while Corinne was still sound asleep? He could just waltz into the house and wake them up with a pot of coffee and tell them how silly they'd been.

Mama and Corinne's relationship had always been marked by unspoken expectations and unspeakable disappointments. Tensions that simmered until they exploded. *That's part of what happens*, he thought, *when your granddaughter is born a grown woman*. Harold hated it, but he didn't know how to fix it. All he knew how to do was be there. He loved them enough to see how much they loved each other, even if they were bad at it. He just wished they could make room for each other. A love that walked on eggshells couldn't stand.

It was tempting to write off their dysfunction as a grandmother and granddaughter so similar they were bound to clash. But that was too simple. The truth was Mama and Corinne *wanted* to be more similar than they were. And the things that made them different were the things that terrified them. Corinne's courage scared Mama. Mama's angst scared Corinne. Both looked at each other and saw what could be or could have been. Corinne was scared of hurting Mama, and Mama was scared of losing Corinne. They didn't know how to talk about it, so they took it out on each other in outbursts— with Harold in the middle, drawn and quartered.

But they meant the world to him.

After a blur of a drive, he pulled into Mama's driveway. Only then did he realize he'd made it the whole trip without any music, no sound at all. He'd never driven all the way home without even the news on in the car. He turned the ignition off, took a deep breath, and went toward the back door. He expected to find his mother slumped in her bed, sobbing and rocking. Or draped in black, lighting candles on her altar, now overtaken with pictures of Corinne, with Cameron and Yvonne and his grandparents pushed to the back. Instead, he found Mama sitting on her swinging bench in the backyard, smoking a cigarette and laughing one of her deep reverberating cackles. Her eyes were closed and her whole body was shaking. *Great*, he thought. *She's finally lost it.*

He walked over to her slowly, like he was afraid of startling a bird. She saw him when he was halfway across the yard, just in front of the vegetable garden, and she didn't get up to hug his neck like usual.

"Harold!" She smiled. "Come sit with me, son!" She patted the open seat on the bench next to her.

"I ever tell you about the time Grandma Cindy got them ducks drunk?" She took his hand in between hers after he sat down.

"Tell me again," he said with a wary smile. She had told him, over and over, but he liked the story. And he knew she only told it when she was in a good mood.

Mama started to talk but then busted out laughing so hard she almost choked on her cigarette. Then she took a deep breath. "So Grandma Cindy used to make home brew—that's what they used to call beer that you made in your house."

Harold nodded. One day, he'd tell her about the times he'd tried and failed to make his own home brew, but he didn't want to interrupt.

"Well, this time, she thought it didn't smell quite right, thought it was a bad batch. So she poured it out in the backyard to get rid of it." Mama choked back another laugh. "Next thing she knew, she looked out in the backyard and there were all these ducks laid out. She thought they were dead. And, you know, she felt bad for killing all the ducks, but she figured she'd feel worse if she let them go to waste, so she came out and plucked off their feathers to make some pillows."

"By dinnertime"—Mama was crying now—"Grandma Cindy looked out here and there was a whole slew of naked ducks walking 'round in this yard." She gestured right in front of them. She finally doubled over in laughter.

Harold laughed with her, but more out of relief that he hadn't found his mother broken and beside herself. When she'd finally gathered herself, Harold asked, "Corinne here?" He was hanging on to the faintest sliver of hope.

"No." Mama sat back up straight. "She took off to Vicksburg. They picked her up hours ago, but you knew that, didn't you?"

"Yeah, I knew she was supposed to go, but I was hoping maybe she didn't." Harold could hardly believe how calm his mother was. "You been sitting out here this whole time?"

"Where else would I go?" She took one more drag on the cigarette and then turned to look Harold in the eye. "Let's go on and get you fed. It's going to be a long, long day."

—

Harold and Mama watched the phone like hawks for word from Vicksburg. Corinne had been arrested around 8:00 a.m., Daphne called to tell them. She said that they expected her to

stay in for about three hours and that it was all under control. She even promised to bring Corinne home as soon as she
was out. But when the clock struck 12:00 p.m. and the phone
hadn't rung again, Harold texted Daphne that they were on
their way. He didn't see the response until they were pulling
out of the driveway.

Daphne: Okay

"You know sometimes I think I just about failed," Mama
said as soon as they were out of Port Gibson's city limits.

"What are you talking about, Mama?"

"It's just . . . I lost Yvonne, I lost Cameron, and now look
at Corinne! Just about *throwing* her life away."

"You know that girl's always had a hard head, Mama."
Harold tried to be comforting, but he hated when she got like
this. She saw everything as a reaction to her. It was like she
thought she had superpowers.

"But then what about Yvonne and Cameron?"

"Mama, those were *accidents*! And, yeah, they were awful
and I don't understand why they keep happening to us either,
but they're not your *fault*!"

"But there had to be *something* I could have done." Her
voice cracked on the last word.

"Mama." Harold reached out for her hand. "First of all,
we don't know what's going to happen today. Cori might be
just fine and go on and live all those dreams you dreamed
for her." He paused. "Or maybe she has different dreams. But

if you failed, then what am I? I'm just as much your son as Yvonne was your daughter and as Cameron was your grandson. And I'm still here. Do it look like I'm going somewhere?"

"No, but you hauled off to New Orleans!" She chuckled through her sniffle.

"Mama, I went to *New Orleans*, not the *moon*." He laughed. "Plus you know good and damn well you don't want me in your house, woman! All up under you. We'd be done drove each other up the wall."

"You know I really do appreciate you, and I *am* proud of you," Mama said softly.

"Aww, woman! Don't you go getting sentimental on me!" Harold didn't know if he had the emotional energy for this right now.

"I'm being serious, Harold! I don't tell you enough how good of a son you are. You always have been. I don't know what I'd do without you."

Harold blinked back a tear. He hadn't known how much he needed to hear that. "I love you, too, Mama." He pulled her hand closer and kissed it.

Mama squeezed his hand back and let out a sigh. "Why did she have to go off and do this?"

"I haven't the faintest idea, Mama." Harold shrugged. "But maybe it's not for us to understand. Maybe it's just for us to accept?"

"Accept her throwing away her life over a damn bridge?" Mama shrieked. "There are things I can forgive but can't accept, Harold. That girl has put us through hell."

"Okay, Mama." He smiled on the side of his face she couldn't see. Mama didn't forgive easily. This was progress.

When they pulled up to the Vicksburg jail, they saw Daphne and Alex waiting outside of a silver station wagon with two other white people Harold didn't recognize. They almost looked like they were at a tailgating party. As soon as he parked his truck, Harold barreled through the midday humidity straight toward them with Mama close behind. When they saw him, all four of them stood at attention, putting away their coffee cups. And when the white boy reached out to shake his hand and introduce himself, Harold swatted it away and went straight for Alex.

"How y'all out here and Corinne ain't?" Harold was breathing so hard it sounded like a growl. He was so angry he could barely see straight, until he looked at Daphne, who looked like she had the whole world in her belly.

"Harold." Daphne's voice was gentle, soothing. But neither Harold nor Mama returned her careful smile. "We don't know why she's still in there. They haven't let me talk to her, but I called the lawyer, and he said to call him back if she wasn't out by five."

"*Five o'clock?*" Mama hurled the words back at her.

"It's twelve forty-five now," Harold reminded her. "Plus, that still don't answer my question: How am I looking at these two white boys and not my niece?" He looked directly at Alex and hissed, "*Where is Corinne?*"

"She's inside." Alex was doing that "calm down" motion with his hands that white boys do when they're scared of Black men. "I don't know why they let us out and not her—except we all know why. They didn't book me and Mercer here." He gestured to the teenager Harold wasn't interested in knowing. "They drove us around for a little bit before they let Mercer call his father, kept us just long enough for the sheriff here to talk to the sheriff there."

"They were out in about an hour." Daphne was staring down at the parking lot gravel.

Harold fixed his eyes on Mercer. "You forget to tell your daddy you had somebody else with you? Somebody's granddaughter? Somebody's niece?"

Mercer rose from his slump against the car, and Harold noticed he was the only one who wasn't eating. "No, I told him about Corinne. He said he was going to call to have her let out too."

"Well?" Mama's voice was high-pitched now. "And?"

"And he said he'd call for her too. I'm just as confused as you are that she's still in there!"

"Oh, you *confused*?" Harold asked sarcastically. "Well then, that's half the problem right there."

"I'm not confused," Mercer admitted. "I'm frustrated. I'll call my father back right now. Maybe he needs to call again." He pulled out his phone and stepped away.

"You do that." Mama cocked her head to the side.

"I'm really sorry about all this." Daphne came closer to them and whispered, "We really are doing everything we can, but there's parts of it we can't control."

Harold could feel his heart rate slow. He knew she was right, and it was nearly impossible to stay mad at a pregnant woman in this kind of heat. As he looked at the sweat on Daphne's temples, he realized he probably shouldn't have Mama out in the heat much longer. He wrapped his arm around her shoulder and guided her back to the truck.

"Come on, Mama. Let's go sit in some air."

"I'll let y'all know as soon as we hear something," Daphne called after them. "I promise."

Just as soon as he closed the door to the truck, Mama handed him a cigarette and a lighter before he could even turn the air conditioner on. They smoked their cigarettes in silence with the door closed and the windows up. Harold turned on the public radio station, and they both went into their private worlds.

As the smoke swirled around him, Harold wondered what Cameron would think of Corinne doing all of this in his name. Cameron had never been one for politics or protest. Mama even had to force him to register to vote. Harold could still hear her screaming at her grandson about the people who had died for his right to the ballot, and she'd be damned if he didn't use it. Cameron would probably think Corinne was doing it for the attention. But to be fair, that was why Cameron thought Corinne did everything. According to him, Corinne read books for attention, made the honor roll for attention, washed dishes for attention, braided her hair for attention, went to college for attention. In the past, Cameron's incessant taunting of his little sister had exhausted Harold. Right now, he'd give anything to have Cameron tell them that Corinne was self-centered and ridiculous, even if it wasn't true.

Harold had always seen himself in his nephew. They'd both loved working with their hands, for one thing. When Cameron had gone to work on the oil boat, it had reminded Harold of how much his nephew had loved being on his fishing boat. He missed taking him fishing out on the creeks, smoking weed, and sitting in silence. He missed calling his nephew at halftime during the Saints games. He missed taking him to the games at Alcorn and yelling at the field until they were hoarse. He'd watched his nephew grow into his anger and had wanted to watch him grow out of it. Now, Harold wished he'd tried a little harder to get him out of his funk. Maybe that would have kept him off the boat, put him on a different boat, or even helped him keep his feet steady during the storm.

Harold was so lost in his memories that he didn't see Daphne approaching with a giant smile on her face. When she knocked on his window, he nearly jumped out of his skin. Then Mama nearly choked on her cigarette as she tapped him on his elbow and pointed toward the door of the brick building. There was Corinne, small and proud, in the doorway.

His breathing stalled, and all the resentment and anger that had built in his chest floated away. He got out of the truck as though he were in a trance. He couldn't take his eyes off Corinne. He saw so much of her mother in her, it could have knocked him over. The sister he had shared secrets and jokes and scars with. The one he had teased and fussed and fought with, the sister he'd fought over. Harold would have done anything to bring Yvonne back. And seeing Corinne there, he finally understood why she'd done what she did for the brother she'd lost.

When Corinne saw him and Mama, her face flashed from stunned to embarrassed. She paused before she walked toward them. As she approached, Harold saw time cascade as her face morphed into the many versions of her he'd known: her screaming baby face, her petulant toddler face, her self-conscious preteen face. And now, she'd fully taken on Yvonne's face. *That's the thing about having children in your life*, Harold thought. *It forces you to confront the realities and surrealities of time.* She'd never looked so beautiful and he'd never felt more proud.

"Come here, baby!" Mama stretched out her arms. Harold watched as Corinne and Mama melted into each other. Their embrace was different this time. Now, Corinne was holding Mama, not the other way around. He'd wanted so badly to protect his niece, but now he saw that, though she was still precious, Corinne had outgrown the limits of his protection. And it hurt.

When Corinne let Mama go and came over to him, he held and rocked her like he had when she was still a little baby girl.

He wanted to tell her how proud he was, that he knew her mother would be too. That he'd always known she had a lot in her, but not quite this much. But instead he said, "Go on and say your goodbyes. Let's go home."

AFTER THE STORM

August 5, 2014

Corinne opened her eyes slowly, like she didn't trust them. It took a few moments to accept that she was, indeed, lying in a bed and not on a bench. It took her even longer to recognize it was *her* bed, in *her* room, in Grandma's house. As she sat up, she relished the comfort of her books and pictures and stuffed animals.

She had to concentrate to distinguish between what was real, what she had made up in her dreams, and what was left over from the very real nightmare that had happened earlier that day. Yes, she remembered, she really had broken the law today. Yes, she really had been arrested and had sat in a jail for upward of six hours. No, it hadn't stopped the oil boats or the refineries or global warming. Yes, it had been worth it.

Miss Daphne had promised her that whatever had been put on her record today could get taken off, but Corinne didn't care about that anymore. She cared about the general principle. She was glad that Miss Daphne had said that in front of Grandma, though, because she'd been convinced that Corinne would get kicked out of Oberlin if she had a record. She hadn't believed Corinne, but for whatever reason, she trusted Miss Daphne.

When she picked up her phone, Corinne saw she had more text messages than she cared to read. Some from Mercer, some from Cleo, Ashley, and Marcus. Some even from her coworkers at the museum. *Word moves around Vicksburg faster than it does on Twitter*, she thought. She didn't open them because she didn't want to find out whether she was fired. She looked for a message from Daphne and, of course, there it was.

Daphne: You doing okay? I'm proud of you. Call me whenever.

Corinne felt her resentment melt away, and she wrote back.

Corinne: I'm okay. Thank you for everything. I'll call you in the morning. Hope you made it back to New Orleans all right.

Outside, the sun had begun to fall, creating beautiful ribbons of orange and purple in the sky. She'd napped much longer than she'd planned to.

She hadn't slept much at all the night before, or the night before that. She couldn't remember the last time she had slept the whole night through. Certainly not since Cameron died. From their own admissions on the quiet, smoky car ride back home from Vicksburg, Grandma and Uncle Harold hadn't been sleeping so well this summer either. So, when they'd gotten home, they'd all gone to their separate rooms to lie down.

Before that, though, Corinne noticed that the noxious tension that used to hang in the air had been replaced with a sweetness Corinne had never known. It felt like they each remembered how precious—and fragile—they all were. And so they'd moved around each other gingerly and spoken to each other gently.

As soon as Corinne had seen the smiles on Grandma and Uncle Harold's faces in the parking lot, all the guilt and fear she'd built up inside the jail washed away. Now she felt triumphant, taller even.

When Corinne opened her bedroom door, Grandma's cackle and Uncle Harold's howl pulled her into the kitchen.

"So, Harold." Grandma was wheezing. "Gerald would bring out the hose and just run it all over the front yard! And then Dandy would chase the water! 'Cause he didn't know what it was!"

Corinne recognized the story. It was another one of the ones Grandma told her whenever she asked about her childhood. She'd go on and on about Dandy, the best dog on earth, and how her brothers used to play with him all day, but he would only sleep in her room because he loved her the best. Or about how Uncle Bobby would put on whistling concerts, and she and her cousins had to try not to laugh in the middle of them. Or about the baby chickens her father would bring home from the post office, and how they'd cause pandemonium around the house. Or all the shady things Grandma's mama—who'd died before Corinne was old enough to remem-

ber her—would whisper to her when they visited other people's houses: *"I wouldn't wear that to a dog fight."* Or *"That
dress is tighter than Jack's hat band."* Or *"Pass me a piece of
that tacky little cake."*

Corinne loved those stories. She loved how happy Grandma
was when she told them. She could tell that they were like a
trapdoor to escape from the more painful parts of her childhood. Corinne had seen pictures of Dandy, and she knew he
was a German shepherd, just like the police dogs they'd used on
children in Birmingham. When she'd visited the park across the
street from 16th Street Baptist Church, she'd seen the sculptures
that showed the size and scale of the dogs the police had used to
terrify children. Corinne was sixteen, and the sculptures placed
the snarling snouts at her collarbone. They must have towered
over the children, but they went anyway. Day after day. She
wondered if there had been dogs outside of the school Grandma
integrated. But she knew better than to ask. At least not tonight.

When Grandma saw her lurking in the kitchen door, she
tilted her head sarcastically to one side. "Well, look who woke
up from the dead!" she said.

"We been waiting on you!" Uncle Harold teased. "If it
ain't our very own little Fannie Lou Hamer!"

"No," Grandma said with a smile, a tear glimmering in
her eye. "She gets that from *my* daddy. Her *great*-granddaddy."

"Y'all not mad?" Corinne was confused, and she must
have looked it.

"Naw, we not mad, little girl. Too glad to have you in one
piece to be mad." Uncle Harold kissed her hard on the cheek

and pulled her in close for another of his rocking hugs. "We're proud of you."

"Really?"

"Girl, yeah!" Harold assured her. "We got a few phone calls about you and your little Thriller on the River, though. Half of town laughing their heads off wondering what the hell you thought you was doing. Mr. Rob across the street called over here wondering if it was all about oil, why you didn't go after the gas station. So you might got some explaining to do."

"Of course I didn't think that. Nothing that big ever comes down that easy," Corinne muttered. "Nobody ever asked why racism didn't come tumbling down after the March on Washing—"

"Okay, Corinne!" Grandma waved her hand at her. "We get it. You don't have to explain yourself to anybody. We love you anyway."

"Grandma, *you* not mad?" It wasn't like Grandma to pass up a good moment to tell her she'd told her so.

"No, I'm not mad, baby," Grandma said softly. "You hungry?"

Corinne had to think about it. She hadn't eaten since morning, but she was surprised to find that she was still, in fact, full.

"No. But I'll eat if you want me to."

"It's fine, suit yourself. But why don't you get yourself a glass of tea and come out on the back porch with us. It's cool enough now." Grandma picked up her cigarettes and whiskey and headed for the back door.

"Okay," Corinne whispered, still in shock. Grandma was so calm, so cheerful, it was almost eerie.

"And, Corinne?"

"Yeah?"

"There's two photo albums sitting out on my dresser. One of them is pink and brown, the other is green and brown. Bring them when you come out, you hear?"

Corinne nodded as she poured herself a glass of tea. When she went into Grandma's room, she saw the two albums Grandma described and realized she'd never seen them before. Grandma was usually obsessive about her photo albums—both maintaining and sharing them. She would take them out like they were old friends and carefully point out distant relations to try to make sure Corinne knew her family. But these looked like they hadn't been touched in ages. Their edges were fraying and the plastic from the pages inside was coming loose. Corinne picked them up carefully for fear they'd turn to dust.

When Corinne went out back, the sun had gone pretty much all the way down. Grandma and Uncle Harold had the overhead light on, even though they usually sat in the dark and watched the fireflies.

Grandma patted the empty chair next to her. "Come here, baby girl." She hadn't called her that in years. When Corinne handed her the photo albums, Grandma held up her hand to refuse them. "No," she said. "I want you to open them. The green one first."

Corinne set her drink down on the table between her and her grandmother. When she opened the green book, she saw a brownish newspaper clipping from the *Nashville Banner*. It was dated August 27, 1957, but it had held together remarkably well. The headline read: "80 White Children Out to Make Way for 2 Negroes at Glenn Elementary." The black-and-white picture showed a Black man clutching the hands of two little girls as he crossed the street in front of a white woman who looked like a crossing guard on a residential street.

Grandma leaned over her and pointed to the little girl on the man's right, closest to the white woman. "You know who that is?" she asked softly.

Corinne felt a chill over her whole body. She looked from the picture up to Grandma's pained smile. "Is that you?"

"Mm-hmm." Grandma took a drag on her cigarette and then exhaled. "That's me, all right."

Corinne looked closer at the picture. The little girl wore a plaid dress that came down past her knees. Her hair had been greased, pressed straight, and styled into pigtails with bangs. In her right hand, she clutched a folded piece of paper. Corinne couldn't tell if the paper looked gigantic because of Grandma's tiny frame or if it was actually larger than usual. Little girl Grandma was wincing away from the crossing guard, holding the folded sheet of paper up like a shield.

"You were so *little*!" Corinne couldn't hide her horror.

"I was five," Grandma said, staring out into the backyard toward her hummingbird garden.

Corinne's throat went dry. She'd known that Grandma had been a child when she went to the White Folks School, but she didn't know she'd been *that* young. She thought she must have been in middle school, or at least third grade. But *five years old*?

"Is that your daddy?" She hovered her finger over the man walking next to her.

"No, that's Mr. Griffith. Jackie Faye's daddy. They lived next door. He was taking us to school that day."

Corinne felt a strange mix of horror and joy. She'd dreamed of the day Grandma would tell her these stories. She looked over at Uncle Harold, and he looked just as shocked.

She chose her next question carefully. "Were you scared?"

"Mama, we don't have to talk about this tonight." Uncle Harold watched her closely, like he was ready to take a bullet for her.

"It's okay, Harold." Grandma turned her eyes away from the darkness that had overtaken the backyard and looked at her son. "I want to talk about it. And she needs to know. She *deserves* to know." She breathed deep before turning to Corinne again. Her voice cracked as she said, "Yes, I was scared. More scared than I've ever been in my whole life, then or since. Before I went to that school, I barely knew what white people were. I barely knew what hatred was. I definitely didn't know anyone hated *me*." She took another drag of her cigarette. "But it wasn't like that the whole time.

After a couple of weeks, one of the schools got bombed, and then things calmed down. It didn't get *easy* after that, but those big old mobs weren't out there anymore."

"When did y'all decide you were going to do it?" Corinne made her voice as soft as she could.

"*Decide?* I didn't have a choice, Corinne." Grandma's voice went up an octave. "I didn't *decide*; I *found out*. And you're looking at the moment I found out right there. I found out when I went to that school, when I saw those lunatics waiting for me."

Corinne looked at the second black-and-white picture farther down on the page, where there was a sea of white people so pale it was hard to tell where one face began and another ended. Their mouths were snarled and their nostrils flared. Their eyes were narrow like a snake's and their veins popped out of their temples. They had signs that said "Keep Our Schools White KKK" and "Honor, Fight, Save the Whites" and "What God Has Put Asunder, Let No Man Bring Together."

Corinne had seen pictures like it a million times, and somewhere in her mind she knew that Grandma had faced mobs like this. But she had imagined Grandma much older, much bigger, much badder, with her shoulders slid back, head high, marching into that crowd proud and defiant. Corinne had always imagined a brave little girl. But here on this page, she could only see a scared little girl.

"Your parents didn't tell you what you were about to do?" Corinne asked breathlessly. "Y'all never talked about it?"

"What was there to talk about, Cori?" Corinne could see

that Grandma was trying—really trying—to be patient. "It wasn't like I could argue with them. Daddy had decided this was what I was going to do, so that's what I did. We talked about it some after it had already kicked off, but that was more because Daddy always wanted me to be the best. He wanted me to *show* those white kids. Every time I got anything wrong, he'd get the strap and just tear me up. Tell me I wasn't trying hard enough. That I was letting those white folks beat me after all he did to get me into that school. It took a long time for us to get past that. A *long* time."

"Did he ever . . ." Corinne paused. "Did he ever say he was sorry?" Corinne thought about the pressure Grandma put on her and Cameron to get good grades and go to college. It seemed so frivolous now. She couldn't imagine having the weight of the race placed on her shoulders in elementary school.

"He did." Grandma let out a wry laugh.

"What kind of father . . ." Corinne couldn't get the question out.

"He was a *good* father, Corinne. You hear me? A good one. You don't know what it was like to live in that world. Even I don't know what it was like for *him*, growing up in Mississippi in the 1920s and '30s. He didn't want me to know. He didn't want *you* to know. That's why he did what he did. My daddy was a good father and a brave man."

Corinne still didn't understand how her great-grandfather could spring something like that on his five-year-old daughter, but she could tell she was hitting a nerve.

"What about Grandma?" Harold asked.

"She didn't give me a warning either, if that's what you're asking, but she wasn't as hard on me as Daddy was. She tried to calm him down." Grandma paused. "Mama was my rock. She was the one who insisted they send me to a Black middle school. She saw the toll it was taking on me."

Corinne tried to think of a more artful follow-up question, but all that came out was, "What kind of toll?"

"My personality changed." Grandma looked out to the hummingbird garden again. "I used to be real talkative, outgoing. I used to laugh a lot. Made friends easy. But then I just shrank into myself. I started to be nervous all the time. I started to stutter, and that made Daddy even angrier, so I nearly stopped talking altogether. Every little sound, every movement somebody would make near me would just make me jump out of my skin."

Watching Grandma wince, it occurred to Corinne that Black women—celebrated the world over for their extraordinary ability to bend and bend and bend—can, in fact, break. Into a million little shards. And no one would come to put them back together again. Corinne wiped the tear from her eye and went to sit at her grandmother's feet to better gaze at her face. If she squinted, she could see the little girl from the picture in Grandma's face today.

"What kinds of things happened, Grandmama?"

"You know, it's hard to talk about." She breathed deeply. Corinne didn't breathe at all. "For one thing, it was lonely, but at the same time, I stood out. I couldn't blend in or escape. I did everything alone—played alone at recess, ate lunch alone.

Everything. And there were Black lunch ladies who tried to make it easier. They'd save me extra treats like chocolate milk 'cause they knew I'd be the last one to come through the line. But the other kids were just . . . I guess they just didn't know how to react to me. I wasn't what they expected. You know, they were expecting somebody like Buckwheat. You know who Buck-wheat was, right?"

Corinne nodded. She remembered seeing him once when *The Little Rascals* had played on that black-and-white chan-nel Grandma liked. He was such a caricature that it turned Corinne's stomach, but Grandma didn't even react. "But the other kids didn't play pranks on you? Tease you?"

"Not as much as you might think. It was more that they just acted like I wasn't even there. It was like they talked through me." She paused. "But there was that one little white-trash boy who spat on me. I remember that."

"What happened?"

"This was sometime in the third grade, and the teacher left the classroom for something. And this little asshole, who wore the same pair of pants every damn day, stood up and yelled, 'The teacher's gone now! Let's jump on her!'"

"What did the other students do?"

"One of the other white boys said something like, 'No, leave her alone. My daddy said she's special.' But that little piece of trash still managed to get up close to me and spat right on my face."

"And what did you do?" Corinne wanted to go back in time and fight that little boy.

"I told the teacher, and she let me go call Mama. And Mama had him suspended. When he came back, he never spoke to me again."

There was a long pause as Corinne and Uncle Harold watched Grandma's face, but she kept staring out into the backyard. Corinne thought about asking another question but didn't want to push Grandma too far. Finally, it was Harold who punctured the silence.

"How old were you when you stopped?" Harold asked.

"After the fourth grade," she said with a sigh. "That was four years at that school. Longest years of my life. I'd never wish that on my worst enemy. Except I'd wish it on those people who stood outside yelling and spitting at me and Jackie Faye." She paused. "You know, we were *children*! They just looked like *demons* to us."

"With all that, it's a wonder you managed to pass your classes," Corinne said. She tried to imagine learning her times tables in that atmosphere. "What were the teachers like? Were they nice to you?"

Grandma let out a wry laugh. "No, indeed. And a couple of them did try to hold me back a year, but Daddy wasn't having that." She paused a moment. "You know, I wish I could tell you the sorts of things they said, but I honestly don't remember. It's like I can see their mouths move, but I can't hear the words. I just know it made me feel bad. Real bad."

"I'm so sorry, Grandmama." Corinne reached up for her grandmother's hand and kissed it. "I'm so sorry."

"Don't you be sorry, baby." Grandma moved her hand to Corinne's chin and tilted her face upward. "I did it for you. I know I said I didn't have a choice, and that's true. I didn't. But the thing that kept me going was knowing that at least my daughter wouldn't have to do this. But now here my *grand-daughter* has to do it, and . . . I just can't help but feel like I let you down. You weren't supposed to have to carry this burden. I'm telling you all this as a way of saying . . . *I'm* sorry."

"No! Grandmama! No, you didn't let me down!" She kissed her hand again, furiously. "You're the reason I *can* do what I did today. It's because of you that I can go to a school like Oberlin across the country and not . . . be *afraid*. I'm so proud of you. I'll *always* be proud of you. And . . . I'm . . . I'm so *grateful*." She laid her head in her grandmother's lap, and the tears came flooding out. "Thank you, thank you," she whispered again and again. There was something liberating about finally being able to say those words and mean them.

"You're welcome," Grandma whispered as she stroked Corinne's hair. For a moment, only the crickets and the frogs filled the air as the two of them swayed in the breeze together.

Finally, Corinne pulled back and looked up. Grandma reached down to wipe the tears from her granddaughter's eyes before she cupped her face. She felt a roughness on Grandma's fingers she'd never noticed before. She remembered Grandma's hands as she cut the butter into the bowl of flour as they made breakfast that morning. The same way she had for years, but with more intention, like it was fortification itself. She remembered her shuffling around the kitchen with less grace, more gray hair, more wrinkles. Breathing heavier than she used to.

"I never told you all this because, well, it *hurts*, but also because you were never supposed to know. But now I know that you need to know." She sighed. "I know you did what you thought was the right thing to do today, Cori. I don't all the way understand it, but I'm proud of you anyway, and I need you to know that too."

"I know, Grandmama." Corinne placed her hands on top of Grandma's. "I guess I avoided talking to you about it too much 'cause I didn't want you to worry, and I felt like you'd already been through enough . . . I figured this was *my* battle, and I didn't want to drag you into it. I wanted to show you that I had it too."

"That's just the thing, Cori. There's no such thing as 'it.' I know everybody wants to think the kids who went into those schools were so courageous, never felt an ounce of fear. And maybe that was true for some of them. But it wasn't for me. I couldn't pretend it was easy, so I just pretended it never happened." Grandma pursed her lips. "You remember when you got that poster of Ruby Bridges?"

"Yes, ma'am." Corinne's stomach sank as she thought about the memories that poster must have brought back for Grandma.

"I'm sorry I reacted like that, but the reason I did it is because . . . when most people see that painting, they see a brave little girl, but when I look at it, all I see is those marshals at her side, and I have to wonder . . . where the fuck were they when I was going to school? When those white folks were screaming in my face? Threatening to tie me up by my shoelaces? Threatening to kill my mama and my daddy in front of me? Measuring my pastor for a casket? They were burning crosses and hanging Black men in effigy—hell, they bombed a school to bits—and not once did the U.S. Marshals or the National Guard or any-fucking-body come to Nashville!"

"Fucking cowards." Harold spat out his beer.

"Corinne." Grandma looked her in the eye. "I hope you know that whether you win or lose, if this world does come to an end, it's the white folks that did it. We been trying to wake them people up ever since we got to this country, ever since we laid eyes on them, and it's . . . it's on them. I don't want you to fall into that trap of trying to save white folks, 'cause you'll run yourself ragged. You can't save nobody from themselves, you understand me?"

"Yes, ma'am." Corinne nodded.

"Truth be told, there was a small part of me that was trying to do that even back then, even before I knew much of anything about white folks. When I was walking through those mobs shouting and spitting and throwing eggs on me. They were so worked up into a frenzy like that at *children*. They looked scary, *evil*, but they also just looked like somebody in *pain*. I just couldn't believe that the sight of little five-year-old me and Jackie Faye could drive somebody to *that*. I guess I just felt sorry for them."

Uncle Harold nearly choked on his cigarette. "*You* felt sorry for *them*? You better than me."

"I know it sounds crazy. Believe me, I know. But those people looked like they were in a prison more terrifying than anything I'd ever wind up in. It was like watching an elephant run from a mouse. Just didn't make sense. And they were the ones with all the power. That got clearer as I went through school, and it was crystal clear by the time I left. So I knew if I wanted to save myself and the people I loved, I was going to have to save them, too, whether I liked it or not. Whether I liked *them* or not."

"Grandmama," Corinne whispered after a pause. "Believe it or not, that's exactly how I feel about global warming. I know it might not look like it, but I couldn't care less about saving these white folks. If I could save Black people—if I could save *us*—without saving them, I would. In a heartbeat. But I can't."

"Now, that I believe." Grandma chuckled and then sighed. "You know how they say history repeats itself? Sometimes I wonder if that's really true or if it's just that white folks never learn. And since white folks are the ones who get to write history, it just looks like it's repeating itself."

The three of them stayed up later than they ever had, until just before dawn. Grandma showed Corinne and Uncle Harold pictures they'd never seen, told stories they'd never heard, bared the scars she'd never shown. She told them about the really bad days at the beginning of first grade, about waking up in the arms of a neighbor as he carried her next door because it was too dangerous in her bed. She told them how her mother lost ten pounds in the first month and her father started parking the car behind the house so no one could put a bomb in it. She told them about her mother getting fired from her job at PET Milk and going to work at Fisk.

She told them about the bombing at Hattie Cotton Elementary School and how the mobs went away after that. But the bombing had also made Jackie Faye's parents take her out of the school, leaving Grandma all alone. At the same time, no more mobs had meant no more national press—no more photographers jumping in her face demanding to know, *"Which one of you is Cora?"*—and that left her alone in a whole other way. She never met any of the other children who integrated the other schools.

She told them about the stale tension that had lingered for years after the bombing. She told them about the second-grade play and picture day. She told them about walking home alone after the mobs had disappeared and her lingering fear of being followed home. About how her classmates were afraid to be outright evil because their parents wanted to think of themselves as civil and they didn't want to be a headline in a northern newspaper, so they found subtle ways to let her know she wasn't welcome.

The three of them sat together, troubled by the weight of history and the messiness of the truth. Corinne would never see her grandmother the same way again. This was the first time she'd ever truly seen her. She finally saw the trauma behind her family drama, and she began to understand the depth of words like *forgiveness* and *sorrow* and *regret* and *love*.

After many drinks and tears, hugs, and curses, Grandma stood. "Come on, y'all. That's enough. Let's go in before these mosquitoes eat us all the way up."

When Corinne rose from the floor, she felt lighter than she ever had. She looked into Grandma's bloodshot eyes and saw herself reflected. The two of them held hands all the way to the back door and left Uncle Harold to lock it behind them.

For the first time in a decade, Corinne slept in Grandma's bed, her arms wrapped around her shoulders like a cape. Before they surrendered to sleep, she leaned over Grandma's ear and whispered, "Grandmama, would you do it again?"

"Yes," Grandma whispered back and kissed Corinne's hand. "Again and again. But only for you."

After the Word

On August 27, 1955, Mahlon Jerome Griffith and Mary Clyde (Syler) Griffith braved angry, throbbing mobs to register their youngest daughter, Jacqueline Faye, for the first grade at Glenn Elementary School in East Nashville, Tennessee. Two years earlier, in 1955, they'd tried to do the same thing with their eldest child, Belinda Julia, my mother. A few years later, in 1959, they sent their youngest child, Harvey Steven, to Glenn as well.

You see, there are ways in which this story was writing itself before I was born.

I was named after my grandmother, who died before she got to meet any of her grandchildren. When Granddaddy heard I was named for her, he cried. He never cried. When I learned who she was, I finally had a name for that protective presence I felt all around me: Grandmama.

Since I was a small child, I remember hearing that my grandfather was a great man, an "activist." When I tried to find out more about what that meant—including by asking him directly—I got either terse bits and pieces or explosive reprimands for questioning my elders and digging up painful memories. They told me to watch a movie, read a book, so I did. Once or twice, I even caught glimpses of them in documentaries—quick clips of Grandmama clutching Aunt

Jackie's hand as she guided her down the school stairs. But I never saw their names in a book. Thus, family history functioned like a family mystery.

Like Corinne, I committed to what I call "climate work"—taking a firm, unflinching look at the climate crisis and dedicating my talents to solving it—in 2014. I, however, have never, ever been as brave as Corinne. My commitment was from a desk, crafting advocacy and editing policy. Through years of doing that, I found myself alarmed by the ever-worsening projections and bewildered by the nonchalance all around me—including from (mostly white) colleagues in my own field. Were they not seeing the same data I was seeing? Did they not live on the same planet? I grew tired of the "best practices" for climate communications that never seemed to work and dominant narratives that were nothing more than assumptions.

So, I set out to destroy them.

I started writing and publishing essays on my own. I tweeted, lectured, podcasted, taught. All the while, trying to deconstruct the mythology that kept us from having honest conversations about the crisis in front of us.

One of the most insidious, bedeviling, and outrageous narratives I heard went something like this: "our grandparents and great-grandparents didn't know what they were doing when they got us into this mess." I heard it everywhere: in blogs, at rallies, in speeches. And every time, it hit me like a brick. Whose grandparents and great-grandparents were they talking about? Certainly not mine. My great-grandparents were trying to get land to farm as they saw fit and pass on to their children. My grandparents were fighting for full citizenship. None of them had the time, power, or gall to dig up fossils and set them on fire!

Once or twice, I tried to attack this assumption in my nonfiction, but I soon realized that the story was too big. I also wanted to talk about the awkwardness—and even the guilt—of trying to talk to your forbears about the enormity of the climate crisis when they lived through Jim Crow (that slick name for American apartheid). I needed to talk about the conversations that you are simply *unqualified* to have with your parents and grandparents when they are older than integration. How can I fuss at my grandfather about plastic in the ocean when he's seen lynch mobs? How can I tell my mother how scary climate data is when she saw Emmett Till's swollen face when she was barely seven years old? This wasn't a story I could tell, it was a story I had to show. And something I needed to show *myself*.

Early in 2019, Corinne presented herself to me as a fully formed person, bold and resolute. Soon, I saw her everywhere: in the park, on the way to work, at the grocery store. I heard her voice in the wind, felt her breath on my neck. She whispered her story in my ear, and demanded that I make her real.

When she told me about her scheme, I was taken aback.

You want to do what? I asked.

Yes.

Have you thought about—?

I don't care.

And what if—?

I. Don't. Care.

I listened, but I didn't sit down to write until June 29, 2019: the day my Uncle Harold died. I was at the beach in Sonoma County, California, when I felt his spirit drape over me like one of his hugs. We walked and talked through the sand and wind just like I was sitting on his back porch in Birmingham. When the cell service came back on my phone, I learned that my mother had been frantically calling me. Uncle Harold had died of a heart attack.

With a raw throat and tears still streaming, I started writing what would become *Troubled Waters* that night.

All writing is an act of self-discovery, but this was an act of self-excavation, self-evolution. This story took me generations deep into myself, forcing me to re-ask the questions that had gotten me in trouble as a child. To get the full answers that had been lost to time and trauma and death, I went down rabbit holes and into the stacks of library archives. This story led me from the North to the South in so many more ways than one.

There are pieces of my family woven throughout these pages, in the stories and the characters. My great-grandmother really did make a bad batch of "home brew" that wound up getting the ducks drunk. She thought they were dead, so she plucked their feathers. A little while later, she looked up to find a yard full of naked ducks.

When my mother was little, Granddaddy really did bring baby chickens home from his job at the Post Office. My mother really did set a Confederate flag on fire at a bar in Vicksburg. On another occasion, she left a penny for a tip at a

Shoney's. My aunt really does explain my veganism as, "Mary doesn't eat food, she eats what food eats." And my mother and her siblings really did have a dog named Dandy, and I've heard stories about him all my life. My Uncle Harold, who was technically my cousin, really did laugh big enough to fill a house. As you might expect, there are parts of me infused in the characters too.

But at the same time, this is not my family, and this is not me. This is as much an homage to my family as it is a work entirely of my imagination, at Corinne's insistence. Corinne, Cora, Harold, Daphne, Cleo, and all the others are their own people—just as real as my own family—and I am so honored to have been chosen to bring them into this world.

DEVOTION

For Mahlon Jerome Griffith and Mary Clyde (Syler) Griffith, known to me as Granddaddy and Grandmama. For their children: Belinda Julia, George Jerome, Jacqueline Faye, and Harvey Steven. Known to me as Mama, Uncle George, Aunt Jackie, and Uncle Stevie.

For the Griffiths and the Nalls, the Sylers and the Maxwells. Thank you for your stories, your laughs, your auras—so much of what makes me who I am. For the ones walking this earth and the ones guiding us from the other planes. I feel you everywhere.

To the places that inspired this story: Nashville, Port Gibson, Vicksburg, Oberlin, Winchester, Birmingham, New Orleans. To the places that held me while I wrote it: the Bronx, Harlem, New Orleans again. To the places that made me: Mississippi, my heart, and Birmingham, my soul.

To my comrades. The ones who listened to me as I talked through each character, each setting, each storyline. The ones who read the early drafts, full and partial. The ones who talked me through my anxieties and imposter syndromes. There are too many of you to name, but you mean more to me than I could ever write.

To my informants: the activists and archivists and lawyers and academics and journalists who influenced and challenged my thinking. Thank you for your time, grace, and patience.

To my accomplices: my agent, who believed in me from the very beginning; my editor, who saw the vision; and the entire team at Harper Muse. There's so much more to come.

To Corinne Jewel Sterling, Cora Mae Sterling, and Harold Sterling. Thank you for coming. Thank you for choosing me. I will carry you with me forever.

DISCUSSION QUESTIONS

1. Have you ever been personally affected by a natural disaster, such as a flood, tornado, or hurricane? What was your experience, and did you consider the role climate change may have had in the event?

2. Have you had an experience where a family member or friend challenged a lifestyle choice you made? For example, Corinne's decision to become a vegan was met with resistance from her uncle and grandmother. How did Corinne handle it? And how did (or do) you handle pushback you may receive from friends or family?

3. Cora faced high expectations from her parents, particularly her father, and Corinne deals with the expectations of her grandmother. How does this influence their relationship?

4. How has generational trauma affected the Sterlings' relationships with one another and their views of the world?

5. The effects of systemic, environmental racism are seen throughout the book—from the Great Flood of 1927 to Cora's childhood experience of desegregation of the schools, to Corinne's experiences as a Black student at Oberlin. Which one of the threads did you connect with the most?

6. Cora finds solace and guidance in her hummingbird garden. How do you find solace when grieving?

7. Do you share Corinne's concerns about climate change? Do you find that you encounter a dismissive attitude regarding your concerns, much like Corinne did? Why do you think that is?

8. What did you think of Uncle Harold? What was his role in the story and in Cora's and Corinne's lives?

9. What are your thoughts on Mercer and Corinne's protest on the bridge? What did you think of Corinne's motivations, goals, and the outcome of the protest?

10. The book closes with self-discovery, revelations, and repair to relationships. What did you think of the ending? What affected you the most?

11. How did the author bring this quote to life through her characters: "Black women—celebrated the world over for their extraordinary ability to bend and bend and bend—can, in fact, break. Into a million little shards"?